THE FIRST LADY OF DOS CACAHUATES

ALSO BY HARRIET ROCHLIN

So Far Away

Pioneer Jews: A New Life in the Far West

The Reformer's Apprentice

THE FIRST LADY OF
DOS CACAHUATES

A novel

Harriet Rochlin

FITHIAN PRESS, SANTA BARBARA, 1998

Copyright © 1998 by Harriet Rochlin
All rights reserved
Printed in the United States of America

Published by Fithian Press
A division of Daniel and Daniel, Publishers, Inc.
Post Office Box 1525
Santa Barbara, CA 93102

Cover photograph courtesy of the Arizona Historical
Society/Tucson, Upham Collection, AHS #62,883

Book design by Eric Larson

Rochlin, Harriet, 1924–
    First lady of Dos Cachuates: a novel/ by Harriet Rochlin.
    p. cm.
    ISBN 1-56474-265-2 (cloth: alk. paper).
    —ISBN 1-56474-264-4 (pbk.: alk. paper)
    I. Title.
PS3568.O3247F5   1998
813'.54--dc21   97-44159
                                                      CIP

In memory of my parents,
Sarah (Holtzman) and Mike
Shapiro, who came west to shed
heavy clothes, rusty restraints,
and slavish habits.

I remember the devotion of your youth,
The love of your bridal days,
How you went after Me in the wilderness,
In a land that was not sown.

Jeremiah 2:2

THE FIRST LADY OF DOS CACAHUATES

Fresh from the Rabbi

FRIEDA LEVIE GOLDSON stood on the Oakland train platform with her husband of three hours, her family and three longtime residents of Levie's Kosher Boardinghouse. Cautionaries whizzed around her like agitated birds.

"Don't talk to strangers."

"Eat only the *kosher* food from the picnic basket."

"Don't forget to light the *Shabbes* candles."

"Don't drink the water unless it's been boiled."

"Watch your pocketbook and valises."

"Write the minute you get there."

"If he doesn't treat you nice, don't be ashamed to come home."

Come home? Frieda thought. After her father almost had Bennie arrested to keep them from marrying? Her eyes shifted to her husband. Did she love him, really love him, as much as she'd thought? She barely knew him. He was so burly, freewheeling, unpredictable. And his hair, it was the color of blood oranges. She'd never seen a Jew with hair like that. What if their children looked like him? What if they behaved like him?

"Listen to what I'm telling you," her Aunt Chava cried, shaking Frieda as if from a deep sleep.

"Listen?" her father, Abram, muttered. "If she listened she'd be married to Gimel, not to a stranger, from a place that ain't even on a map."

For the fifth time, or was it the tenth, Bennie was assuring her father he would protect her, love her, look after her. She wanted to nudge him to stop, but didn't dare get close enough. He might put his arm around her, or worse, kiss her. Had she made a mistake? If she had, it was too late to rectify. Now that they were married, he could carry her off like a valise, and no one would lift a finger to stop him.

Her gaze darted from her family to a placid-looking blonde girl of ten or eleven in a neighboring party. She stood two feet from her elders, concentrating on weaving a long coil of multi-colored yarn on a small spool. Overlooked by the adults, she seemed oblivious to their excited babble. Oh, to be that ignored child, unseen, unchided, unlamented.

A high, familiar giggle floated down the platform. Rising on tiptoes, Frieda spotted Rosamund Cohn and her daughter Minnie, swathed in full-length cloaks and veils, slipping past the Levie party to Minnie's train, three cars away from the newlyweds. Frieda had warned Bennie that Minnie was too sickly, spoiled and attached to her mother to pioneer in an Arizona–Sonora border outpost. But Bennie would not be dissuaded. They had a wife for his brother, an influential new investor, seats on one of the Southern Pacific's inaugural trips to the Arizona Territory as a wedding present, and no cause for worry. The Arizona sunshine would do wonders for Minnie; Minnie would do wonders for Morrie, and Mrs. Cohn would do wonders for the International Improvement Company, Dos Cacahuates Division.

When the engineer sounded a departing whistle, Bennie seized her elbow and started toward Car 22, her relatives trailing. There must have been more warnings and parting embraces, but she didn't remember. Suddenly, she was in her seat, watching Bennie arrange their valises and food baskets in the rack above. Moments later, he was settled beside her, getting acquainted with their fellow passengers. She was about to caution him not to tell people they were newlyweds, when a stone struck her window. On the platform beneath her stood her brother, Sammy, with another stone in hand; Sylvia, the second of the three Levie daughters, supporting her weeping mother; Ida, the youngest, clutching Aunt Chava's arm; and her father, his face set in a disapproving grimace. Frieda lifted her hand half-heartedly, reluctant to acknowledge, even to herself, that she was the object of their distress.

The train lunged forward, then back. A whistle blasted and the wheels began to rotate, slicing Mama, Papa, Aunt Chava, Sylvia, Sammy and Ida from view. Slowly the wood-sided cars, rattling and rocking, chugged out of the station. Her body vibrating with unfamiliar sounds, movements, emotions, Frieda closed her eyes and flattened her palms against the seat.

"Your first train, little girl?" Bennie teased. Did he have to talk so loud? His arm dropped protectively around her shoulder. Frieda twisted out of his grasp.

"You're so beautiful," he whispered, leaning against her. "I can't take my eyes off you."

Was Bennie complimenting or mocking her? Some schoolfriends had admired her curly brown hair, short, round nose, deep-set blue eyes, full bosom and narrow waist. But as boardinghouse mainstay for five years, working sixteen hours a day, fending off randy boarders, arguing with heavy-thumbed grocers and settling family squabbles, she'd grown as plain as porridge.

"Hardly beautiful."

"Beautiful," he insisted, loud enough to incite a look from the man in the seat ahead.

Bennie didn't notice. He was busy removing her glove and kissing her fingertips.

In one swift move, Frieda yanked back her hand, wrapped it around his, and hid them under the folds of her skirt. Recapturing her hand in his, Bennie settled down and began commenting on the countryside.

Before the railroads were in, he'd traveled the terrain in every season, by foot, horseback, wagon. At Martinez, he leaned in front of her to point out a crease in the oak-dotted hills where he was robbed by an Australian highwayman. At Antioch, she had to see a landing where he'd worked unloading ocean vessels. At Tracy Junction, he showed her Mount Diablo, bragging that he'd once climbed to the top.

"Why?" she asked.

"For the heck of it."

Frieda looked straight at Bennie for the first time since they boarded the train.

"Don't you like doing things for the heck of it?"

"I haven't had much chance."

"Nothing better. Try it." His brown eyes held hers in a meaningful gaze.

"I will," she blurted. Reddening, she turned and pressed her flushed cheek against the window.

"Soon," Bennie said, pressing his chest against her back.

"I said I would," Frieda muttered into the glass.

Nuzzling his head into her shoulder, he playfully licked a narrow band of exposed flesh between her stiff collar and her ear.

"Bennie," Frieda protested. "If you don't behave, I'm going to sit somewhere else."

"Just couldn't resist. No offense meant." He straightened, folded his hands, and fixed his gaze on the seat ahead.

When the sun dropped behind the Coast Range to the west, Bennie rose, pulled down the stiff window shade, then stepped out into the aisle to take down their picnic basket. As they ate, Frieda studied their fellow passengers, recalling a line in the *Pacific Travelers' Guide*: "On the road, thieves are as apt to look like college graduates as college graduates might look like thieves."

When she repeated the warning, Bennie bounced with laughter. "After you've done some traveling, you get a sense of who people are and where they're headed."

Leaning into the aisle, he demonstrated. The Mexican señora with the three rambunctious boys and two Indian maids was a rancher's wife returning to La Puente following a visit to her family in the north. The middle-aged lady coughing into her handkerchief was probably headed for San Gabriel, the best place in California for tuberculars. The bald-headed, irritated-looking fellow at her side was her husband, a doctor. Why did Bennie think so? He was reading a medical journal, carrying a small black bag and was bored with his wife's distress.

Looking around the car for more material, he found a couple of drummers who had just refilled their merchandise cases in San Francisco and were on their way to Los Angeles to peddle their wares. In front of the drummers were two young new immigrants on their way to relatives in southern California or the Arizona Territory. How did he know? They spoke in a foreign language, only to each other, and kept checking their inside pockets for their passports and billfolds.

"They're as fresh off the boat as you're fresh from the rabbi," Bennie said, caressing her nose.

"Is it really obvious that I'm a...."

"In your new suit, with your adoring new husband, a new ring on your finger, eating chicken and *challeh*?"

Frieda thrust the drumstick she held back into the basket and lay her right hand over her left. Leaning her head against the black plush seat, she tried to relax. A moment later, she stiffened with a new concern.

"Is this a sleeping car?" Frieda asked Bennie.

He assured her it was.

"And this is how we're going to sleep?" she asked leaning back and lowering her eyelids.

"Naw, this is a Silver Palace car. Look," he said, pointing down the aisle, "they're starting to make up the berths."

Frieda stood up to see. Porters were sliding down seats and stringing up black curtains. She watched an old lady, her hand clutching the back of one seat and then another, make her way from the ladies' toilet at the rear of the car. Her gray hair was plaited for sleep and she wore a flannel wrapper over her nightgown.

A group of strangers bedding down together? People cautioned not to speak to one another? Other passengers were rising from their seats, bumping and swaying their way to the toilets, bags in hand. Soon she too would go take off her green serge traveling costume, slip into her white cambric bridal nightgown decorated with Valenciennes lace and laven-der ribbons, put her old coat over it and inch her way back down the aisle to her berth.

Husbands and wives sleep together, so Bennie would climb in after her in his…in his what? She couldn't imagine him in anything but a green suit, boots and Stetson.

"I'm not tired," Frieda whispered. "Do we have to go to bed now?"

"Heck no," Bennie responded. "It's only nine. Let's go to the parlor car and have a glass of champagne."

I do love him, Frieda thought, jumping to her feet.

Bennie in the lead, they moved through the sleeping cars, where the gas lamps were already lowered and quiet prevailed, to the parlor car where nocturnal festivities were underway. At a table under a swaying kerosene chandelier sat two viva-cious middle-aged women with two gentlemen. Their faces were as rosy as the wine the waiter was pouring into their glasses. At another, a monte dealer was playing cards with the two drummers from their car. And near them sat three men in business suits swapping jokes, slapping their thighs and banging the table.

Bennie found two booth seats in the rear corner of the car. The space was tight and they sat thigh to thigh, a rattling table in front of them.

When the champagne arrived, Frieda took a sip, her face puckering. "It looks better than it tastes."

"The more you drink, the better you'll like it," Bennie said.

She emptied the glass and issued a deep sigh, letting her-self fall back against the upholstered booth.

"You sound like a soldier taking off tight boots."

"Exactly." Frieda reached for her husband's hand.

"You're trembling," Bennie said. Laughing, he held up his hand. "So am I." He smoothed her blazing cheek. "Oh, Frieda, I want the best for you." Tears magnified his ma-hogany brown eyes.

"And I want the best for you, Bennie." Her blue eyes were earnest, teary.

"Let's drink to that." Bennie lifted his glass to meet hers. Their faces solemn, ceremonial, they clicked and emptied their glasses.

"I was so scared I'd make a mistake, I didn't hear a word the rabbi said. *Now* I feel married," Bennie told her, "or almost."

Things began to pound and surge in her. She raised her glass for more wine. As she sipped, Bennie kissed and fondled her hand and, floating on alcohol and emotion, she let him. Her goblet was nearly empty when a gruff voice broke in on them.

"Champagne Bennie, at it again." A chorus of male laughter followed.

Frieda glanced up to see three men standing alongside their table. Their skins were sunburned, their hats broad-brimmed. The one on the right was big, dark-haired and brawny; the one in the middle was slight, sandy-haired and bespectacled; the one on the left was stocky and balding.

Bennie hooted and jumped to his feet. "Tucson friends," he said in Frieda's direction, as he squeezed out from behind the table. He and the men pumped hands bawling out their pleasure.

"Couple of years at least," said the balding man.

"Just about," Bennie agreed.

"Heard you and Morrie got yourself a little store down on the Arizona-Sonora border."

"And a few other things."

"Such as?" the sandy-haired one asked Bennie, his tone playful, almost mocking. He leaned around Bennie to address Frieda, one small blue eye coming down in a suggestive wink.

"I never met ole Goldson, *Hijo del Oro,* we call him, when he didn't have a line on something really big."

"Struck it rich, this time," Bennie said, turning toward Frieda. The men leaned in to hear. "Meet Mrs. Bennie Goldson. Frieda, this is...." The men's boisterous exclamations drowned out the names he recited.

Casual good humor draining from their faces, they saluted her with respectful bows.

"Mrs. Bennie Goldson," said the tallest man in a baleful tone. "Marks the end of the Wild West."

"You'll have to excuse us, ma'am, we're mourning the passing of an age," the balding man told Frieda. "Hijo here, he's the last to go." He turned to consult his companions. "Got to get a bottle of champagne, men, and toast the happy couple."

Bennie started to decline, but Frieda interrupted, saying they'd be delighted.

When the champagne arrived, Bennie proposed a toast to the First Lady of Dos Cacahuates.

The men chuckled. "Dos Cacahuates?" one of them repeated. "Two peanuts?"

"A big new enterprise," Bennie said.

Sipping champagne, Frieda watched the men's eyes light up as he told them about the International Improvement Company, Dos Cacahuates Division.

"Dos Ca-ca-wah-tes," one of them sounded out, "kinda catchy." He held up his glass, "Here's to Dos Cacahuates."

Frieda and the men lifted theirs too.

"And to its *beautiful* First Lady," the tallest man said, gesturing in Frieda's direction.

"*Charming* First Lady," the one with the spectacles added.

"*Courageous* First Lady," the balding man joined in.

Frieda accepted their tributes with flushed cheeks and a self-conscious smile. When they ran out of adjectives, the men turned back to Bennie.

"What do you have down there now?" the balding man wanted to know.

"The store, an adobe house, a construction crew working on a hotel."

"Other settlers?" the tall man asked.

"Half-dozen on the American side and about five hundred on the Mexican."

"Is that where you're taking this little lady?" the tall man questioned, his eyes avoiding Frieda's.

"Sure," Bennie said. "Now that the Southern Pacific's up and running, we'll put together a short line and we'll be in good shape."

The sandy-haired fellow grinned. "Good shape and up to your knees in ca—" He stopped abruptly, as though kicked under the table.

"Time for us to turn in," Bennie said, rising.

"You can't go yet," the tall man objected. "You ain't even played the organ. You'll have to get used to it, ma'am," he told Frieda. "You've gone and married the life of every party."

In a flash the three were on their feet, propelling Bennie toward the organ.

"Just a few," he called over his shoulder to Frieda.

Light-headed, woozy, fearing at any moment she might rise like the smoke curling from the men's cigars and spread across the top of the car, Frieda remained in her chair, clutching the arm to secure herself.

It was too much to take in. Frieda Levie on the inaugural Southern Pacific train from San Francisco to the Arizona Territory. Frieda Levie in a plush parlor car drinking champagne, conversing with strange men who toasted her beauty, charm and courage. Men who spoke directly to her, listened to her responses, frankly admired her and envied her husband.

Her husband. What a charmer. Broad-shouldered, red curls crowning his leonine head, teeth glistening, his thick, outdoorsman fingers playing the organ the same way that he played life—by ear.

Bennie caught her eye. He raised a hand to his heart, then put both hands back on the keys, chorded and sang:

Believe me if all those endearing young charms,
That I gaze on so fondly today,
Were to fade by the morrow and flee from my arms
Like a fairy dream fading away....

Frieda joined him:
Thou will still be adored as this moment thou art,

Let thy loveliness fade as it will,
And around the dear ruins....

She was singing a love song to her husband, in front of strangers, in a voice she'd never heard before. It was sure, melodious, unashamed.

CHAPTER TWO

Car 19

BENNIE'S SANDY-HAIRED friend tapped Frieda's hand and, when she didn't look up, shook her arm.

"He's looking for you, ma'm," he said jerking his thumb at the stringy, grim-faced conductor standing behind him. The conductor stepped in front of Sandy. "Mrs. Goldson?"

It was the first time someone addressed her by her new name. Squaring her shoulders, she rose. "Yes."

"I've been searching for you. Your friend in Car 19 needs you."

Bennie had moved on to a jaunty, western tune. "My friend in Car 19?"

"Miss Minerva Cohn."

The name and the image of the person who bore it collided with a sickening thud. Minnie, three cars away, summoning her. "Is it urgent?" Frieda asked with ill-concealed irritation.

"She has Car 19 in an uproar."

Bennie had risen and was at her side, the markings of their musical union still on his face—lovestruck eyes, flushed cheeks.

"Minnie has a problem. She sent the conductor for me."

"Tell her we'll see her in the morning."

The conductor eyed Bennie. "It won't wait."

"I'll go see what it is," Frieda told her husband.

"I'll go with you." He took her elbow.

"No, you stay here. If I go alone, I'll get away faster."

His eyes clung to hers. "I don't want to let you out of my sight."

Squeezing his upper arm, she murmured, "I'll be back soon, I promise."

Leading Frieda through the rolling cars, the conductor outlined Minnie's plight. Coming down the aisle, after preparing for bed, she'd tripped on her nightdress, fell and hit her head. The bruise was not serious. Brushing aside assistance, she'd risen on her own power and had hurried to her berth. If the injury was as minor as he said, why had Minnie summoned her? The conductor's tone was cool, businesslike. Was he minimizing the injury to protect the railroad against a possible lawsuit?

When the lights had dimmed, the conductor continued, she started to cry. Several people had tried to find out what was troubling her, but Miss Cohn had ignored their queries and had gone on bawling. After a while, the passengers had begun to complain.

"I tried myself several times to get her to say what was wrong, but she held her berth curtains closed and wouldn't say a word. I finally warned her that if she didn't quiet down, I was going stop the train and put her off."

"You shouldn't have done that," Frieda chided him. "You terrified her."

"Lady, we have fifty passengers in that car, and not one of them is asleep."

"But you wouldn't put her off the train."

"I've put passengers off before."

"A frightened girl?"

"You know her pretty well?"

Frieda nodded.

"See what you can do with her."

The situation in Car 19 was worse than Frieda had expected. A number of passengers were in the aisle grumbling about the noise. Disconsolate sobs led Frieda to Minnie's berth.

"Minnie, open up, it's me," she called, tugging at the curtains.

The heavy black cotton parted and Minnie peeped out.

She gestured for Frieda to join her, and as soon as she had, snapped the curtains together. By the light of the full moon beaming through the open window shade, Frieda made out her distraught friend. Her nightgown tucked under her, Minnie sat crouched on her haunches. Her hair was tangled and matted with perspiration, her green-white skin glistened and her eyes were wide with fear.

A wave of nausea shot through Frieda. She closed her eyes, inhaled, then gathered Minnie's trembling body into her arms. Patting her bony back, she coaxed forth her friend's version of the accident. She'd tripped, fallen and hurt her head. It wasn't the bruise that bothered her, it was the way people leaped at her. One man grabbed her elbow. An older woman seized her handbag, and an impudent young man had actually tried to put his arm around her.

Her mother cautioned her to steer clear of the other passengers and, under no circumstances, to trust anyone but Bennie and Frieda. A bearded man pretending to be a doctor tried to get her to take some sleeping powder. And when she refused, he urged the conductor to force it on her. The two were in cahoots, they wanted to drug and kidnap her, Minnie said, her voice rising to a wail.

"Shush, shush," Frieda tried to quiet her. "You're scared, and your imagination's running wild."

"That's easy for you to say. You have a husband to look after you, and I'm all alone."

"You're not alone, I'm here." Frieda soothed, massaging her friend's tense shoulders. "Now, now, you're all right."

As she talked, she eased Minnie into a reclining position, then curling up behind her, sat smoothing her damp hair. Minnie lay still for several minutes, then quietly began to weep again. Everyone in Car 19 was furious with her. Frieda was angry with her too. She didn't want to disturb her on her wedding night. The words wedding night emerged in a prolonged squeal.

Frieda placed her fingers on Minnie's lips. "Don't talk," she whispered.

Pushing Frieda's hands away from her mouth, Minnie continued her dirge. Bennie would hate her too. His brother wouldn't like her either, and she'd have to go back to San Francisco all by herself. "My mother's planning to leave for Europe in three days, and if she does, I'll have to stay in that big house all by myself."

She didn't hate her, she loved her, Frieda told Minnie. So did Bennie, and his brother would too.

"You're lying," Minnie said. "You know you hate me, and so will they. I'm going to get off the train in Los Angeles and wire my mother to come get me."

"You're tired and overexcited. You'll feel better after you get some rest. Take the sleeping powder," Frieda urged. "You'll be all right after a good night's sleep."

"I know it's your wedding night, but I need you, Frieda. Please," Minnie begged. "I can't stay in this berth all by myself. I'll go crazy."

"Take the medicine, and I'll stay with you until you fall asleep."

"Not until I go to sleep, all night."

Frieda didn't see how she could.

"Then I won't take it." Minnie closed her eyes and opened her mouth wide. She looked like an infant about to scream itself blue.

"I'll go talk to Bennie," Frieda said, her tone quiet, measured, her heart pounding. Cross Minnie, and she'd spurn Bennie's brother as speedily as she'd agreed to marry him. With no less speed Mrs. Cohn would scotch her much-needed investment in Bennie's company. Frieda pushed her legs through the curtains.

Minnie grabbed two fistsful of Frieda's jacket and hung on, crying, "Don't go. Send the conductor for him."

The conductor agreed, if she promised to keep Minnie quiet until he returned. Ten minutes later he reappeared with Bennie, apprised of the dilemma, yet seemingly undismayed. He greeted his new wife and his future sister-in-law with the buoyancy of a slightly drunk charmer accustomed to winning over difficult men, women, children and animals.

Through the parted curtains, her voice lowered to a whisper, Bennie clutching her hand, Minnie holding her ankle, Frieda explained their predicament. In the shifting shadows of the dimmed kerosene fixture, she watched Bennie's expression graduate from confident to tenacious. They could all go to the parlor car for a drink. They could both stay with Minnie until she felt better. He would find a trustworthy person to guard her berth while she slept.

"No, no, no," Minnie screeched. "I won't go anywhere. I'm afraid. I want Frieda, only Frieda, to stay with me all night. Please. Pleeease." The second plea rose into an eery wail.

The conductor returned. This time he addressed Bennie. "Are you going to take care of her, or shall I?"

"We're trying to reason with her," Bennie told the conductor.

"It won't work. Give her what she wants or I'll throw off the three of you. The other passengers won't stand for this. They paid good money for an inaugural trip on a Silver Palace car, not a night of misery in a crazy house."

"But this is our..."

Frieda tugged at Bennie's arm and, when he turned, shot him a silencing glance.

"But, Sweetheart..."

She put her finger to his lips. "He means business, Bennie. Bring me my train bag, please."

He searched the car like a trapped animal looking for an escape, then, surrendering to the unavoidable, did as she asked. When Bennie returned, he stayed with Minnie while Frieda went to change into her nightgown. Just before she climbed back into the berth, he gathered her into his arms and whispered, "Soon as she's asleep, come to me."

Frieda didn't see how she could, but she nodded, if only to see his face brighten.

Worn by the long siege and lulled by the sleeping powder, Minnie dropped off within minutes. Soon, the car was as quiet as tight quarters for fifty sleeping, or at least supine, people could be. Frieda lay wide awake, monitoring Minnie's breathing and staring at the black curtains. Squeezed to the edge of the berth, each time the train swerved, she had to clutch the railing to keep from falling out. With groans and sighs, Minnie heaved her thin body from side to side. Then just when she was sure she was stuck for the night, Frieda detected a light snore. She parted the curtains, stuck her head through and looked down the aisle. A cold draft blew through the narrow passageway. One passenger's cough, another's snore, blended with the clatter of steel against steel. Bennie was three dark, cold, rocking cars away. She had her coat, but her slippers were in her bag. If she did risk leaving Minnie, dare she walk through those dark cars in the middle of the night, by herself, in her nightgown, barefooted?

Then there was *it*. Did she really want to do *it* for the first time in a curtained berth on a train? She'd allowed Bennie physical liberties she'd granted no other man. And several times, his hand had grazed her breast and lingered there, stirring within her sensations of alarming intensity.

The train went around a curve. Minnie's leg flopped over onto Frieda's. She kicked it off, bolted upright and peered through the dark at her sleeping charge. Slipping one foot and then the other out of the berth, she peeped into the darkened passageway. For several moments, she let her trembling legs dangle over the side, then pulled them back in again.

Stay, go, she was sick with indecision. Just as she was that evening in Dr. McManus's dental chair. McManus, a short, thin man with a waxed mustache and an oily manner, examined her infected tooth and told her it had to come out at once. He'd give her a few whiffs of gas and, before she knew it, she'd be on her way home. Unconscious, unprotected, in that tiny, dark office, at the mercy of that waxed mustache? Frieda wavered. She was about to jump up and run, when he put his hand on her shoulder, eased her back into the chair and arranged the cone on her nose. Breathe in, breathe out. The last thing she felt was his belt buckle cutting into her shoulder, and the last thing she heard was the click of his steel instruments. Then true to his word, before she knew it, her decayed tooth was wrapped in a handkerchief in her handbag and she was on her way home.

Frieda sat up, gathered her coat around her and lowered her feet to the Brussels carpet. Barefoot, crouching, senses vibrating, she crept like a savage through the darkened train. The further she got, the less concerned she was about Minnie. By the time she entered Car 22, blood pulsing in her head, throat, heart and groin had washed away thought of everything but her destination.

She moved slowly down the aisle, sniffing for Jockey Club toilet water and Pollack's stogies. Alongside a lower berth near the end of the car, she hesitated, scenting the air. Then she yanked back the curtain and flung herself on the sleeping occupant. With a cry of alarm, then joy, Bennie drew her into his arms. His lips wet her face, throat, ears.

"Am I dreaming? If I am, don't wake me."

Frieda laughed. "If you're dreaming, so am I."

He pulled off her coat and ran his hands over her. Shivering with cold, Frieda tried to pull back the blanket and join him beneath it. He gripped the edges.

"I ain't got a stitch on," he muttered, shy as a boy.

Shamed by his shame, Frieda reached for her coat.

"Am I crazed?" Bennie cried, flinging back the cover and pulling her against his naked body.

"I been dying to get you unwrapped. Ummm, delicious."

His mouth found hers and stayed until she pulled away, struggling for air. He felt heavy, hard, driven. Like the bartender in her father's wine shed, but different. Bennie loved her. Pinned in place, her mind stilled, her body said things it had never said before. Emitting a final shudder, Bennie fell against her gasping, then rolled to her side. When words came, they tumbled out in bits and pieces, light, moist, sweet, like crumbs of a delicious cake. He said he never loved a woman the way he loved her. She said she never trusted a man the way she did him. From the present they drifted into the future. Life with her was going to be more fun than a county fair. Life with him was going to be a true partnership, the only kind of marriage she ever wanted.

The berth was still dark as a subterranean cave when Frieda eased herself out of Bennie's embrace, pressed a parting kiss on his lips and slipped through the curtains into the aisle. Gathering her coat around her, she made her way through the cold railroad cars. When two hairy, bare legs and a bald pate poked out of a berth, she shuddered, thinking for the first time of what might have happened had she chosen the wrong berth.

Back in Car 19, her toes resting against Minnie's shoulder, she reflected on her altered body and her altered life. A part of her had been torn away and replaced with a dull throb. In a day or two, the pain would be gone and forgotten. But that impulse (stronger than fear, shame, modesty) that drew her to him, his delight in her and the dawning of hers in him, would linger. They were tokens of the new, unimaginable territory she was traveling toward.

CHAPTER THREE

Welcome to Dos Cacahuates

"MOHAWK STATION ain't much," Bennie warned as they got off the train.

Their luggage piled around them, Frieda and Minnie stared at the jagged, dead-looking mountains that dwindled to lava-bed hills, and then to sand and ash. Frieda's mouth dropped open, and a disappointed whimper floated out. She felt as if she were standing in the middle of a cold campfire, surrounded by a ring of charred rock, witnessing the aftermath of a disaster.

The stationkeeper, a flinty, grizzled man with a Scottish accent, attended Bennie's inquiry, rolled it over and shook his head. "Spoke to someone from Dos Cacahuates? Can't say I have. Fact is, never heard of Dos Ca-ca-wah-tes."

Frieda shot Bennie a questioning glance.

"Mac knows it as Goldson. What I'm wondering is why Morrie ain't here. I wrote more than a week ago asking him to meet us at Mohawk Station."

Minnie's fatigue-grayed face turned a shade grayer. "He doesn't want me," she concluded.

"Yes, he does," Bennie assured her. A puzzled look flitted across his face like a fast-moving cloud. "Well, girls, looks like you're going to have yourself a stagecoach ride, too. Have space for us on the next coach, Mac?"

The stationkeeper assessed the trunks, valises and boxes. "Three passengers and a couple hundred pounds of luggage. Guess they can handle you. All's they got now are a Mexican rancher and his wife bound for Altar."

At five-thirty, the five passengers left the stationkeeper's shack to board the stagecoach. The Mexican couple took the seat facing forward, and Minnie, Frieda, and Bennie settled opposite them. Bennie tried out his Spanish on the aging pair, but the rancher had a bad toothache, and his wife was too travel-worn to talk. The Mexican driver, Yermo, and his helper, Pepe (Bennie knew them both), finished loading the baggage. Then they swung up into the driver's seat, and with an "*hasta luego*" to Mac and an "*adelante*" to the horses, they set off.

After a fiery, carmine sunset that silhouetted the jagged ridges and tinted the scorched surfaces pink, a full moon rose, illluminating the desert and silvering the road. Minnie and Frieda exhausted, the Mexican couple ailing and withdrawn, silence prevailed inside the coach. Failing to kindle conversation, Bennie tilted his Stetson over his eyes and sank into a deep sleep.

Minnie slept fitfully. Each time the coach slammed into and out of an arroyo, she woke with a startled cry. And when she breathed in more dust than her fragile lungs could tolerate, she coughed, tears streaming, gasping for air. Then, eased by Frieda's reassuring words and sips of water, she was soon dozing again.

Frieda spent the entire night wide-eyed and upright. From time to time, she pulled back the canvas curtain to gaze out at the mysterious-looking desert. The immense sky was a midnight blue studded with blazing stars that seemed to be advancing earthward, like marchers in a candlelight parade. Out of the feathery chaparral rose palo verdes and mesquites huddling together like neighbors seeking companionship, news, protection, while the solitary saguaros reminded her of giant soldiers, their arms outstretched in welcome or warning. By the end of the long, dismal, dark night, Frieda tended toward the latter.

A little after dawn the driver made a comfort stop, assigning one side of the stage to the ladies and the other to the gentlemen. The blue-white air was sweet and only a little chilly. Frieda drew in several deep breaths and instantly perked up. On the east side of the road, sunlight bounced off a wall of mountains—the Growlers, according to Bennie. To the west ran another two ranges, the Mohawk and the Quitobaquito. Frieda gazed around the newly lit valley awestruck. The slopes of the surrounding hills were ablaze with splashes of color: a stretch of orange, a blanket of purple, blending with a patch of blue.

"Wildflowers," Bennie said, "poppies, verbena, lupine."

"Is it always like this?" Frieda asked.

"No," Bennie replied. "This is a spring show after a rainy winter. But the desert's always got something to get excited about."

Back in the coach, Minnie pulled out her combs and handkerchief and with a tiny mirror began to tidy her straggling hair and clean her dust-streaked face. Frieda looked on concerned. Excitement darted and dimmed in Minnie's red-rimmed eyes, and her pinched face was the color of a withered mushroom.

"Look, you can see Mexico," Bennie announced, pointing south. Frieda peered into the distance, unable to detect an iota of difference between the Mexican and American desertscapes.

The coach swerved westward, then bumped along a thin trail through raw desert for a half-hour.

"See that plateau ahead?" Bennie said, stretching his finger a tad north of due west. "That's where we're building the hotel. The store is down on the desert floor. You can't see it yet; it's hidden in the cottonwoods."

Frieda and Minnie looked out the window, narrowing their eyes, attending, nodding.

"We're putting the hotel up on the hill alongside the hot springs so the guests will have a short walk to the baths and a grand view of the valley from the front veranda."

Slowing, the stage entered a clearing.

"Welcome to Dos Cacahuates," Bennie cried. "I'll go find Morrie." He threw open the door, jumped out and ran to-

ward a small frame building with a false front and a big sign
that read GOLDSON BROTHERS, GENERAL MERCHANDISE and beneath that in handwritten script, "If we haven't got it, we'll
get it." By the time the coach halted at the hitching post in front
of the store, Bennie was coming out of the door. Frieda
watched him stop, slap his head, turn and run back inside,
then emerge again holding a brown bottle—the medicine
he'd promised the rancher for his sore tooth.

Pepe helped Frieda, then Minnie, alight. Blinking in the
strong morning sun, the two exercised their numb limbs and
looked around. From the grove behind the store came the
sound of birds greeting the new day. Frieda tracked the chorus through the trees to a dark green pond. A giant trunk of a
fallen cottonwood extended like a peninsula into the water.
Tule reeds, thick green bushes, bright yellow narcissi ringed
the water.

"Minnie," Frieda called, her voice full of quiet awe,
"come see." Standing near the water's edge, she and Minnie
watched as hummingbirds whizzed from bloom to bloom and
wildfowl glided over the still waters. When Bennie came up
behind them, they turned, faces aglow, bubbling with their
discovery.

Bennie nodded, preoccupied.

Peering past him, Frieda saw the coach heading back
down the narrow trail.

Slipping away from Minnie and to her husband's side,
Frieda whispered, "What did Morrie say?"

"He's not in the store. I'll have to look around for him."

"That's good," Frieda responded. "Minnie and I will have
a chance to tidy up before we stand inspection."

"I'll take you to the house, then go get Angelina and
Ramón. Have I told you about them? We hired them the day
after Yancy Nunes and International Improvement arrived.
They'll fix you up with warm water and towels." Hooking
arms with Frieda and Minnie, Bennie guided them across the
deserted clearing.

"Wait 'til you see the house," Bennie said. "It was just a room we used to store things the Papagos and Seris brought to trade or sell. Someone got busy on the place while I was gone, painted it, dug up some furniture."

Bennie left them in the doorway of the low, whitewashed adobe. The interior was also newly whitewashed, and the mud floor was covered with Indian rugs. A double bed dominated the room. The ponderous carved mahogany frame reminded Frieda of the bedroom suite in Rosamund Cohn's bedroom. It looked absurdly out of place in the Indian hut amid hanging baskets, pottery, wood carvings and strings of beads. A small dilapidated iron cookstove and a peeling cupboard took up the other wall. In the center of the room was a rough-hewn, handmade table and two cross-legged benches. There was a pungent fragrance of honeysuckle from the vine that hung around the single window, which, to Frieda's delight, framed a view of the pond just beyond the clearing.

Minnie had fallen exhausted onto the bed and lay looking around the room. "It's crude," she decided, "but sweet."

Frieda silently tested her own adjectives: exotic, quaint, interesting, homelike? No, not homelike.

A tap sounded at the door.

When Frieda opened it, a man and woman entered, Angelina and Ramón. The woman carried a pitcher of water, the man, one of the suitcases; Frieda stared at them. They were like the pond—composed, tranquil, exquisite. Were they brother and sister, husband and wife, or simply co-workers? Short and slender, they were no taller than Frieda, but so narrow-boned and erect that they appeared tall. Their skins were less swarthy than Minnie's. The woman's eyes were green, and the man's a soft, coffee brown. How old were they? Older than she (twenty-two), but younger than Bennie (thirty-three).

"*Café?*" the woman asked.

Frieda nodded. Angelina went back out to the yard where a small cooking fire burned. Ramón followed. As soon as they were gone, Frieda and Minnie burst into giggles.

"They're so beautiful and dignified," Frieda said, "I feel as if I should be waiting on them." She started to take off her dust-stiffened dress. "Come on, Minnie, we've got to wash and change before Bennie and Morrie get here." Swaying with fatigue, Minnie forced herself to her feet. "My heart is beating so loud I can hear it." Frieda helped Minnie lift the dress over her head and took the hairpins out of her dust-streaked black hair. By then, Angelina was back with two cups of coffee on a tray. She set it on the table and stood waiting for her next assignment.

Minnie picked up the wrinkled, pink lawn dress she had just dug out of her suitcase and slid an imaginary iron over it. Nodding, Angelina took the dress and left with it over her arm. Minnie inhaled, as if drawing in resolve, then made her way to the basin of water on the table. Scrubbed clean, her face looked more tired than it had when dirty. She raised her arms to her hair, but soon dropped them, her face puckering like that of a weary child. Would Frieda comb her hair?

By the time Frieda had Minnie's black mane tamed, Bennie was at the door.

"Don't come in," called the girls in unison.

"Then you come out, Frieda."

"I've taken off my dress."

"Put it back on." Bennie's voice sounded measured, somber.

Frieda did as he suggested. Starting for the door, she thought to ask, "Are you alone, Bennie? I haven't had a chance to tidy up yet."

"I'm alone."

"Where is everyone?" Frieda asked as she stepped through the door.

"Yancy's in his tent, but he's not feeling well."

"Something happen while you were gone?"

"Well, yes."

"To whom?"

"Morrie."

Frieda gasped. All the frontier perils she'd refused to think about rushed in at her. Morrie had been killed by hostile Indians, Mexican bandits, or he'd been bitten by a rattlesnake or scorpion.

"Is he dead?" She whispered the last word, surprised she had got it out at all.

"No," Bennie said. A blank space followed, as he forced his eyes to meet Frieda's. "He's married."

Frieda reached behind her to slam the door shut. "Married? You wrote to him saying you were bringing a bride for him."

"He went to Tucson last week and missed the letter."

"Who told you?"

"Yancy Nunes. He went with him. Morrie got married in Tucson on Monday."

Frieda's shoulders sagged. "Two days ago?"

"He and Nunes went to Tucson to talk up Dos Cacahuates at the Southern Pacific celebration. They set up a table in front of the Palace Hotel and did pretty well passing out handbills and drumming up interest. According to Yancy, they sold six lots."

"What's that have to do with Morrie getting married?"

"A girl at the hotel came to them for help. When Morrie found out she was Jewish, he did all he could for her. She was in big trouble."

"What kind of trouble?"

"Some roughnecks were trying to force her out of the Arizona Territory."

"Why didn't she go to the sheriff?"

"He's related to the men who were out to get her."

"So Morrie married her?"

"Not right then. He proposed on Saturday, with some nudging from Yancy, I suspect. It isn't like Morrie to fly off and do something like that in a big hurry."

"Marry a girl in trouble right off the streets, a perfect stranger to everyone?"

"Not to everyone."

"He knew her before?"

"No, I did."

"She's a friend of *yours?*"

"Yah. Lollie Friedman—that's her name—and I worked together in Charleston, up near Tombstone. First at Diamond Jack's Saloon and then at Heavenly Harry's. She's a singer and a dancer. A good one, but she's...." Bennie broke off.

"She's what?"

"Mrs. Morrie Goldson now."

He was sending her a message she refused to accept. "Where are they?" she asked, fixing her gaze on his.

"He went up to Charleston with her to pick up her things. They'll be back in a day or so."

"Minnie's mother is already on her way to Europe. We can't send Minnie back to San Francisco alone."

"I brought her down here to get married," Bennie said. "I'll find a husband for her."

He appeared cool, but he didn't know how unreasonable Minnie could get. "Is Mr. Nunes married?"

"I already asked him and he declined. He's a sick man, a lunger."

"Frieda." It was Minnie calling.

Frieda looked at Bennie, tears forming. "Poor Minnie."

"I know we'll be able to work something out."

"I'm afraid for her, Bennie. She's tired and overly excited. If she starts having a tantrum, she won't be able to stop."

"Let me handle..." Bennie started to say. But it was too late. Minnie was standing in the open doorway, smiling and refreshed in her newly ironed pink lawn dress with little white daisies on the bodice. She had added a wreath of artificial white daisies to her hair. "How do I look?" she cried, twirling her skirt.

Frieda hung on to Bennie's hand as he guided Minnie back through the open door, saying, "Minnie, dear, I have something to tell you."

CHAPTER FOUR

Devil's Highway

Dos Cacahuates, A.T.
March 29, 1880
Dear Family:
    I hope you received the short letter I sent you from Yuma. I apologize for not writing as soon as I arrived in Dos Cacahuates and hope I have not caused you concern. Once we left the train at Mohawk Station, our journey became considerably more arduous. Yet as you can see, we arrived intact and grateful to have been spared the harrowing conditions earlier pioneers, Bennie among them, endured when hostile Apaches and other outlaws ruled the roads, such as they were.

Frieda lay down her pen and rose to shut the front door. Several Mexican construction workers were heading for the store, and their voices resounded in the clearing. If the noise woke Minnie, who was taking a *siesta* (they were already calling the afternoon rest a siesta), the tri-weekly stage would arrive and depart once more without her letter.

Frieda rose to check on the small mound under the pile of *serapes* on the bed. When Bennie told her his brother had married during his absence, Minnie fainted and had been ailing ever since. Nothing agreed with her, not the food, not the climate, not the water, not the people. Frieda tried to lure her out of bed, but Minnie resisted except when she had to go to the outhouse, which she often did, since she was suffering from diarrhea. By the end of the first week, she lay inert, too weak to cry or complain.

Frieda leaned down to make to make sure Minnie was still breathing, then she returned to the table, eager to complete her letter home while her charge dozed.

> To my great surprise, dear family, my new home is more verdant than I had imagined desert land could be. We are situated in an oasis in the midst of the Sonoran Desert. Twenty feet from the store is a pond fed by an underground river and warmed by dripping hot springs. This time of year birds abound. They're migrating north for the summer and stop at the pond for rest and refreshment. Bird-watching is a popular pastime here. The locals have set up several bird feeders and watch these feathery sojourners the way reporters cover the comings and goings of prominent guests at elegant hotels. Orioles, doves, wild geese pass through daily, and yesterday a blue heron dropped in and caused quite a stir.

Frieda had tried to interest Minnie in the birds, to no avail. The only time Minnie perked up was when the stagecoach arrived, with, she kept hoping, a letter from her mother. Bennie begged her not to despair; he was searching for another bridegroom and was certain to find one worthy of her soon. But Minnie no longer wanted a husband; she wanted to go home.

> By the time you see Dos Cacahuates, the ordering efforts of man will have been added to the wondrous works of God, so let me describe my new home to you as I found it. A short distance to the west of the pond, which I have described, is Bennie and Morrie's general merchandise store, a frame building with living quarters in the rear. It's stocked with a wide assortment of merchandise for ranchers, farmers and miners, and their families. "Everything," says Bennie,

"from Earling Fig Laxative to buckboard wheels."
Next to the store is our house (temporarily), a one-
room adobe, formerly used as a trading post. During
Bennie's absence his brother Morrie and Yancy Nunes
(Mr. Nunes is vice president of International Improvement, but everyone is on a first-name basis
down here), assisted by Angelina and Ramón, the
maid-laundress and the handyman, whitewashed and
furnished it. Yancy lives in a tent just across the clearing. Another tent serves as the sales office until the
hotel is completed. The hotel site is on a plateau
above the clearing, alongside the dripping hot springs.
A Mexican construction crew lives and works up
there, and Angelina and Ramón have a small stick-
and-mud hut down beyond, opposite the store. Surrounding the settlement, as far as the eye can see, is
this vast desert plain....

"Frieda," Minnie cried, sitting up with a start.
"Frieda!"
"I'm here. Try to sleep a bit longer, dear," she urged.
Minnie let her thin body fall back against the pillow.

...of great beauty. Being here, one understands
why Colonel Leighton chose to develop this charming site as a gateway between nations. I haven't had a
chance to visit the Mexican town across the border
yet. It was formerly known as Cacahuate. The town
was settled by Padre Kino, who established missions in
northern Mexico in the late seventeenth century.
Bennie says there's supposed to be a buried treasure in
the mission here....

"Frieda—quick."
Frieda helped Minnie out of bed, found her a shawl, then
guided her to the outhouse between the store and what was
now known as Frieda and Bennie's. Minnie shuffled along

slowly, bent over and clinging to Frieda's arm.

"Don't go away," Minnie called, as the outhouse door closed behind her.

Frieda assured her she wouldn't.

"Are you still there?"

"I'm right here."

When they returned to the house, Frieda guided Minnie, still clutching her stomach, back to bed. "Try to relax, dear, you'll be all right."

Minnie heaved herself onto her side and pulled a serape up over her head. Frieda returned to her letter.

> Bennie's brother Morrie is drilling for water at their ranch, along an underground river. Several years ago, the territorial legislature passed something called the Desert Land Act, which entitles the finder of a steady supply of artesian water to a reward of $3,000 to $5,000. Morrie hopes to claim the reward and get a truck garden and citrus orchard going. Most of the fruits and vegetables we get now come in on the stagecoach from Tucson or Yuma or from across the line. I haven't had an opportunity to get to know Morrie yet. He spends much of his time out at the ranch. And when he's in Dos Cacahuates, we never seem to be in the same place at the same time.

Minnie refused to be within shouting distance of Morrie and his wife, and since she wouldn't allow Frieda out of sight, Frieda'd had little chance to get to know her brother- and sister-in-law, or anyone else in Dos Cacahuates. Bennie spent the first few nights in a bedroll alongside the double bed where Frieda and Minnie slept, then, in disgust, set up a tent a short distance from the house. They knew something had to be done, but what? Mrs. Cohn might be away for months. Frieda was afraid Minnie wouldn't last that long, and if she did, their marriage might not.

Lying awake at night, Frieda mulled over solutions. Ask

Minnie's father, who lived in Virginia City, Nevada, with his second wife and family, to come for her. Take her back to San Francisco and, if need be, stay with her until her mother returned. Write to Mrs. Cohn and apprise her of Minnie's plight. Bennie vetoed all of them. He was determined to preserve the good will of his investor and keep his promise to find Minnie a husband.

Dear ones, I almost forgot to tell you, Morrie had quite a surprise for us. Two days after we arrived, he got off a stagecoach with his own new Mrs. Goldson—the former Lollie Friedman. Her father is a prominent hardware merchant in Los Angeles. The only living quarters available for the newlyweds was a room in the back of the store, but no one heard a word of complaint from Lollie. She took a bolt of cloth from the shelf, found scissors, needle and thread, and whipped up a bedspread, tablecloth and curtains. In no time she claimed to be as "comfy as a coot."

Minnie had risen and was standing at her shoulder, peering down at the letter.

Frieda spread her hand over the paper and coolly said, "Minnie, dear, I can't write when you hang over me like that."

Minnie's face crumpled. "You wish I'd die and get it over with."

"That's not true, dear. But if I don't get this letter off to my family, they're going to send a search party out for me. Lie down for a few minutes, then I'll read to you."

Her tone was gentle, her gaze unyielding. Minnie slunk back to bed, leaving Frieda pen in hand, discarding unmentionable subjects until she hit on Yancy Nunes.

The unexpected abounds here in Dos Cacahuates. Not the least curious is seeing a tent flap draw back and Yancy Nunes step into view. One hardly need be told he is a Jewish gentleman of background and education. A southerner by birth, he also has family connections in Newport, Rhode Island, his mother's birthplace. Yancy was caught up north during the Civil War, when he was attending Harvard College, and there he remained for the duration, traveling between Cambridge and Newport, where his maternal grandfather, a spice merchant and lay rabbi, lived. He is one of the handsomest men I have ever seen, barring my own dear husband, who is an entirely different type. He is extremely tall, delicate-framed, with a long, slender face, huge brown eyes, a cap of long, straight, black hair and one of those luminously pale eastern complexions. But alas, the tragedy of this impressive figure is that he is very ill. Fortunately, his health has improved somewhat since he arrived. At present he is engaged in establishing a community newspaper. An old Washington hand press arrived on the stagecoach and he has been working on it, trying to get it into operation. He's going to call it the Dos Cacahuates *Selah*, which, according to Yancy, is a Hebrew word meaning a voice lifted in praise.

Speaking of praise, there is one more thing I must tell you. We are going to hold a Passover celebration right here in Dos Cacahuates. I mentioned to Bennie that the holiday was approaching; he told Yancy, and they began planning a *Seder*.

Not out of piety, Frieda soon discerned. Yancy was banking on the religious holiday to attract investors, make the camp appear larger, more civilized than it was, and maybe even draw a bachelor or two for Minnie.

We sent out invitations and have already received acceptances. It is heartening to see how our people stay in touch in the Territory.

All in all, Dos Cacahuates is more and less than I

had imagined. I can't deny we have all the inconveniences of any infant community, but they seem minor when one feels one is serving Mankind. My love to you, dear family, and to all the boarders.

Yours for a Better World,
Frieda

P.S. If you speak to someone who would like to invest in the most promising townbuilding venture in the Arizona Territory, tell them to write to Mr. Yancy Nunes, Vice President, International Improvement Company, Dos Cacahuates, A. T.

The letter sealed in its envelope, Frieda turned to Minnie with a cheery, "Now, let's...."

Minnie was on her knees alongside the bed. Her tiny brown face was green, her brown eyes were rolled back in terror and the nostrils of her thin nose fluttered. Her hand was planted under her left breast. In one quick step, Frieda was at her side.

"Come, let me help you up," Frieda said softly. "We'll go outside, get a little air." Step by step, Minnie allowed herself to be drawn into the yard.

"If I do die here, Frieda," Minnie said, straining to get the words out of her pulsing throat, "promise me you'll see that my body gets back to San Francisco."

She had heard about the bleached bones of fallen travelers strewn over *Camino del Diablo*, Devil's Highway, that ran behind the Goldsons' store. She was afraid she, too, was going to die in the desert and be left there to be picked clean by buzzards and yowled over by coyotes.

"You're not going to die here, or be abandoned. Bennie is going to find you a nice husband."

"I don't want a husband. I want my mother," Minnie whimpered.

CHAPTER FIVE

Seder Songs

ON THE MORNING of April 1, Frieda helped Minnie dress and led her to the sales office tent, purportedly to help Yancy Nunes with the company's bookkeeping. Disregarding Minnie's wary expression, Yancy took her arm and guided her to a chair alongside his at a paper-strewn oak desk. Flipping open an accounts book, Frieda heard him tell Minnie, "I've been told you're admirably well-trained in business practices. I've fallen shamefully behind in my bookkeeping, and would be everlastingly indebted to you if you could...." As he spoke, behind Minnie's chair he energetically signaled to Frieda to leave.

Side-by-side at a counter at Goldson Brothers General Merchandise, Frieda and Lollie composed a menu, then summoned Angelina and Ramón to determine which of the ingredients were locally available, which they could send for and which they would have to do without. Away from Minnie, and in the company of her sister-in-law, Frieda's spirits rose. Billowing blonde hair, jaunty step, flashing smile, alert, green eyes, Lollie fairly crackled with vitality. At Levie's Kosher Boardinghouse, Seder preparations were laborious, painstaking, exhausting. With Lollie, it was like planning a grand ball—guests, food, attire, music, entertainment.

They started to cook on Tuesday morning. Ramón and Angelina built a Mexican stove outdoors—a ring of rocks covered with an iron grate, and on the grate they set an army-size pot Bennie bought from a cook at Fort Yuma. Morrie put on a *yarmulke* and went to Ramón's chicken coop, new butcher knife in hand. One by one, he dragged out five chickens and, reciting the appropriate blessing, slit

44

each of their throats, then turned the chickens over to Ramón and Angelina for plucking and cleaning.

The sisters-in-law, wearing calico housedresses, their hair bound in cloths, began preparing the *gefilte* fish in Frieda and Bennie's makeshift kitchen. As they worked, they exchanged life stories.

"I'm the youngest of six girls," Lollie began. "Poor Papa. More daughters, more trouble."

Frieda nodded. "I know what you mean. I'm the oldest of three daughters and a son."

"Papa was so fed up when I arrived, he wanted to drown me in the Los Angeles River, but it was dry."

"When's your birthday?" Frieda asked.

"All Hallow's Eve, 1858. Fonsie, my family's Irish cook, says I'm a Jewish witch."

"Then I must be a Jewish leprechaun. I was born on St. Patrick's Day, the same year," Frieda said.

"Sure and begorra, a wee bit of Irish is all to the good, especially when it comes to high jinks," Lollie said, heeling and toeing a jig.

"Bennie told me you're a singer and dancer."

"To the Friedman family's disgust. I was raised on 'Stop prancing around like a circus horse!' and 'Stop yowling like an alley cat!'"

"Families," Frieda said with a sigh.

Lollie shrugged, uncaring. "The Turnverein Hall was around the corner, and I started slipping over there to watch the performers rehearse. By the time I was twelve, I was filling in for actors who were sick or off on a toot."

Frieda rested her chopping knife against the bowl and shot Lollie a questioning look. "Your father didn't object?"

"That's why I ran off with Emil Pride."

"You ran off with Emil Pride?"

"No, silly. With the Emil Pride Troupe."

"Just like that?"

"Just like that. I rolled up a few dresses, climbed out of the bedroom window and left on the company's stagecoach."

"What did your father do?"

"He tracked us to Yuma, but I raised such a fuss, he decided to let me stay."

"And you were able to support yourself as a performer?"

"That, and a few other things," Lollie said.

What things? Frieda wondered. *Lollie'd been driven out of Charleston. By whom? Why?*

"Bennie told me you and Morrie met in Tucson."

Lollie chopped vigorously, her eyelids fluttering. "The dumbest of dumb luck. He's the sweetest, most appreciative man I've ever known. A perfect match for me."

Strange, Frieda thought, *those two didn't seem to have a thing in common.*

By late afternoon on Wednesday, eleven guests had arrived. Alf Kredel, a prospector who had a small mine in the Ben Nevis Mountains near Quijotoa, brought mining investors from San Francisco, Sam Schwartz and Henry Label, both men in their fifties. Abe Beisel, who ran a freight line between Guaymas and Tucson, came with his nineteen-year-old son Irving, and an old peddler named Finklestein they'd picked up along the way. Sadie and Ike Silverstein, proprietors of a general store and a boardinghouse in Gunsight, pulled in a few minutes after Beisel. The last to arrive were Don Herman Rosán and his three sons, Umberto, Ernesto and Panchito, ages nine, seven and six. The Goldson brothers came to the Arizona Territory in 1863 with Herman, their second cousin. Seven years later, Herman married a Mexican woman named Rosita Suarez and moved to Hermosillo in Sonora, Mexico. The most Jewish thing about Herman now were his cousins, Bennie and Morrie.

At four-thirty, Yancy invited the guests to the sales office tent, where, with the help of maps and renderings, he and Bennie explained their ambitious plans for the development of an international community and two short line railroads linking the west coast of Mexico to the Southern Pacific Railroad and, in so doing, to the west coast of the United States.

Next they showed off the townsite, marked with sticks and string in the chaparral. Then they marched the visitors up the steep path to the bluff where a small, red brick hotel was in construction. There they pointed out the adjacent hot springs, the fifty-mile-wide view of mostly untouched desert, and below on the flat, the Garden of Eden oasis, where under the cottonwoods and willows alongside the pond stood cloth-covered tables and chairs for the Seder guests.

At five o'clock, Frieda arranged on the main table the ceremonial objects her parents had given her as wedding presents. The heavy old silver summoned images of holidays at home, moving Frieda to tears. Yancy must have been similarly touched. As meticulous as a high priest, he began ticking off the pieces: "Candlesticks, Kiddush Cup, Elijah's Cup, Seder Plate." That done, he picked up the sole Haggadah and rehearsed a few lines. Frieda listened, heart pounding at the sound of his impeccable Hebrew and mellifluous chant.

As the sun set, Dos Cacahuatans and their guests clamored to the tables. Once there, they fell into an uneasy silence. *Had something gone wrong?* Frieda wondered. *Or like her, were they just nervous?*

She'd enjoyed the preparations; they were festive, high-spirited. But as she and Minnie walked out of the house in their best dresses, skirts held up out of the sand, Frieda shook with self-doubt. Would the others see her as a presumptuous San Francisco girl trying to herd strays back into the corral? Or accustomed to a more traditional Seder, would they be offended by their ceremonial compromises—tortillas for matzah; chiles for bitter herbs; wine sanctified, not by a rabbi, but by the Brothers of the Holy Cross.

The other locals were also showing signs of strain. Excited by the presence of so many brethren, Bennie kept jumping out of his chair to tell another joke, or deliver one more *abrazo*. Eyes lowered, hands folded, Lollie looked like a six-year-old threatened with a whipping should she misbehave. Twitching and trembling, Minnie clung to Frieda until, desperate to get on with her duties, she pressed her charge into a seat alongside Yancy. Morrie, his dream of Jewish community realized, albeit momentarily, gazed around in disbelief. If nothing else, the setting was tranquil and reassuring. The falling sun had tinted the surrounding mountains and nearby hills to soft pinks, and glazed the pond so it looked like rose-colored glass.

Assuming a patriarchal stance and tone, Yancy began the service. At his request, Frieda recited the blessing over the candles, then shyly retreated to her place alongside Bennie. Eyes half lowered, she surveyed the diverse gathering. All the men had dug up yarmulkes from somewhere, except Don Herman, who covered his head with a handkerchief, while his Catholic sons, wearing gold crosses at their throats, sat bareheaded. The Mexican construction crew, seated slightly apart, were also hatless.

Yancy cleared his throat, placed the Haggadah in the circle of the candlelight and read in Hebrew, then translated the passages into English and Spanish. When he completed the blessing over the wine in three languages, they drank, some decorously, others thirstily. At that point, Frieda offered Yancy a basin of water for the next ritual: the washing of the hands. A light wave of conversation erupted. Yancy called for order and began the blessing over the *karpas*, the parsley, symbolizing the first fruits. In its wake, Yancy slipped into his own eulogy of spring in a new land. To make this desert bloom with new life and activity, he told the assembled, was a sacred undertaking.

"Grow the parsley out here, Nunes?" called spry, hairy Alf Kredel.

Impatient with the interruption, Yancy ignored Kredel and raised his hand, a tortilla resting on the palm: *"Ha lachem aneeya dee ahloo avatanu b'orra d'metzrayem."* He continued several more sentences in Hebrew, then translated into English. "Behold this is the bread of affliction which our ancestors ate in the land of Egypt. Let all who are hungry come eat. Let all who are in need come celebrate the Passover. *Mira, este es el pan de aflicción,*" he translated into Spanish.

"Bread of affliction is a good name for it," Abe Beisel called out. "Especially when you got nothing to go with it. But it ain't half bad with some beans and a little chile." Beisel spoke in a comical singsong, more Mexican than Yiddish. A rush of comments went up concerning the best way to eat tortillas. When the platter was passed for the Blessing Over the Matzah, most of the guests seized a whole tortilla or two and stuffed them in their mouths, their eyes shifting away from Yancy and toward the cook fires where large pots steamed forth the unaccustomed fragrance of gefilte fish and chicken soup. Frieda overheard Don Herman describing the tasty concoctions to his sons, promising they would soon taste real Jewish food.

Yancy persisted. "The *Ma Nistanah*, the four questions, comes next. Will the youngest guest come forward?"

Don Herman shepherded Panchito, the smallest of his sons, to Yancy's side.

"*Por qué distinta esta noche de los demás de las noches?*" Yancy read, his hand resting paternally on the boy's thin shoulder. His lisping archaic Spanish evoked a look of curious amusement from the boy.

"*Porqué,*" Don Herman called out, "*esta noche comemos con la gente de su Papá, y no con la gente de su Mamá.*"

Laughter broke out at the Spanish-speaking end of the table. Don Herman translated for the others. "I explained to my son that this night was different because he is eating with his father's people, not his mother's."

When the rest of the table quieted, the grinning Panchito repeated Yancy's words aping his accent, evoking more chuckles. A natural comic, Panchito turned to the leader for more lines.

So it's innocent merriment they want, Frieda could all but hear Yancy say to himself. He fed the boy the rest of the questions and stood by relaxed as Panchito experimented with dialect and gestures. When the Ma Nistanah was completed, Yancy decided it was time to eat.

"You forgot the bitter herb," Schwartz called.

"No, we haven't," Frieda cried, seizing the platter of yellow chile and passing it around the table, while Yancy accounted for the substitution. The bitter herb, he explained, was included in the ceremony to heat the mouth and bring tears to the eyes reminding Jews of the tears shed by the Hebrew slaves in Egypt. "The yellow chile," Yancy guaranteed, "would do the job just as well."

Frieda went to help Ramón and Angelina serve the meal, while Lollie started, "*Dayenu*," the most popular of the Seder songs. She sang slowly, enunciating the words, then began again, urging the others to join in. By the time she got to the second refrain, the group was chorusing and clapping happily. "*Di-di-a-nu, di-di-a-nu, di-di-a-nu, di-a-nu, di-a-nu.*" Face aglow, Lollie strolled behind the guests, bending in close, drawing back, repeating the words, clapping in time to the melody. Even the members of the construction crew overcame their shyness and joined in.

Yancy sang along, noticeably relieved that the burden of the ceremony had been lifted from his thin shoulders. Champagne suddenly appeared on the table, compliments of Abe Beisel, who had amassed a cellar-full during his Guaymas days. "Let all those who are thirsty come drink," invited the freighter. No longer waiting to bless each sip, the bottles moved quickly around the table as glasses were filled and refilled. Even Minnie, sitting between Nunes and Alf Kredel, emptied several glasses of the bubbling wine. Giggling like a thirteen-year-old, she slid first against Yancy, then against Alf. In a gallant mood, the miner took Minnie's hand and lamented that he had a wife back east. Minnie rolled her eyes flirtatiously, feigning regret. Then Alf thought of a prospector in Quijotoa with a real eye for ore who was looking for a wife.

Yancy leaned in front of Minnie to say, "Tell him she's not only the prettiest single Jewish girl in Dos Cacahuates, she's a first-rate bookkeeper and a clever letter writer."

About the meal, all agreed. The fare was the finest Jewish food they'd ever eaten in the Arizona Territory. The gelfite fish, matzah ball soup, roast chicken, potato pudding, carrot and prune tzimes, applesauce, compote were all superb. Toasts went up to each of the Mrs. Goldsons. Boulder-broad, rock-strong, leather-tough Sadie Silverstein, an oldtimer in the Territory, welcomed the newcomers. "These two are going to keep everyone on their toes."

As the plates were cleared away and the wine glasses refilled, Lollie jumped to her feet to start "*Had Gadyo*," another Passover favorite. As they wound down on the Hebrew version, Yancy remembered the words in Spanish and went to teach them to the Rosán boys. "*Un chivito, un chivito, mi padrecito compró un chivito....*"

Then Abe Beisel had a request—a song Lollie used to do in Tombstone and Charleston—"None Can Love Like An Irishman." Lollie begged off; she wasn't doing that kind of thing anymore.

"You ain't seen nothing 'til you see Lollie sing that song," Abe persisted.

Ike Silverstein rose to assist Abe. Each taking an elbow, they pulled Lollie to the head of the table. The campfire blazing behind her and the moon lighting her face, Lollie gave a helpless shrug, then undid her apron, cast it aside with an abandoned gesture, crying, "If I'm going to do it, I might as well do it right."

She lifted her skirts and skipped to a spot closer to the table. A hand reached back and undid the ribbon restraining her blond hair. Ruffling her mane, she dropped her head for a moment. When her chin came up again a light radiated from her green eyes, her teeth flashed in a roguish smile, her head tilted back at a bold, provocative angle and she began to sing.

The turbaned Turk, who scorns the world
May strut around with his whiskers curled
Keep a hundred wives under lock and key
For nobody else but himself to see
Yet long may he pray with the Alcoran
Before he can love like an Irishman.

For almost an hour the group kept Lollie onstage with cheers and wild applause. She sang, danced, recited, played both parts in a scene from *Rosie's Last Stand*. She even did some acrobatic tricks, her arms and legs flying, revealing, to Frieda's astonishment, her stockinged limbs, her petticoats, even her underdrawers. Frieda looked over to see how the Goldson brothers were taking the display. Bennie was as raucous as the rest; he clapped, chanted and shouted for more. Morrie sat, eyes lowered, clearly embarrassed by his wife's immodest performance.

When Lollie finally slid into her seat exhausted and perspiring, others took over. Don Herman recited, with arms flailing, "Oda a la Libertad." Then the Mexican construction workers tuned up a couple of guitars and sang a lengthy medley of songs—"La Paloma," "Cielito Lindo," and "El Abandonado."

The air was still mild at almost eleven o'clock. The Rosán boys were falling asleep in their chairs; the youngest, Panchito, was whimpering for his mama. One by one, their father lifted each of them and carried them off to their bedrolls, recalling on one trip that the same had been done for him until he was old enough for his *bar mitzvah*. Minnie, too, had fallen asleep and had to be led to bed by Frieda. Sadie wanted to help put away the food, but Frieda insisted she was a guest.

The older woman eyed Frieda. "If I know anything about a cook's legs, yours feel like two hot lead pipes by now. Be sure you get your sister-in-law to help."

"Oh, Lollie'll do her share," Frieda assured her, "soon as she catches her breath."

"I hope you're right," Sadie replied, starting toward the tents. "When you get up at five, it's hard to stay awake after dark."

After the tables were cleared, the men sat talking about the new twin towns, the hotel, the railroad. Soon a deck of cards appeared.

Gambling on a religious holiday? She didn't want to be like her father, a fanatical defender of the old faith in a new land. But some lines had to be drawn, some laws obeyed. Or did they?

A bird call struck Frieda's ear. She listened as it sounded again. The calls of the owl, dove and hawk were already familiar to her, but the sound that cut the night air was one she'd never heard before. The yowl of a coyote joined the bird in a duet. Frieda shivered and hurried back to her house to get a shawl.

Once there, Frieda gazed longingly at the place waiting for her alongside her snoring friend. Sadie was right, her legs did ache, from hip to toe. Lollie had to be worn out too. The poor thing must have been too exhausted to say good night. Water and towels for Sadie, then she'd slip away too.

The candle was out. Frieda entered the dark tent, calling the woman's name. Sadie was on the cot. She reached up and put her hand to Frieda's lips.

"Shush," she ordered. "Listen to this."

Frieda dropped to the edge of the cot. A man's voice wafted through the dark from somewhere behind the tent.

"You didn't recognize me?"

"Not until you did your bird call, you crazy Irishman," came the reply.

Lollie. Frieda rose, but Sadie pulled her down.

"Oh Sweetheart," Lollie crooned, "I thought I'd never ever see you again."

"Why did you marry him, Loll?"

"I hoped it would put an end to us." Lollie's tone was plaintive, regretful.

"Not as long as we're both alive." There was a full silence, followed by gasps and sighs.

"I missed you so," Lollie said.

"And I you. I need you, Loll. Where can we be alone?"

"On the other side of the pond. But not tonight, it's a Jewish holiday."

"All the more reason."

Lollie laughed. Another prolonged silence followed, punctuated by more sighs and groans.

"It's Passover, right?"

"Yes."

"Then let's you and me pass over to the other side of the pond."

"But I'm married to...."

"I don't care who you're married to, Loll, you belong to me."

"I know it, may God help me, but Morrie...."

"Please, Loll. I love you so."

"And I love you."

"Let me hold you, darlin'."

After another silence, Lollie said, "I can't think straight when you kiss me like that."

"Come on, show me the way."

"I can't."

"Yes, you can."

They were kissing again.

Staring at the canvas wall, Frieda listened to the pair moving off through the Mexican hay. When she looked down at Sadie, she found the woman's eyes were fixed on her, appraising her response.

"How could she?" Frieda asked.

"Things happen out here. All kinds of things."

"I admired her free spirit," Frieda said.

A sly smile stretched across Sadie's dry lips, but she remained silent. Frieda waited, searching the tanned, wrinkled face and sharp blue eyes for a clue. Finally, the older woman offered one.

"Sometimes, being free one place only means that you're tied up somewhere else."

CHAPTER SIX

Out of the Sandstorm

THE DAY AFTER the last of the Passover guests had left, a sandstorm rose in the valley and swirled down on Dos Cacahuates. The grit-laden wind threw over the tents set up for the guests, turned over barrels and boxes, knocked dry branches off the cottonwoods and willows, swept sand through unsealed windows, uneven door jambs and chinks in the adobe walls.

The disturbance quickly separated the able-bodied from the ailing. Morrie rode his horse out to the ranch to reinforce the covers on the excavations for the new artesian wells. His wife, Lollie, stationed herself in the store, shielding the merchandise with tarpaulins, dispensing supplies and preparing food from the shelves for the crew battling to keep intact the newly divided townsite and the just-begun hotel. Bennie was everywhere, up on the construction site, in the corral with the animals, off to give Morrie a hand. Yancy holed up in his tent where, as he put it, he could hide his uselessness and cough his fool head off. Minnie started the day with a pounding headache and a sick stomach and by three o'clock had added to her infirmities a racking cough, sore throat, shortness of breath, smarting eyes, a rash and the galloping fear that the howling winds and the banging shutters were driving her mad.

And me with her, thought Frieda, who was once again locked in with Minnie around the clock. Oilcloth nailed over the windows, rags stuffed around the door frame, the one-room dwelling was as dark as the chicken coop at the boardinghouse and, after the outhouse blew down, smellier. Also more oppressive. Give the chickens food and water, gather their eggs, and Frieda had been finished. Minnie kept at her day and night, her thin, weepy voice cutting into her like wire restraints. Unvented, Frieda's irritation exploded in violent images: *throw her outside and bolt the door; take her to Bennie (bringing Minnie was his idea); tie rags over her mouth; threaten to shoot her. Shoot her.* Ashamed of her unloving impulses, Frieda hovered over her charge, cooing reassurances, offering tea for her raw throat, cool cloths for her aching head, cough tonic and more cough tonic until Minnie, lulled by the opium-laced medicine, slept. During these respites, Frieda tidied the house, washed clothes, prepared meals and brooded over her interrupted marriage.

On the morning of the third day, the winds calmed and the sand settled on the rearranged landscape. *Peaceful as a baby sleeping off a temper tantrum*, Frieda thought, gazing out the window. After Minnie was bathed, breakfasted, medicated and dozing, Frieda tied a cloth over her hair, seized a broom and swept the mud floor. She was in the front yard shaking out a red and black Navajo rug and taking in the soft, sweet air, when she heard Bennie shouting her name.

Turning, she peered across the sunlit clearing. Her husband was rushing toward her, red-eyed, stubble-faced, excited. *What now?* Frieda wondered, as she went to meet him, rug over her arm.

"Where's Minnie?" he called.

Without so much as a hello for her? "Minnie's inside. Why?"

"Miner's here and wants to meet her."

"Who's Miner?"

"A suitor. He came a long way."

"In a sandstorm? Where'd he come from?"

"Up near Quijotoa. Alf Kredel told him we brought Minnie from San Francisco for Morrie, but it didn't work out, and she's up for grabs."

"Up for grabs? Is that what Kredel told him?"

"More or less. Go get her."

"Not so fast, Bennie. Who is he?" She may want to kill Minnie, but she didn't want to hurt her.

"He's been in the Territory for years. I've run into him in Clifton, Globe, Tubac. I had no idea he was in Quijotoa."

"What does he do?"

"He's in mining."

"And his name is Miner?" Frieda eyed the open door, went to close it, then returned to say, "Sounds like a made-up name to me."

"It is made-up. Mendel's his first name, and he has a long last name no one can pronounce, so folks started calling him Mendel Miner. Go get her."

"A man with a made-up name travels nearly eighty miles in a blinding sandstorm to meet Minnie? What's his hurry?"

"The Arizona Territory is not exactly crawling with single Jewish girls from well-to-do San Francisco families. Get her, or shall I?"

"She's asleep."

"Wake her. He's a bona fide suitor. Alf told him Minnie can read and write English and keep books."

"Can't he read and write English?"

"Truth is he can't. But that doesn't mean he's not smart. He's got a nose for ore and that makes him a big man in these parts. He needs a wife who can help out with the reading and writing."

"And a little capital?" Frieda guessed out loud.

"Capital never hurts," Bennie said.

"Three thousand from Mrs. Cohn, how much from Mr. Miner?"

"I'm hoping for a thousand or so, but we haven't got to it yet. Dos Cacahuates is a good investment; Mendel will want to get in on it."

"He doesn't sound like a match for Rosamund Cohn's daughter."

"I think he's a perfect match. I wouldn't introduce them if I didn't. I'm counting on Mrs. Cohn."

For more capital and other investors, Frieda knew.

"Get her, sweetheart. I told him I'd be right back."

Frieda threw the rug on the doorstep. "I want to have a look at him first."

"You won't take my word, huh? Come on, he's in the store." He grabbed her arm and started toward the Goldson Brothers.

She drew back, pulling the cloth from her head and smoothing her hair. "I can't go looking like this."

"He came to meet Minnie, not you."

"I won't be introduced to anyone, not even an illiterate miner, looking like a char woman."

Bennie thought for a moment. "Have a peek at him through the store window."

One foot in Bennie's cupped hands, the other braced against the side of the frame building, Frieda peered through the murky glass, then signaled to be lowered.

"What's wrong?" Bennie called as she started back across the clearing.

"I'm not getting Minnie out of bed to meet the likes of him." Her tone was adamant, bitter, to her ears, shockingly bitter.

"All right, be stubborn and spend the rest of your married life sleeping with your poor, little, coughing, complaining friend." He started back toward the store.

Frieda whipped around and followed him. "She's not my choice as a bedmate, Bennie, but she has feelings and, when she's not scared out of her wits, some sense too."

His face tightened with anger. "That's my bed you two are sleeping in, and I want it back."

Their gazes locked. She'd never seen Bennie as riled. He scared her, but she spoke her mind.

"You met her mother, you saw how they live, how could you think of introducing Minnie to that filthy creature?"

"He has two days traveling dirt on him. Cleaned up, he's a nice-looking fella, and doing better than most in these parts."

"Where's he from?" Frieda thought to ask. "If he's from Germany, Mrs. Cohn might consider him."

"From one of those Balkan places."

"Are you sure he's Jewish?"

"He says he is and—." Bennie stopped.

"What?"

"He's circumcised. I'm telling you, he's a decent fella. Doesn't drink, smoke, gamble or chase women." He moved closer. Their chests touching, he put an arm around her shoulder, lifted her chin and lamented, "Married three weeks and no more than a few stolen hours together. What kind of marriage is that?"

I warned you Minnie wasn't for pioneering, Frieda thought. What she said was, "Push her too hard and she'll throw a tizzy."

"Don't I know it. Now go get her." Bennie slid his hand from her shoulder to her waist, down to her backside.

"If she doesn't like him, he'll hear about it, and so will we, forever and ever."

"She'll like him. When I get through with him he'll look like the Prince of Wales."

"Bennie, the magician." Her tone mocked, but the expression in her blue eyes was amused, conspiratorial.

He winked, started off, then whirled around, as if he'd forgotten something. Seizing Frieda's hand, he pulled her to him and pressed a long, hard kiss on her upturned mouth. Drawing back, he whispered, "When am I going to have you to myself again?"

"Before we're old and creaky?" She caressed his stubbled cheek, saying, "Let's see if I can get Princess Minnie up and presentable."

The princess did not want to get up. Her chest felt as if it'd been stepped on by a heavy boot.

"Alf Kredel praised you to the skies," Frieda coaxed. "His friend can hardly wait to meet you."

Minnie remembered Mr. Kredel. "He was terribly fresh.

He put his hand on my knee. When I reminded him he was a married man, he said his wife was too far away to know or care."

"This man is single and eager to marry."

"I'm not going to get out of a sick bed to meet an absolute stranger."

"He's not a stranger," Frieda said. "Bennie and Morrie have known him for years."

At the mention of Morrie's name, Minnie winced. "Haven't you and Bennie humiliated me enough, Frieda?"

"We're doing our best to make amends, dear."

Minnie pulled herself to a sitting position and, tossing her head, announced, "I don't need your help. I've found the man of my dreams."

"You have? Who?"

"Yancy Nunes."

"He's very sick, Minnie."

"I've never met anyone like him. He's not only an enterprising businessman, he's a journalist, scholar and a poet. Alone and ill, he needs someone, Frieda."

"Be sensible, Minnie, he won't marry you. And your mother won't let you stay in Dos Cacahuates unmarried."

"My mother is off in Europe having a wonderful time, and I'm here on the Devil's Highway disdained by everyone except Yancy."

"He appreciates your help in the office, Minnie, but he can't look after you. He's dedicating what little strength he has to building Dos Cacahuates."

"And I'm dedicating myself to helping him."

"How?"

"Writing his letters, keeping his books. Yancy was amazed at how fast I caught on. He says I'm a woman of remarkable abilities."

"Mendel Miner thinks—."

"Mendel Miner? What kind of name is that?" Her words were stiff with scorn.

"What kind of name is Yancy Nunes?"

"Southern and Sephardic. It's very aristocratic."

"That's exactly what Mr. Miner said about your name. He told Bennie it echoed in his ears all the way from Quijotoa: Minerva, a Greek goddess; Cohn, of priestly lineage."

Minnie sat up. "I don't believe you."

"I wouldn't lie to you. You're my best friend."

"Admit it, Frieda, you hate me."

"I've spent my honeymoon looking after you. What more could I do to prove I care for you?"

"You're interested in my mother's money. You can't stand me."

"I think it's the other way around. Why else would you refuse to grant me a tiny favor any well-bred houseguest would be pleased to do for her hostess?"

Minnie folded her arms against her chest, wriggled her rear-end into the mattress and studied the wall.

Dire threats? Physical force? Trickery. "The man says he won't leave Dos Cacahuates until he sees you. Come meet him, say you're sick and excuse yourself. Bennie will tell him someone else has claimed your affection, and he'll be on his way."

Exasperated, Minnie threw herself against the pillow. "All right, but only for a minute."

Frieda rushed for a wash basin and a hair brush.

Grains of sand coated Minnie's scalp and dotted her wiry, black hair. Unable to tame the tangled mass with its owner fighting each brush stroke, Frieda resorted to a long braid wrapped around her head like a coronet. As she eased Minnie's pink dress over her newly arranged hair, Minnie thought to ask, "What's he look like?"

"I haven't seen him yet."

"I like tall, fine-boned, dark-haired men like Yancy, with melancholy brown eyes."

"A tall man makes a woman feel small and insignificant," Frieda responded. She preferred a man closer to her own size so she didn't always have to look up at him.

Minnie stood pat. Tall, slender, dark-haired, with pale, pale skin.

Frieda favored fair- or red-haired men like Bennie with a healthy, masculine look. In the selection of a mate, health was the most important of all attributes—particularly if one hoped to have children. And what was a marriage without children? Besides, a woman with a sick husband or sweetheart had to be exceedingly strong herself.

"You may be right," Minnie said, "but the heart beats so loud the head can't reason."

Frieda smoothed down a stray strand of Minnie's hair, then stepped back to appraise her handiwork. "You're absolutely regal, Minnie. Look at yourself." She gave her a small hand mirror.

Minnie squinted at the glass, nodding approval and testing a smile. As a final touch, Frieda bounced a powder puff over Minnie's face, then took her elbow and guided her toward the door. As they stepped out into the light, Minnie balked.

"I'm just doing you a favor. Don't get your hopes up," Minnie said, voice atremble.

Frieda was having second thoughts herself. Doll up a friend like a mail-order bride for the inspection of a woman-hungry illiterate? What had possessed her? She was about to suggest they wait inside for Bennie to come get them when she looked across the clearing and spotted her husband and a man dressed in a bright blue suit and white shirt coming toward them. "There they are," Frieda whispered, jerking her head at the pair.

Tightening her hold on Frieda's arm, Minnie narrowed her myopic eyes and croaked, "Where?"

"There," Frieda said, starting to walk toward the advancing men.

Minnie wouldn't budge. "I feel sick. I've got to lie down. Take me back to the house."

"Lean on me, and *move*. You don't want him to think I'm dragging you."

"I don't care what he thinks. Yancy needs me."

"To hell with Yancy. Mr. Miner wants a wife."

"I don't want a husband."

"Yes you do. You're just nervous," Frieda said as she and her barely ambulatory friend inched along.

The four met alongside a red wheelbarrow in the middle of the clearing. Frieda stared at Miner, then turned to Bennie in disbelief. He responded with a self-satisfied grin. Mendel Miner looked like a prince, if not of Wales, then of the Balkans, and now of the Arizona Territory. His newly washed hair was blonde and wavy; his freshly-shaven face, smooth and high-colored; his eyes, alert and slate blue (like his suit); his nose, straight, short and well-shaped; and his mouth and teeth neither added nor detracted to his otherwise pleasing countenance.

No less astonishing was his response to Minnie. He was examining her feature by feature, as if she were a pedigreed animal, a rare work of art, or a precious metal. Then he stepped back, and holding up his hands, framed her like a portrait painter fitting his subject into the landscape. After several moments, or was it minutes, he came toward her with the singleness of purpose of a person who spends most of his time alone and rarely consults others before making up his mind.

Standing toe-to-toe, he took her right hand in both of his, lifted it to his lips and pressed on it a long, reverent kiss. Then releasing her hand, he stepped back and sought her eyes. Without a word, he seemed to be pledging his adulation and pleading for hers. The intensity of Mr. Miner's attraction mesmerized Frieda. When she recovered sufficiently to check, she noted that Bennie (mouth agape) and Minnie (eyes wide, hand clamped to her braided crown) were equally enthralled. Especially Minnie. She looked as if the power of the man's gaze was about to lift her off her feet and carry her away. When Frieda put a reassuring arm around her quivering shoulders, Minnie, without a word or glance, shrugged it off. Her eyes stayed fixed on her suitor's, and his on hers, even as he whispered in Bennie's ear.

"Mr. Miner wants me to tell you, you are so beautiful, he can barely speak," Bennie told Minnie.

When his spokesman was finished, Miner explained. "Excuse, excuse please, no good Angleesh." Placing his right hand on the left side of his chest, he added, "Heart speak good."

Minnie batted her eyelids, curled her lips in a coy smile, fanned her burning cheeks, then studied the effects of those flirtatious gestures on her swain.

Judging from his next act, he took them to mean she was as pleased with him as he was with her. "We talk over dair," he said, offering her his arm. With his free hand he pointed to the cottonwood-shaded pond, west of the store.

Frieda watched them go, her heart pounding at having witnessed—participated in—a phenomenon she'd read of, but had never seen: love at first sight. Or was it, Frieda wondered as she watched the pair disappear into the cottonwoods, a remarkably effective ploy to ensnare a wealthy, love-starved neurasthenic? What did Bennie think?

Bennie thought Mendel was the answer to their prayers. For now, maybe for good. Head bent so their cheeks touched, he wrapped his arms around Frieda and rushed her toward the flaking adobe. When she cast a concerned look over her shoulder, he dismissed her fears. "They've got their business to attend to, and we've got ours."

Later that night, as the women settled in bed, Minnie reported that Mendel had two silver mines in full operation and had just hit a rich new vein in Quijotoa. He'd shown her a clipping about it from the Tucson *Daily Citizen*.

"Mendel says all he needs now is a smart American wife to work with him." She paused to reflect. "It's extraordinary, Frieda. I remind him of his mother, and he reminds me of my father."

Leopold Cohn was in mining too, Frieda remembered. Also, that he'd abandoned Rosamund for his French mistress when Minnie was three.

"Mendel's not only gifted, he's ambitious. He's going to be a lot richer than my father ever was. Best of all, he's crazy about me, Frieda. He is, he really is."

"I know, Minnie. He couldn't take his eyes off you."

There was just enough light in the small, adobe-walled room for Frieda to make out Minnie's face. Her head was tilted toward the ceiling, her eyes, closed and her mouth open. She looked like she was in pain, but she wasn't. She was ecstatic. In the five years they'd known each other, Frieda had never seen Minnie look genuinely happy before. The closest she'd witnessed was a spiteful pleasure in someone else's misery. Frieda squeezed her hand.

"He asked me to marry him," was Minnie's response.

"What did you say?"

"I don't know. Mendel said I said yes."

Three days later, the tri-weekly stagecoach appeared with Yermo at the reins. While waiting for the stage, Mendel drew up plans for their marriage and honeymoon. When they reached Tucson he'd rent one room for Minnie and another for himself at the Cosmopolitan Hotel, then speak to Sam Drachman, the local lay rabbi, about arranging a first-class Jewish wedding with Jewish guests, Jewish food and Jewish music. After the wedding, he'd hire a carriage and they'd travel to Quijotoa, Globe and Phoenix to put his business affairs in order before they boarded the Southern Pacific for San Francisco where they'd honeymoon in the Cohn mansion and be on hand to greet Mrs. Cohn upon her return.

When Yermo was in his seat, Minnie bestowed on Frieda a perfunctory embrace, then dismissing Dos Cacahuates and its inhabitants with a sweep of her hand, she allowed her fiancé to help her board. Frieda watched the stagecoach roll off, Minnie's head nestled against Mendel's bright blue shoulder. Clouds of dust rising behind it, the departing vehicle looked like the last picture in a book of fairy tales. *Dear God, let them be happy ever after,* she prayed.

Us too, she added, when Bennie sprang at her like a bridegroom let out of quarantine.

CHAPTER SEVEN
Was She Happy?

FOR THE NEXT THREE days Bennie and Frieda honey-mooned. They made love, slept, ate, bathed in the hot springs (she in her petticoat at midnight), strolled, nuzzled, exchanged memories, made love, slept, ate. Her husband's sole request was that she allow him to delight in her company. It was like being emancipated from slavery and enthroned by a single proclamation. Was she cold? Was she warm? Was she comfortable? Was she hungry? Was she happy? *Was she happy*. Bennie loved her as no one had before, ardently, openly.

As family lore had it, her mother, with Frieda in her arms, crept off the boat in San Francisco homesick and remained in that state thereafter. Her enterprising father hit the dock running and ran nonstop until he crashed into the Panic of '75. Then he dropped business and, with equal energy, devoted himself to his religion. The only time Frieda recalled Abram embracing her or her mother was when she was a toddler. They were still living in Grass Valley.

Late one night, after a long absence, she and Bella woke to the sound of his wagon rolling up to their shanty. They scrambled out of bed and dashed into the chilly, pine-scented air to greet him. Elated by their welcome, he leaped from the wagon, lifted Frieda in one arm, put his free arm around Bella and hurried them out of the cold. Frieda had the impression he held her in his lap and smoothed her hair while her mother set out bread, cheese and tea. About one thing she was sure: he'd never kissed her or, in her sight, kissed her mother.

The Sisters of Service discussed sexual relations between

wives and husbands at length, but only as it pertained to a woman's right to reign over her own body. Of amatory pleasures, neither Miss O'Hara nor the Sisters had anything to say. Except Minnie, who occasionally shared (unwanted) erotic tidbits from her French governess.

"Has anyone ever told you you're a passionate woman?" Bennie asked sometime during their first entire night together.

Superior, stern, aloof was more like it, except for the man who said she had passionate lips (and she'd come to despise him). "Am I?"

"Very."

Was he teasing? She couldn't tell. What she did know was that parts of her throbbed at his touch and yearned to be touched again.

When Bennie's business duties could be put off no longer, he insisted she accompany him. Thereafter they awoke at the call of Ramón's roosters, dressed (Frieda behind the sheet her husband had strung across a corner) and cooked breakfast. Together they tidied their one room, then hand-in-hand went to do what needed doing.

Their first stop each morning was at Goldson Brothers. When an itinerant well-driller agreed to a joint venture for a percentage of the government reward, Morrie asked Lollie to tend the store for him. A member of a large Los Angeles wholesale mercantile family, Lollie went at storekeeping as if she'd never done anything else. She reorganized the shelves, swept the floors, fawned over the customers and came up with new ways to expand the stock and increase the sales. When she wrote home to tell her parents that she'd married a Jewish gentleman in general merchandising and ranching, the Friedman clan was so relieved, they flooded the newlyweds with gifts, best wishes and the offer to ship the Goldsons hardware (her father's line), dry goods (an uncle's), and furniture (another uncle's) at cost, no payment or interest due for six months.

With Bennie, Lollie was good-humored, but businesslike.

While the two discussed customers, orders and deliveries, Frieda roamed the dark, merchandise-packed store at Bennie's behest, helping herself to whatever she needed—a knife, mirror, lantern, frying pan, chopping bowl, strainer. With Frieda, Lollie became a devilish schoolgirl cutting up to amuse her chum. One morning, she got more carried away than usual. It began when Bennie asked her to find a sunbonnet for Frieda.

"Right this way, ma'am," Lollie drawled. "I'll fix the little lady up so's you won't recognize her."

To the bonnet, Lollie, stifling giggles, added a Fat Man's Special shirt, a miner's slouch hat, Wellington boots, a buggy whip to hold in one hand, and a kerosene lantern in the other. When she led her back to Bennie, Frieda obliged by crossing her eyes and poking her front teeth over her bottom lip. "Now ain't that the purtiest thing you even seen, Mister?" Lollie demanded.

With Bennie guffawing and banging the couter, the sisters-in-law pranced around the store, trying on one of these and one of those, until, overcome with mirth, they collapsed in each other's arms.

The next stop each day was the construction site. As Bennie conferred with the workmen in a lilting Spanish shot with laughter, Frieda noticed the men's eyes kept darting to her. Was she doing something wrong?

"Wrong?" Bennie responded. "Your visit's the high point of their day. They call you *la mayordoma* or *Doña Fridita*. Lollie is their *Doña Lolita*. They've studied your attributes and each picked his favorite. Some prefer *la rubia con los ojos verdes*, the blonde with the green eyes; others, *la castaña con los ojos azules*, the brown-haired one with the blue eyes."

Thereafter, Frieda distanced herself from the men as they conferred and avoided the workers' eyes, particularly those of Harrigan, the mason in charge.

"Arri-gahn," as the Mexicans called him, was a half-Irish, half-Mexican young man in his twenties. Only a little taller and heavier than Frieda, he had green eyes, light brown hair

and a sun-toasted complexion. Bennie brought him from
Tucson to lead the crew. Harrigan had learned masonry in
Los Angeles and knew how to mix, mold and fire American-
style bricks. His familiar-looking Irish face and his unexpected Mexican accent and gestures intrigued her. But his
eyes sought hers more often than the others, and lingered
longer—especially after Bennie had inspected the brick work
and pronounced that day's efforts "*magnífico.*"

Then it was over to the sales office to see Yancy Nunes,
who either leaped at them with his latest idea or stared past
them from his camp stool as if they were intruding strangers.
When his eyes were dull and his expression morose, Frieda
presumed he was in pain and offered him tea, a tonic, a poul-
tice. He ignored her remedies, clearly annoyed that she noticed his discomfort. On his better days, he treated her with
the respect due a college girl (untrue, but she didn't correct
him) and a metropolite. "As a San Franciscan, you'd be interested in…" he'd say, handing her a book, a newspaper, a poem
in a magazine. Rising to the station granted her, Frieda responded with attitudes and opinions.

Despite his mercurial moods, Yancy won her respect.
Neither his poor health nor his workplace—a tent in the
Upper Sonoran Desert—slowed him down. On good days
and bad, his pen sped: ads for newspapers, handbills, articles
on Dos Cacahuates for eastern magazines; letters to United
States Congressmen and Customs Service officials, territorial
legislators, American and Mexican railroad executives; reports
to his employers, Colonel Leighton (who was still in Europe)
and the colonel's Guaymas, Sonora partner, Alejandro
Ramirez; "Dear Horace" letters (Dear Horace: I have a fabu-
lous investment opportunity I'm passing on to a few of my
most substantial…); and recently, the first issue of his newspaper, the Dos Cacahuates *Selah*, due for the printing press
on May 1.

Afternoons, Bennie, with Frieda seated beside him in the
wagon, peddled merchandise to mines and ranches in the
foothills and the valley. The longer trips to Quitojoa, Pirigua,

Coral, Cabeza Prieta, or south into Mexico to Puerto Peñasco, Altar, Santa Ana and Caborca, Bennie—unwilling to leave Frieda, or to expose her to a long, tiring and potentially dangerous journey—passed on to Ramón.

As they rolled over the bumpy roads, Frieda, feet pressed against the floorboard, braced herself against the jolts and drank in the friendly April air and the blooming desert. Each day there were new things to see—the lemon-colored prickly pear blossoms, the waxy bloom on the tall saguaro, the red buds tipping the wands of the ocotillo.

But where were their customers? Did they live in holes in the desert floor like jack rabbits, in mountain caves like gnomes? Clutching the seat handle and refusing to look down as the wagon ascended and descended steep mountain trails, she peered out into the unpeopled expanses, sure that sooner or later people would materialize. And they did. High in the mountains at mines like the Sweet Patootie and the Make Me Proud, Mary, and down in dark canyons at the Queen Frederika, and the Spencer, et al., at the sound of Bennie's bell, they came running out of mine shafts, tents and splintery one-room houses. Each got a cheerful greeting, an introduction to the new Mrs. Goldson, an invitation to examine the merchandise in the back of the wagon and a handbill describing the big new townsite and short line development.

Better times were on the way, Bennie assured his customers. The miners listened in silence, until one big fellow in a striped canvas coat said what Frieda suspected others thought.

"Tell it to the big boss, mister. I work for wages."

In the seventies, Bennie explained as they drove off, promising discoveries excited a rush of prospectors and miners into the area, but much of the ore was of inferior quality and most of the newcomers sold out to large, absentee mine operators. "They'll perk up once the railroad's in and hauling costs go down."

The ranches ranged from complex operations—ranch house, bunk house, barn, corral, well, windmill—to single, crumbling adobes, the size of hers and Bennie's, surrounded by ocotillo fences. Their inhabitants, a smattering of women and children among them, gathered around the wagon. Some welcomed the new Mrs. Bennie with friendly questions. Others settled for a shy or indifferent how-de-do. Only old Mr. Sitton was openly hostile.

Sitton's place was on the east side of the valley, at the base of the Ajo Range. It was little more than a well, an adobe house and the ruins of two other buildings. Sitton was a dried-up whip of a man in his seventies, toothless, bearded, squinty-eyed. He carried a shotgun under his arm.

"Where ye from?" he snarled at Frieda when Bennie stepped behind the wagon.

"Umph," was his reply. "Treat you purty good, uh?" He jerked his thumb at Bennie.

"Oh yes."

"Like a queeeen?"

Frieda nodded.

"That's what you city girls think you deserve." His tone was nasty. "Queens. Who's going to do the work, will you tell me that?"

She looked around to see if Bennie was coming yet. "Come out here to lord it over everybody."

"Mr. Sitton, I...."

"I guess they treated you like a queeeen up in San Francisco, too?"

On the way home Bennie told Frieda old man Sitton's story. He'd come out before the Civil War and was one of the few who stayed during the war after the army pulled out. His first wife returned home to have their first child and never came back. The second, a common-law wife, was with him ten years, had six children, then after two disappeared in the desert—no one ever found out what happened to them— took the four remaining kids and went to live with her sister in California. His third and last try was a middle-aged Mexican woman from Cacahuate. After a couple of years, a priest persuaded her that since Sitton couldn't marry her, they were living in sin.

"He's likely to die out there and nobody will know," Frieda said.

Bennie shrugged. "Not even Sitton."

CHAPTER EIGHT

Across the Line

FIVE WEEKS ON THE border and Frieda had yet to visit
Viejo Cacahuate, as the Mexicans still called the old town.
With Minnie gone, the Passover flurry over, their love feasts
down to regular repasts, the novelty of being unemployed di-
minishing, Frieda began eyeing Mexico like a crusader looking for a cause—especially after a nocturnal visit from some
Sonoran neighbors.

Late one night, the clatter of horse hooves, men's voices,
then pistol shots woke her. Bennie leaped out of bed and ran
for the rifle propped up against the fireplace. Trembling, she
watched him wait near the door, rifle raised, listening. As the
horse hooves receded, he put back the rifle and returned to
bed.

"What was that?" Frieda whispered, still shaking.

"Probably *rurales* after *bandidos.* Sounds like they gave
them the slip," Bennie said, gliding his hand under her nightgown and drawing her to him.

Rurales? Bandidos? Frieda wanted to know more. But her
husband's attention had shifted from Sonoran lawmen and
thieves to more pleasurable pursuits. His lips on hers, his
hands everywhere else, he soon persuaded her to forget them
and join him.

Most of Goldson Brothers' customers were Mexicans.
Regretting her baby Spanish, Frieda observed them like an
anthropologist studying the buying habits of a native population. Almost every day, a few rode into Dos Cacahuates on
horseback. Occasionally, an entire family or a party of villag-
ers piled out of a wagon in front of the store. They came

from all over Sonora and as far south as Sinaloa to buy American mining and farming implements, clothing, furniture and household staples at Goldson Brothers. Bennie, and Lollie by example, greeted, attended, fed and quartered them like long-awaited relatives or visiting dignitaries. Most responded amiably—more like friends than customers—made their purchases and departed. They had duties elsewhere.

Unlike the beggars from the across the line who, like biblical gleaners appeared day after day, silently picked through the Dos Cacahuatans' garbage, then vanished. One morning, a thin, old woman, her back as round as a cup handle, directed a wordless appeal at Frieda. She was seated on the ground in front of the house when she came out. Their eyes met: the woman's, supplicating; Frieda's, commiserating. She went back into the house and returned with tortillas, supper leftovers and coffee. The next morning, the old woman was back with a ragged middle-aged couple, and the day after that, six pairs of eyes fastened on her as she stepped through the door. As Frieda was distributing tortillas, beef jerky, dried fruit and coffee, Ramón arrived with a load of fire wood.

"Como perros a la puerta," Ramón pantomimed a dog scratching at the door. *"Cada día más,* every day more," he warned Frieda. For the next few days, he stationed himself on the road into the settlement each dawn to turn back the mendicants before they reached Doña Fridita's.

From the hilltop hotel site, Frieda could make out the environs of Old Cacahuate. Looking south past the Devil's Highway was an irregular circle of treetops. Yellow and green fields flanked the ragged green core, and a ribbon of a river meandered toward it from the west. Surrounding these skimpy signs of habitation lay unpeopled plains of chaparral, cacti-dotted hills and blue mountains. Squinting her eyes, she searched for further signs of their twin border community.

"Don't bother, unless you can see through one hundred feet of sandstone," Bennie advised one day. "Cacahuate's behind that butte to the east. It's just an old Mexican town."

Old Mexican town rooted: Catholic church, plaza, bandstand, colorfully dressed strollers; tile-roofed, white-plastered houses; flowers—all the Mexicans she knew in San Francisco grew flowers, if not in a garden then on a porch, landing, or windowsill. Not only the Mexicans. The porch at Levie's Kosher Boardinghouse was loaded with potted nasturiums, lantanas, geraniums. Her mother loved geraniums—she called them *ger-rye-knee-nums*. Tears came, and with them an unwanted thought. She missed her family, the boarders, Miss O'Hara, her friends, even Minnie. She missed San Francisco—crowds, buildings, commotion, seascapes. At home, especially at the boardinghouse, there were too many people for comfort; in Dos Cacahuates, too few.

She couldn't see her Sonoran neighbors, but she felt their presence. The roosters crowing in the distance each dawn were theirs. The faint strains of music she picked up outdoors some evenings—strumming guitars, scratchy violins, a wailing horn—theirs. The morning aroma of burning mesquite and frying lard drifting north into Dos Cacahuates, theirs, too.

On the morning of April 29, Frieda waited on the front seat of the wagon as Bennie harnessed his horse, Tomaso. In honor of her first visit across the line, she had on her green traveling suit and her black kid dress boots. Eyes closed, she pictured herself in various settings: in the parlor of a hacienda (there were crosses and plaster figures of Jesus on the wall) having tea with four generations of a gracious Sonoran family; in a forest, reading Emily Dickinson's poems with a group of enthralled dark-haired girls dressed in Sisters of Service uniforms, white blouses and black bombazine skirts; in a kitchen with a winsome, young Mexican woman preparing *frijoles, salsa fresca,* and *enchiladas* in Mexican clay pots.

Once the wagon was rolling, Frieda began searching the landscape for fascinating particulars. During her four years with the Sisters of Service, one Sister moved to the Sandwich Islands, another to Malaysia, and a third to the Oklahoma Territory. All wrote long letters to the group describing their exotic new homes, and their experiences helping needy natives.

Miss O'Hara read their accounts aloud at meetings, then enjoined the Sisters to emulate their courage, hardiness, ingenuity and dedication.

It took no more than five minutes to get from the front of the store to the triangular stone marker on the American side, and to the four-feet-square adobe guardhouse on the Mexican side of the international border.

A portly, white-haired, dark-skinned Mexican filled the doorway. "Ha, *Don Fuego*," he greeted Bennie, the words whistling through his absent front teeth.

Frieda made a mental note to comment on the Mexicans' penchant for nicknames. They called her la mayordoma, the boss's wife; Bennie, with his red hair and lively ways, Don Fuego, Mr. Fire; and his brother, Morrie, pensive and obsessed with artesian wells, *Don Agua*, Mr. Water. Together they were *Los Hermanos Fuego y Agua*, the Brothers Fire and Water.

"*Mi mujer*," Bennie introduced Frieda. A second Mexican appeared from behind the first. Shorter and thinner, he leaned around the side of his bulky companion to get a look.

"*Ella es de San Francisco*," Bennie bragged.

"San Francisco, California?" asked the shorter man.

"Sí, California."

The two men bowed to Frieda. "*Mucho gusto, Señora*," said one, then the other.

"Mucho gusto," she repeated.

Pleased with the exchange, Frieda waved to the men as Bennie signaled Tomaso to move on. The road soon turned and cut through a massive hedge of oleanders. It was as tall as a two-story building and ran some fifty feet along the international boundary, screening the outskirts of Viejo Cacahuate from the American settlement. As the vehicle moved through the opening, Frieda peered ahead, quivering with anticipation.

Several hours later, the Goldson wagon pulled up again in front of the guardhouse. The guards ambled over to admire the plants Bennie brought back, and to greet Don Umberto and his son, Ignacio, crouching in the back of the wagon with the purchases. The four men conversed at length, presumably about the orange seedlings growing in gunny sacks; the sets of radishes, carrots, onions, celery and lettuce in clay basins; and the work the Sonorans would be doing at the Goldson ranch. Blank-faced, Frieda lay against the backrest as if thrown there. As they headed for Dos Cacahuates, Bennie chatted in his jocular Spanish to sweat-stained, fierce-smelling Don Umberto and his no-thicker-than-a-ruler son. Frieda neither understood what they were saying nor cared. Her gaze lowered, she either tore at the handkerchief in her hands or dabbed her eyes with it. It was not only her mood that changed. While across the line, she'd pulled a faded sunbonnet over her hair, replaced her dress boots with work shoes and exchanged her trim green jacket for a gray shawl.

When the vehicle came to a stop in front of Goldson Brothers, Frieda jumped to the ground and half-ran to the house. Weep, rail, vomit, she had to relieve herself of what she'd witnessed.

The main street of Cacahuate, Sonora, Calle Principal, was a pitted path separating stained and disintegrating adobes and lean-tos. Behind Calle Principal lay an unnamed alley, where people were living in holes dug into an embankment and in makeshift hovels. The church was no bigger than a humble dwelling and in poor repair; several scrawny flowering bushes dotted what passed for a plaza, but most of the square was overrun with Mexican hay. Weathered walls, their tops lined with broken glass, concealed the residences of what Bennie called Cacahuate's more prominent citizens. El Tesoro and La Fuente, Goldson Brothers' competitors across the line, were hardly stores at all. The merchandise lay on the ground in front of the entry—several leather suitcases, a metal trunk, a few black shawls and blankets, piles of used shoes, several women's skirts and men's pants made of *manta,* white cotton, and clay pots of various sizes. Several other "enterprises" had to be saloons—men stood, some reeling, around the entry.

Wherever they stopped, beggars gathered around the wagon, their hands extended. Poverty was not the Cacahuatans most searing affliction. A man with a pendulous goiter; children's faces and limbs dotted with scabies or ringworms; a ranting woman dressed in a torn soldier's uniform and a sombrero; and the most frightening, a dog-man who loped down the road after the wagon on all fours, both arms and legs unbent, his back bowed like an animal, barking and snarling.

As she undressed behind the sheet that night, Mexico lay dark and menacing across her chest. Once in the afternoon and again in the evening, Bennie asked what was bothering her. The first time, she said she was tired; the second, she pretended not to hear.

After Frieda was in bed, Bennie went out to help Ramón set traps around the chicken house to discourage a coyote who'd been making nightly visits. She was tired and the bed felt good, even better, for Bennie's absence. She didn't want him kissing and fondling her, or coaxing her to explain why he shouldn't. The candle out, she was glad to be alone in the dark, sorting out her tangled thoughts.

About, among other things, her husband. He'd taken her to Cacahuate without a word of warning. Didn't he see what she saw? Or did he no longer care?

"Wake up," Bennie was saying. He had his hand on her shoulder. "Folks'll think I'm beating you."

Frieda's cheeks were wet and her throat was raw. She sat up with a start. Pulling the blanket up around her, she searched the room for the terror shaking her.

"You're all right," Bennie said. He tried to draw her to him, but she resisted. "You were having a bad dream."

The dog man. Frieda's hand rose to stay her racing heart.

Bennie patted her upper arm for a while, then in a soft, storyteller's voice, tried to distract her with an account of one of his nightmares.

"Back in '66, I was down south of Tucson, working at a

mine in the Santa Ritas. Once when I was coming back north, a couple of Apaches rode out of the chaparral and went after me. I galloped like all get out and just made it into Pete Kitchen's ranch. During the next year, I kept dreaming I was being scalped, sometimes by red men, sometimes by whites. Once I was camping out alone, with no one to scare but my horse. The poor old fellow came ambling over to my bedroll to see what was going on. Twice I was with other fellows and they had themselves a good laugh. They tell me I screamed so loud in a hotel one night that men in the saloon next door ran for the sheriff.

"Who was chasing you, Frieda? You can tell me."

"Those poor people I saw today."

Bennie nodded.

"It's so awful, the way those people live, Bennie."

After several moments of silence, he responded, "*Así es la vida.*"

"That's not living."

"They're used to it."

"Nobody could be used to it."

"It's not that bad," he tried weakly.

"Living in crumbling rooms, caves, sick, hungry, forced to beg? Not that bad?"

"There's more to Cacahuate than that."

"I didn't see it."

"A number of Cacahuatans are no worse off than you and me; a few, better."

"Then why don't they do something?"

"What can they do?"

"See that their poor get food, clothing, medicine."

"They do what they can."

"It's not enough. If they don't help, we should."

"Three-quarters of the town would rush right over."

"Let them."

"Not yet. We still barely have enough ourselves."

"We have to do something."

"We're doing something," Bennie said. "Building this

townsite, the hotel, pushing to get the railroads. We're making jobs, plenty of them."

She listened, weighing his words.

"It's not charity these people need, it's work," Bennie continued.

"That true, but I have to do something right away."

Bennie leaned over and consulted his big, brass watch. "It's three in the morning."

"You go to sleep, Bennie. I can't." She rose, picked up a shawl from a nearby chair, went to the table, re-lit a half-burned candle and went for paper and pen.

"Aw, Fried'," he complained.

Her shawl pulled tightly around her, her bare feet on the floor, Frieda spread her hands over the paper and thought. The Sisters of Service spent an entire winter collecting clothes, food and medicine for Lilian Latham's Sandwich Islanders. If asked, they'd do the same for Frieda's Mexicans.

Dos Cacahuates, Arizona Territory
April 30, 1880
Dear Sisters:
    I will never complain of my lot in life again after my trip across the border into Mexico yesterday. I was not aware that such terrible deprivation existed anywhere.

A coyote yowled, and Frieda's pen halted. She shivered as if back in her nightmare, then started to write again.

    Dos Cacahuates, Sonora, if it's on a map, probably appears by its centuries-old name, Cacahuate. I've been told it was founded by Padre Kino and has an illustrious history. At present, it has about 500 souls and is as completely lacking in....

A coyote shrieked, a man grumbled, then a rifle discharged. The sounds occurred just as Frieda was writing the word "lacking." She crossed out the smeared letters and began again. Suddenly the window alongside the table exploded and a wounded coyote came through the broken glass, the trap Bennie had set clamped to its left rear leg. The injured and bleeding animal collapsed on the letter. Frieda screamed, jumped up and ran to a corner where she crouched, face covered. She could hear Bennie cursing as he chased the wounded animal around the room. A thump sounded, then silence. Lowering her hands, she saw Bennie near the door. He was standing on something. The coyote. His broad, bare feet were red with its blood. In his hand was a thick wooden mallet, covered with blood too. Frieda shuddered, squeezed her eyes shut and clapped her hands over her ears. Albeit faintly, she heard the door open and close, then water splashing.

She was still cowering in the corner when Bennie, smelling of lavendar-scented soap, gathered her up into his arms and carried her to bed. She lay mute with shock, hearing and not hearing him sweeping up the glass and nailing a board over the broken window.

When he got back into bed, Frieda threw herself in his arms and sobbed until Bennie cautioned, "Use them all up now and you won't have any tears left for real trouble."

As she was drifting off, she reminded herself and him, "There's so much to do, Bennie."

He started to object.

She put her finger to his lips. "In the morning."

CHAPTER NINE

Learning from Angelina

THEY WRANGLED the next morning as Bennie installed new glass in the window and Frieda scrubbed bloodstains from the table, chairs and floor. She worked quickly, humming to drown out his grumbled "awwws" and "gawd almighties."

Why in the hell did she want to stay in camp? They were having a grand time, gallivanting around together. She ought to take in the sights now, while she had a chance. He had to go over to Tucson to pick up a shipment of tools coming in from the east on the Southern Pacific. She could do a little shopping and visit with Minnie. Wouldn't she like to see Minnie before she and Mendel left for San Francisco?

She felt obliged to see Minnie, if only to verify that, in their eagerness to be rid of her, they had not passed her on to a villain. Bennie assured her Mendel was one-hundred percent responsible, but what did he really know about him? Minnie'd written her one inimically brief letter instructing her to forward her mail as speedily as possible. In a scrawled postscript, she added, "Mademoiselle was correct pertaining to *l'amour.*" The resulting image made Frieda smile, blush, then wince with distaste. Given her friend's preoccupation with sex (entirely theoretical until Mendel), her unguarded speech, and her autocratic manner, she was likely to bombard her with intimate details, until Frieda acknowledged Mendel was a more proficient lover than Bennie. Frieda resolved to refuse to listen to, much less speak of, such personal matters. In any case, she was not staying home to avoid seeing Minnie; she had other reasons.

"We could have supper with the Miners," Bennie continued from outside the door, where he was replacing the glass in the windows, "and spend the night at the hotel. The next day, I'd like you to meet some of the Jewish folks in town. Tucson's got itself a *minyan*, quorum, and a half by now. Phil and Rosa Drachman; Phil's brother, Sam, and Sam's wife, Jennie; Isaac Goldberg and his wife, Rebecca; the Goldtree brothers and their wives...."

He wasn't going to stop until he named every Jew in Tucson; he'd done it before. He knew them all and could recite the year each arrived in the Arizona Territory; their means of endeavor; whether they were married or single; who'd married out of the faith; who'd brought wives from Europe, New York, San Francisco; the ages of their children. Some were close friends, some acquaintances, a few enemies; but all were Jews and, as such, family. She looked forward to meeting them, especially the women, and to visiting Tucson, but not yet. She had to start making herself useful, now, while her conscience was still intact.

Unable to sell Frieda on Tucson, Bennie proposed a shorter trip that day, to Tule Tanks. They'd take a picnic lunch, maybe even spend the night camping out. What a show she had in store—a million stars hanging like spangles from black plush.

"Sleep on the ground, like animals?" Frieda reached for the broom and began sweeping.

"Not only sleep," Bennie said, leaning around the door frame to grin at her. Recognizing the light in his eyes, Frieda turned and swept in the opposite direction, until Bennie came up behind her and wrapped her and the broom in his arms.

"We could swim in the tank," he said, dreamily rubbing his cheek against her.

"I don't know how to swim."

"I'll teach you."

"I don't have a bathing dress."

"You don't need a bathing dress."

Her face blazed again. He was always trying to get her to take off all her clothes. She let go of the broom with one hand to push at his chest.

"The things you think of."

"What's wrong with the things I think of?"

"You're wicked, Bennie."

"Not nearly as *wicked* as I'd like to be." His body pressed forward as hers drew back.

"*Stop.* The door's open."

His tongue darted out to lick her cheek. "Do I have to swallow you to keep you with me? Let's go to Tule Tanks." His eyes, playful, desirous, fixed on hers. "Just today."

The man had no sense of propriety—day, night, indoors, outdoors. Even at that time of month he wanted to hold her, caress her. If she didn't watch out, they'd be rolling on the ground naked as jackrabbits. More naked. Jackrabbits have fur coats.

"You're a love fiend."

"When I'm near you," Bennie persisted.

"Left to you, we'd be doing nothing but making love," Frieda said, dropping her voice to a cautious whisper.

"I'll vote for that."

"We have obligations."

"Come with me."

"I have work to do."

"What work?"

"I'm going to start cooking for the camp. We've been eating like savages, any time, any place, any thing."

"So what?"

"It's not healthy."

Bennie looked skeptical.

"It's not civilized."

"What's so great about being civilized?"

"It's more orderly, kinder, more companionable. We'll all sit down at a table together—Yancy, Lollie, Morrie, Harrigan and his men. The whole camp."

"You'll be working all day."

"Not all day. I've cooked for thirty-five, three times a day, for four years."

"That was in San Francisco. You can't walk out to Howard Street for a cut of beef and a bunch of carrots."

"Ramón has chickens and eggs. Morrie will bring vegetables in from the ranch, and Yermo can deliver provisions from Tucson and Yuma. Across the line, I saw fields, orchards and cattle ranches."

"I didn't bring you down to Dos Cacahuates to cook." Bennie's tone was cool.

"I didn't come to be your paramour."

"What did you come for?" His features stiffened with annoyance.

"To combine Marriage and Service."

Bennie groaned.

Silently, she groaned too. In their raw settlement, Marriage and Service sounded schoolgirlish.

"And do other things, too, like help Yancy with the "Dear Horace" letters. I can write to people I know in San Francisco...."

"Suit yourself," Bennie said, reaching for the can of putty he'd set down on the table.

By the end of the second week, the entire camp—stagecoach drivers and passengers, customers, miners and other passers-through—were enjoying three meals a day served in a dining tent set up next to the store. Eager for well-prepared fare, locals began filling the cook tent with beef, lamb, fish, poultry, eggs and cheeses from Sonora, also with fruits and vegetables from across the line and from the Goldson ranch. When freight-hauler Abe Beisel learned Goldson's wife was cooking for the camp, he began bringing her European wines, sausages, cheeses and hard candies from Guaymas.

In the beginning, every meal was a celebration, especially the suppers. Lustily consumed, they were followed by a guitar concert compliments of one of Harrigan's men, then talk, cards, or both. After a week or so, settlers and visitors alike had come to count on vastly improved food and greater conviviality in Dos Cacahuates. Enormously grateful for these previously absent pleasures, they rewarded the provider—Mrs. Goldson, Mrs. Bennie, Frieda, Doña Fridita—with lavish praise during and after every meal.

Lying in bed one night, Frieda told Bennie of another unanticipated reward for her efforts. Angelina was learning English and American cooking and teaching Frieda Spanish and Mexican cooking.

"She's really quite remarkable. Never a day's schooling, out in the fields from birth; separated from her family at ten to serve as a cook's apprentice; the woman of three men, maybe more; the mother of seven children; a worker from the day she was able to walk, yet she's still beautiful, able, and agreeable."

"*Diós lo quiere*," was Bennie's response.

"It's not always easy to do what God wants."

"*Día por día.*"

"Day by day," Frieda translated.

"*Sí. Cada día es otro día encima.*"

"*Otro día encima?*"

"Another day on earth," Bennie translated.

As she was undressing, Frieda sang: "*Ya se fué mi hombre con brazos del hierro, y labios de leche y miel.*"

"*De* Angelina?" Bennie called from the bed.

"*Sí.*"

"You *are* learning a lot from her."

"*Poco a poco.*"

He was waiting, arms outstretched, when she came out in her nightgown. Smiling, she slid in beside him. When their lips met, hers yielded a moist kiss.

"Did Angelina teach you that, too?"

"No, but I suspect she's a mistress of the art."

"In no time and with practically nothing, you two are turning this outpost into a home. How do you manage?"

"*Cada día, otro día encima.*"

"*Y cada noche, otra noche abajo,*" Bennie suggested.

"Abajo? Under?"

"Come here, I'll show you," he said as he snuffed the candle flame with his thumb, splattering the wax.

CHAPTER TEN

The First Lady

"THIS WILDERNESS is *killing* me," Bennie said. He was stretched out on his back, one hand under his head, the other on his stomach, a benign smile on his lips. Matching expressions of contentment echoed from Yancy, Frieda, Lollie and Morrie, all sprawled around him on a canvas tarpaulin under the cottonwoods alongside the pond.

It was Sunday afternoon (May eighteenth) and they'd just completed a huge midday meal in honor of Colonel Leighton's Mexican partner, Don Alejandro Ramirez, and his two sons, who had all driven up from Guaymas to collect Don Alejandro's share of the lot sales to date and pick up handbills Yancy had prepared in Spanish for distribution in Sonora. Their two-day stay crowned with a five-course lunch and toasts to the success of the townsite and the international railroad, the Ramirezes climbed back into their carriage, promising to return for the lot auction in October.

Exhausted by their hostly duties and drowsy with food and drink, the Dos Cacahuatans sought a cool spot to hold what Yancy mockingly called a meeting of the board.

Lying perpendicular to Bennie, Yancy undid his black string tie, opened the collar of his ruffled shirt and rolled up his sleeves. "The meeting of the board of the International Improvement Company and La Cíbola Hotel, Inc., is now in session." As he spoke, his index finger traced a string of ants filing out of a hole and onto the canvas.

"The first order of business is an expression of appreciation for our company's accomplished cook. The Ramirezes were more impressed with that roasted duck, homemade noodles, string beans, creamed spinach, and apricot küchen made with real butter than with their share of the pre-auction sales. Which I may add, they pocketed with unconcealed glee." Raising an empty wine bottle in Frieda's direction, Bennie led with a rousing "Hail to the cook." Tributes floated at her like holiday balloons. Frieda acknowledged them with an ironic smile. She'd prepared hundreds of similar meals at the boardinghouse with no more praise than requests for seconds. A swarm of hummingbirds darting in and out of a nearby honeysuckle vine caught her eye. She inhaled the heady aroma, allowing its sweetness to seep through her like an opiate. Giving, receiving, receiving, giving. How easy it was in this natural setting; one undertaking, one goal, everyone doing his and her share.

The group fell back into a languorous silence, the quiet too sweet to relinquish. A light snore broke the spell. Yancy laughed and sat up. "It's either *that* or reports." He turned to Bennie: "How's the construction going?"

Bennie eased himself to a sitting position. "First-rate on the hotel. Foundations are in; brick walls in place; beams in; doors, hardware and lighting fixtures will be arriving any day."

"And on schedule," Yancy added. "As planned we're going to have a hotel ready for occupancy in October."

"So it appears. By cutting back to twenty rooms, a kitchen, dining room and a lobby, we managed to squeak by on a forty-five-day loan from the Pima County Bank in Tucson. But we've got to pay it off before they'll give us another. International Improvement will have to shell out for the building materials when they arrive."

"Ramirez cleaned us out," Yancy said. "I gave him eight hundred, twenty-five percent of the thirty-two lots sold. And two weeks ago we sent another eight hundred to London to cover some of the colonel's traveling expenses. Promotion and day-to-day living ate up the rest."

Bennie turned to Morrie.

"Don't look at me, Ben," Morrie said. "All my cash went into the wells."

"Dear Horace money?" Bennie asked, turning back to Yancy.

"A trickle. I'm trying to work it up to a stream, but we're not there yet."

"Did we have to turn eight hundred over to Ramirez now?"

"That was the deal. He and his family put up the land, and the International Improvement Company handles construction and promotion. Seventy-five percent of the townsite take goes to I.I.C., twenty-five to Ramirez."

"So how do we stay afloat until the lot auction?"

"Drum up cash," Lollie drawled, her head on Morrie's stomach.

"Got any ideas?" Yancy wanted to know.

"My folks'll send furnishings for the hotel and a piano on credit, but no cash."

"I'm told midwesterners are looking around after that drought last year. Give me a few weeks on the road, and I should be able to sell thirty or forty lots. But who'd look after the construction, and keep up the store?"

"I'll handle the store; Ramón, the route." The suggestion came from Lollie.

"There you go, Loll," Bennie congratulated his sister-in-law. "With Yancy to order materials and keep an eye on things, Harrigan can run the crew." Bennie's eyes swept around the circle to find Frieda's. She gave him what he sought: her approval.

"Business has been picking up at the store," Lollie was saying, "but it takes so long to restock. There's quick money in booze. How about a saloon? Customers are always after me to sell them drinks."

She sat up, legs crossed tailor-fashion; her tone brisk, self-confident. "I'd call it Lollie's. Maybe Frieda could open a tent restaurant. Twenty-five cents for breakfast, fifty cents for dinner and supper. A dollar for a banquet like today's." She turned to face Frieda. "When the word gets out that Dos Cacahuates is wet and tasty, customers will rush in. There isn't a saloon or a restaurant on the border a day's journey east or west."

Yancy liked what he was hearing. "I'm printing the first issue of the *Selah* in a couple of days. I could work up some ads for the front page. Lollie's Saloon and...." He turned to face Frieda, "How does the "First Lady" sound?"

Bennie answered. "Townsite lots and hotel shares, that's where the money is."

"In the long run," Lollie said, leaning toward her brother-in-law. "We need cash now."

Bennie was not convinced.

"I'm cooking anyway," Frieda said. "It makes sense."

"Not to me," her husband responded.

Put to a vote, it was three against one; Morrie abstained.

When the meeting ended, the others drifted off, leaving Frieda and Bennie lying on canvas, watching the western skies redden on the other side of the pond. Frieda's thoughts were on Lollie. As her sister-in-law rose and stretched her arms over her head, she noticed Lollie's formerly flat abdomen protruded. Was she pregnant?

"I'm dead-set against it," Bennie muttered.

Had he noticed the change in Lollie too?, Frieda wondered. "Against what?"

"The restaurant. It will be too much work, especially after it starts getting hot."

"We need to make some money."

"Making money's a man's job."

"What about Lollie?"

"You're not Lollie Friedman."

"Lollie Friedman Goldson. We're all in this together, Bennie."

"She's worked before."

"I have too."

"You'll wear yourself out."

Frieda bent and planted a lingering kiss on Bennie's lips.
"I'll fold my hands and reign after the lot auction."

"Don't say I didn't warn you."

"You warned me."

"I won't have it said Bennie Goldson took a handsome,
high-minded Jewish girl and ruined her."

"Why? I love being ruined."

Bennie laughed, jumped up and pulled Frieda to her feet.
"If that's the case, I'd better ruin you some more."

At four o'clock in the afternoon on May twenty-third,
Yancy came out of his tent calling, "Get your Dos Cacahuates
Selah. Read all about Paradise Found in the southwest."

There were articles about the First Seder, the annual
Cinco De Mayo celebration and the Easter service in Dos
Cacahuates, Sonora. On the front page, left column, was a let-
ter from Colonel Jack Leighton to the Board of Directors of
the International Improvement Company, Dos Cacahuates
Division, reporting intense interest in the development in
Scotland and England and expectation of the same in Ger-
many, where he was headed.

Ads for the two new enterprises in town also appeared on
the front page. For Lollie's, Yancy had drawn a tap room with
a long bar, and well-dressed men and women seated and
standing alongside it. At one side was a large, round gaslight
suspended over a table with a fringed tablecloth. The copy
read, "When in Dos Cacahuates, it's Lollie's for Refreshments
and Entertainment. Proprietress: Lollie Friedman Goldson,
popular Tombstone and Charleston artiste."

The First Lady, was—as Yancy foresaw it—an elegant eat-
ery in a hilltop hotel. Frieda was depicted in an evening
gown, greeting her similarly attired guests at the door. The
caption below read: "Now, in Dos Cacahuates, you are invited
to enjoy the finest of San Francisco fare: turkey, chicken,
steak, roast beef, Guaymas shrimp, oysters, clams, fresh vegetables, homemade cakes and pies, breads and biscuits. Proprietress Frieda Goldson caters to special diets for religious and

health regimens. Sleeping accommodations are also available at a temporary tent hotel until the commodious La Cíbola has been completed."

On page two, Yancy ran an "Arrivals and Departures" section, two columns full of meaty, often humorous, comments about each and every visitor to Dos Cacahuates in April and May. *That Yancy,* thought Frieda as she read it. *He'd transformed their occasional visitors into a clamoring throng, with some hyperbole, but no lies.*

The third page was devoted to a map of the townsite, a drawing of the hotel, voluminous information about diverse opportunities in the area, and instructions on how to acquire a lot at low, pre-auction prices. On the fourth and last page were the names of every lot purchaser, real and imagined, Frieda suspected. Alongside the list was a "Good and Welfare" column that opened: "We're proud to report the distaff side of the community has already initiated efforts to improve health, educational and cultural life in the twin communities of Dos Cacahuates." Below, Yancy elaborated on plans for a monthly musicale, a Ladies' Aid Society, a sewing circle and, "As soon as American Dos Cacahuates has five children of the appropriate age, a school." On the heels of the future school was the assurance that "religious groups of various denominations will also sprout as rapidly here as they have in other burgeoning western communities."

The bottom right quarter of the page was devoted to a boxed letter written and signed by Frieda describing in detail the plight of the poor of their twin town, Dos Cacahuates, Sonora, and asking for contributions of food, clothing and medicine.

Yancy wanted to identify her as "The First Lady of Dos Cacahuates." Frieda objected. She wasn't the first woman to settle in Dos Cacahuates. Angelina had preceded her by several months, and from her she learned of other women who'd lived in the area—Mexicans, Sand Papagos, Seris. She wasn't even the first American woman to settle in Dos Cacahuates; Lollie had as much claim to that distinction as she had. The title was not only incorrect, it was comical when used to signify the leading or most prominent—particularly in a scrawny outpost with a population of four permanent settlers, two of them women.

Frieda placed three copies of newspapers at the bottom of her trunk for historical purposes, sent one home to her family and another to Miss O'Hara. Responses were barely a week in arriving.

The first, from the Sisters of Service, was signed by Miss O'Hara and thirteen girls. The letter thanked Frieda for the historic first issue of the Dos Cacahuates *Selah* and reported that they had already started to collect clothing, non-perishable foodstuffs and medicines for the poor of Viejo Cacahuate. The second was written by her sister, Sylvia, on behalf of her mother and father. Why did she have to start a restaurant and a hotel—in plain words, a boardinghouse? Had Mr. Goldson suffered business reversals? Was she all right? They hadn't heard from her for several weeks.

Frieda crumpled the letter and threw it on the floor. After pacing for a few minutes, she picked it up and read the rest.

P.S. I went to Felicia and Rudy Seiffert's last week with Rudy's cousin, who has been inviting me out. They asked about you and were intrigued to learn you'd married and gone off to combine Service and Marriage building a new town on the Arizona-Sonora border. They were most curious about your role in the undertaking. I told them you are running a boardinghouse like the one you left on Tehama Street. We all had a good laugh.

P.P.S. Mama begged me to tell you that if you're not happy, don't be ashamed to ask Papa for train fare home.

Not if ten plagues hit Dos Cacahuates. Frieda folded Sylvia's letter and put it in the trunk on top of the newspapers to gloat over when Dos Cacahuates was the largest, most active and most attractive twin community on the American-Mexican border.

A week before Bennie left on his sales trip, he gave Frieda a Winchester, a center-fire repeating rifle, and several boxes of bullets. Daily, he walked with her to the other side of the pond to practice shooting until she was able to hit a target and reload. Next, he gave her a sheriff's model Colt, a blunt-nosed pistol, to carry in her apron pocket. All kinds of strangers drifted through Dos Cacahuates these days, Bennie told her, so she'd better take the pistol whenever she left the house. Toward the end of the week, he brought a Bowie knife home from the store. Frieda balked; she'd rather die than use it on anyone.

"Then keep it under your pillow," he urged. "Even if you don't use it, it looks wicked enough to keep an intruder from advancing."

"I know how to take care of myself," Frieda told him, her voice cracking with feigned courage.

"I know you do, sweetheart, but when your life's at stake, you have to take measures," Bennie said. "If you're not careful out here, you'll be dead in a week."

He moved so quickly, she'd barely noticed that Bennie was cautious. He often stopped to listen, step aside, scrutinize an area before advancing, or leapt to his feet to check some sound in the house, in the brush, on the road. He was teaching her to guard herself as he guarded himself and her, Frieda realized, and tried to do what he told her.

The day before he left, he got specific about her movements around the camp. A woman alone had to be careful. She wasn't alone, Frieda pointed out. Lollie, Morrie, Yancy, Angelina, Ramón, and Old Wally—an old wanderer who was helping Lollie out at the saloon—were nearby. In her own house at night she'd be alone, Bennie replied. Don't get too friendly with strangers or venture out alone after dark. As soon as she was through with her supper chores, she'd do best to stay in her house behind a bolted door. Such precautions, coming from Bennie, sounded out-of-character, but sensible, and unsettling.

As the stagecoach driver was climbing into his seat, Bennie dispensed final cautionaries. This time about the weather.

"Take it easy," he advised from the window of stage. "Get plenty of rest, drink all the water you can and take your salt tablets. The heat can knock you over if you're not careful."

"I'll be all right," Frieda said, her fingers entwining with her husband's on the edge of the open window.

"Are you sure?" he asked. His tone hinted that with one word from her he'd abandon his plans.

"Sure," she said, unlacing her fingers from his.

As the stage lurched forward, Bennie leaned his head through the window and called, "I miss you already."

Afraid to scare herself by saying the words out loud, Frieda whispered back, "I miss you."

"Stay out of the sun," Bennie shouted through cupped hands as the coach dipped into the cottonwoods.

Frieda nodded. No need tell her to stay out of the sun; she knew. The tyrant, summer heat had invaded Dos Cacahuates soon after the Ramirezes left and the temperature had been rising ever since. By the third week in May, the thermometer began passing the one hundred mark most days, but mornings and nights remained relatively cool.

The week after her husband left, the real heat descended. It hit Frieda like a severe injury. Her head ached, she felt dizzy and nauseous and couldn't eat. Her legs hurt, too, and her feet swelled so that she could hardly get her shoes on over the blisters on the balls of her feet and on her heels.

She studied Angelina to see how she managed. Emulating her, Frieda began to wear a loose Mexican-style dress of manta, with little under it. She wavered briefly between the fear of scorpions, gila monsters, snakes, and relief for her hot blistered feet, then decided in favor of sandals—worn with a pistol in her apron pocket. Her hair, singed dry and hot to the touch, she braided and wound around her head like her assistant. She also began accompanying Angelina to the pond twice a day where they waded in their dresses, dunked their heads, then waded out and filled the big clay jars with water to hang in the restaurant and in the house.

At Angelina's suggestion, they started to rise at dawn to get the main part of the cooking out of the way early. The roasts, stews, breads and cakes they prepared either at night or first thing in the morning. The main meal they served at midday and, immediately after, retired for a three-hour siesta.

Before long, Frieda caught on. Non-resistance was the only way to survive the siege. As long as she wore what the tyrant permitted, slept when the tyrant allowed, worked only when absolutely necessary and stayed indoors as much as possible, she'd be all right.

CHAPTER ELEVEN

The Heat

SHE WAS LEARNING to get through the days, but with Bennie gone, would she live through the nights? Limp and exhausted, locked in her house, she lay awake listening to yowling coyotes, croaking frogs, buzzing insects, banjos and guitars, men's laughter and shouts. Where the men came from Frieda didn't know, but Lollie's was often as noisy as Market Street on Saturday night.

Brawls erupted outside the tent saloon, and one night a worker from across the line was shot by a drunk ranch hand from Begler's ranch up in Growlers Valley. The next day, on the way to the pond, Frieda walked past the prisoner tied to a tree waiting to be picked up by a Pima County deputy sheriff. He was filthy and disgruntled, still a kid, a handsome one. She was about to go back to the First Lady and bring him something to eat, when he called out to her.

"Hey, pretty lady, there's something I want you to do for me." His voice was low, seductive and rippling with male arrogance.

Eyes averted, limbs trembling, she hurried passed him to her house. Later that day, she asked Ramón to bring the prisoner simple meals—water, tortillas and beans. But she did not breathe easily until the sheriff finally arrived, trussed him up and carted him off.

Harrigan posed a more complex problem. Several days after Bennie left, he approached Frieda after supper, head bowed, sombrero in hand. He wanted her to teach him to read and write the language of his father, and "espeek" *también*. The request, so earnestly stated, reminded her of how she felt when she started school. She looked like a San Francisco girl, starched pinafore, pale hair and skin, blue eyes. But when forced to speak, her Yiddish-accented English marked her as an outsider, an unwelcome one. Harrigan broke into a wide, chip-toothed grin when she agreed. *"Esta noche,* I come your house."

"Not tonight, and not my house," Frieda said, firm as a seasoned teacher setting straight an unruly pupil. "I'll set a proper time and place. *"Un buen tiempo y lugar."*

At each meal thereafter, she felt his eyes entreating her. His insistence alarmed her. She kept making excuses: it was too hot; too late, she had to cook. One night he knocked at her door. She was already stretched out on her bed in a sleeveless muslin nightgown.

"Who is it?" Frieda called. Her heart was beating like a tin spoon on a pie plate.

"Arrigahn."

"What do you want?"

"Una lección."

"I told you not at my house."

"Adónde? Cuando?"

"The dining tent. Tomorrow after supper." She could hear him grumbling on the other side of the door. After several moments, his boot kicking at the parched earth, he softly called, *"Hasta mañana."*

Frieda went to the drawer, found the Bowie knife, slipped it under her pillow, then took the pistol out of her apron pocket and put it in the table drawer next to the bed. The rifle was propped against the side of the hearth, within easy reach. Her arsenal at hand, she lay down again and listened to the crickets, coyotes, frogs, owls, and Lollie's raucous customers. Blood buzzing in her head, her chest heaving, she longed for that time when she, like Bennie, could leap to action, and just as speedily relax.

The next evening, after the tables were cleared, as Angelina and Ramón were washing the dishes, Frieda sat down on a bench alongside Harrigan and opened a *McGuffey's Reader* between them. A hot wind swept through the tent flap. The kerosene lantern on the table swayed and flickered, casting an eery light. Harrigan didn't notice. Brow wrinkled, he was bent on turning letters into words. Her thoughts were not of letters and words, but of the smells emanating from the body two inches from her. It was an aggressive male odor: perspiration, cigars, whisky, garlic, onions-—a workingman's smell. Distancing herself another two inches, she forced her eyes to the printed page.

To her surprise, Harrigan could read English a little. They flipped through the chapters until he found something that interested him.

"Work," was the title of the poem he selected.

"'Work work, mi voy, be not ah-frah-eed, go on.'"

"'Work, work, my boy, be not afraid, go on,'" demonstrated Frieda.

"'Look lah-vor voldlee in the fa-ce,'"

"'Face.'"

"'Face?'" Harrigan questioned.

"Cara."

He smiled. "Tu cara es muy bonita."

"Continue, Mr. Harrigan," Frieda said. "'And blush not for your humble place.'"

"'And blush not for your oombel place.'"

"You have a good ear, Mr. Harrigan."

His eyes shining with boyish pride, he returned to his reading.

An hour later, he walked her to her door, thanked her and left. Inside, Frieda rested her head against the splintery door, weary but pleased with what they had accomplished.

Each night thereafter, they read from *McGuffey's* together. Harrigan was intelligent and ambitious too; he hoped to move to San Diego and become a general contractor. After each lesson, he thanked her, walked her home and, as soon as she was inside, departed. One night, curious about where he went when he left her, Frieda pulled back the yellow and red calico curtain and peeped out. By the light of a full moon, she watched him hurry over to Lollie's where Old Wally—Lollie's assistant—was dousing the lights and closing up.

"*Qué lástima*, what a pity," he called, then started up the slope to the construction workers' tent.

"Are they coming?" It was a boy's voice and it came from behind Frieda, inside the room. The words were whispered in a quivering voice that sounded as if it were about to crack and spill sobs.

Frieda froze in place.

"Look close, do you see them?"

She whipped around and broke for the door. A figure darted in front of her. The first thing she saw was her Winchester rifle. A tall, thin boy held it up across his chest, his back pressed against the door.

"Don't want to go out now," he said. "They'll see you." His voice was low, as if he was afraid someone out there would hear him.

Frieda studied his narrow, dirty face. She'd never seen him before. He was a young man, very tall and painfully thin. His long, straight hair was the color of butterscotch, as was his skin. His hazel eyes burned with fear. He was wearing the remains of a United States Army uniform, a torn shirt and a pair of pants. There were scratches on his throat.

"I know I look a sight," he apologized. "I've been running for days. The black bulls are after me. They almost had me a couple of times."

The buzzing in Frieda's head slowed a little. *How could bulls chase him for days?* "Real black bulls?"

His tone was irritated, but restrained. "Of course, they're real, right out there." He pointed to the window.

Frieda went to the window and pulled back the curtain.

"Be careful, they'll see you and come charging in."

She let the curtain drop and stepped back several steps. "I was just out there. I didn't see any black bulls."

"You didn't?"

"No."

The boy's twitching face relaxed slightly, then retightened.

"They're there, all right. They chased me all the way down here. Would I be running if they weren't chasing me?" That possibility seemed to anger him.

Frieda studied him trying to decide what to believe.

"I wouldn't," he insisted.

"I'll go out and take another look," Frieda said.

His thin body pressed tighter against the door. He lifted the rifle, his finger on the trigger. "I can't let you do that."

Frieda couldn't make her legs stop shaking, but she could steady her voice. "I want you to leave right now."

His head jerked up to look at her again. "I can't leave here now." He seemed amazed she would suggest it. "Not until they're gone."

"Then let me go. I'll bring help," Frieda said. As she spoke, Frieda remembered that Morrie was spending the night at the ranch and that she had not seen Yancy after supper. Old Wally was her best hope; the old frontiersman always wore a gun at his belt. She didn't know where he slept, but Lollie probably did.

"No," the boy straightened with fear, jiggling the rifle in his shaking hands. "Don't get anyone."

"They'll help you."

"They can't do a thing about the black bulls. No one can."

"Why not?"

His face turned angry and evasive. "I've got to wait until they have a mind to go."

"My sister-in-law is coming to spend the night with me. She'll be arriving any minute. The black bulls might follow her. I'd better head her off."

The boy's lips turned up in a half smile. "Lady you don't understand. Those bulls will stomp you to a bloody rag. Stay with me until they're gone. As soon as they wander off, I'm going to slip across the line. Once I get into Mexico, I'll be through with them forever. They don't dare come into Mexico. Too many good bullfighters in Mexico. Make yourself comfortable." He slid down to the floor in front of the door and drew his knees up toward his chest. His back slumped forward wearily, and his chin dropped to his chest. He remained in that position for several minutes.

"Sakes, I'm tired after all that running."

Frieda sat on the edge of the bed. She thought of the knife under her pillow and the pistol in the drawer, but she didn't reach for either. Not as long as he was holding her rifle. The boy was insane, she was quite certain.

"Who are the black bulls?" she asked, after a long silence.

"Who?"

"What are the black bulls?" she tried again.

The hazel eyes darkened and narrowed. It was too hard to explain. "All I can tell you is that they're dangerous, deadly." He rolled his eyes at the thought.

Mr. Grinowitz. He was at Levie's Kosher Boardinghouse all one winter. When something upset him, he imagined his blankets were attacking him. He'd start cursing and yelling, "They're smothering me, they're smothering me." As a Sister of Service, she'd done a month's assignment at the insane asylum, so the boarders always called her when Grinowitz's blankets turned mean. He was big and heavyset, and he'd wrestle with those blankets as though he were fighting for his life. Eventually, she'd persuade him to let her take the blankets outside and give them a good beating.

"I had a friend who was attacked by wool blankets," Frieda told the boy.

He looked skeptical.

"I'd give him foods that helped him fight them off."

"What kind of foods?"

"Beef stew." She had a fresh pot in the cooler in the store cellar.

"Just plain beef stew?"

"Oh no, not plain beef stew. Beef stew with potatoes and carrots, with lots of gravy."

"What else?"

"Freshly baked egg bread, or sometimes white bread would do as well."

"Something to drink?"

"Lots to drink."

"You got any water here?" the boy asked abruptly. "I'm thirsty."

"Drinks were particularly good for Mr. Grinowitz. Ice cold lemonade...."

The boy's dry lips dropped open.

"Cold beer," Frieda tried.

"I don't like beer," he snapped.

"Fruit punch."

"Fruit punch sounds good," the boy said. "Did it help your friend?"

"Cold apple cider was the best."

The boy quietly appraised her.

"I've got some cold apple cider over at the store. I could go get it."

"I can't let you go out; you'd get hurt."

Frieda rose and stood alongside the chair. "I won't tell anyone you're here. I could bring you some stew, fresh bread, chocolate cake and lots of cold apple cider. I could even fix up a package of food for you to take with you to Mexico."

The boy forced his lips together, then parted them to catch his breath.

"Free of charge," Frieda said.

"I'm so thirsty."

"You'll love this cider."

The boy was still thinking it over. "Sit down and be quiet, let me think." The boy cocked his head over to one side, as if he were listening to his left shoulder.

"You can lock the door as soon as I go out. Then you can stay at the window with the rifle ready. Five minutes and I'll be back with stew, bread, cake, cider."

"No more than five minutes?" His eyes were wary.

"Five minutes," Frieda said. "I'll be back and we'll have a nice little supper."

He took a step away from the door as she advanced and let her unlock the bolts. "Hurry, I'm scared," he hissed, his body starting to tremble.

"I'll be right back," she said. "You can watch me."

Snakes, Frieda thought, as she stepped into the hot night with no pistol in her pocket. Then she was off and running. The front door to the store was locked. Frieda looked back at her house. She thought she saw the curtain draw back. She pounded on the door. Lollie should hear her, but there was no response.

"Lollie, Lollie," she called again, loud as she dared. She remembered where they kept a spare key. It hung behind a loose board in the northeast corner of the building. She found it, opened the door, and ran through the store to Lollie and Morrie's quarters in the back room. Lollie was stretched out on the bed in her petticoat. Five or six months pregnant, Frieda would speculate later when the image returned. There was someone with her. Not Morrie. A blonde man, he had his shirt off and was removing his pants. On the table alongside the bed was a gray wig and the heavy black-rimmed glasses Old Wally wore. Frieda whipped around, her back to the couple.

"I'm sorry to intrude," she apologized, "but I need help. There's a crazy boy in my house. I think he's an army deserter. He has my gun...." Without turning, she outlined her plight, and a plan for the boy's capture.

Frieda left the store alone with a bottle of cider in one hand and a pot of beef stew in the other. She walked across the clearing, rattling the pot to attract the boy's attention. In the meanwhile, Wally, as Frieda suggested, came out the back door. Crouching, he ran along the outer edge of the plaza and came around the back of Frieda's house to the corner, where he waited for the boy to open the door for Frieda.

The boy had his hand extended ready to take the cider from Frieda when Wally, wig and glasses in place, seized his forearm, yanked him out of the door, threw him on the ground and planted his boot on his midsection. Pulling a length of rope from his shoulder, Wally cinched the boy's hands and feet as if he were a stray calf. Then he pulled him to his feet and adjusted the ties so he could inch along the ground in the direction Wally tugged.

The boy looked more disappointed than distressed. "Where's my cider?" he asked Frieda.

She went into the house, came out with a tin cup, filled it with cider and placed it in his fettered hands.

The boy drank, lowered the cup for a refill, drank again, then dropped the cup to the ground, his face contorting. "You tricked me, lady. If the black bulls get me, it's going to be all your fault."

"Quiet, there," Wally ordered, tugging the rope to start the boy walking. "More like soldiers going to get you than black bulls. A party of them are camped over on the other side of the pond. They were in the saloon earlier tonight showing around a picture of the boy. He killed a storekeeper over near Tubac, then did in two other soldiers when they came to arrest him. The soldiers say he's out of his head and dangerous as a rabid dog. That was why we closed early."

Frieda stood near the door watching Wally half-drag the boy across the clearing. Yancy's light had gone on at the sound of the scuffle. A rustling noise sounded at Frieda's feet. She jumped and stepped quickly through the open door. For the second time that night, she bolted the door and leaned against it. Fear and adrenalin sloshed through her, dissolving her knee joints, speeding her heartbeat, squeezing her lungs closed. It was as if she had tied her flapping parts together for the ordeal and now that it was over, the ties had snapped and she was flying apart. To whom could she turn? Not to Lollie. Not to Wally. Not to the soldiers. Yancy.

CHAPTER TWELVE

Yancy Nunes

"YANCY, ARE YOU THERE?" Frieda called through the closed tent flap. "Yancy? May I speak to you?" She could hear him moving around inside. Why didn't he answer? She cast an anxious look back at the moon-silvered clearing. Harrigan? She'd have to walk up the slope to the hotel site and look for him in one of the workmen's tents. "Yancy, I must—" she called, her voice thick with a restrained sob. The flap lifted and he rushed out, colliding with her. She rocked back on already shaky legs, her lips forming a childish "Whoops."

He took her elbow to steady her. "Are you all right?" he asked, assessing her dubiously as he spoke.

"I'm fine." She straightened her stained work dress and ran a hand over her straggling hair. "Fine."

"I thought you'd be spending the night with Lollie. I was going to look in on you after I got the story on that boy from the soldiers, but I forgot. I apologize. Are you sure you're all right?"

"Sure." Her smile slid from crazed to conventional and back to crazed. "You talked to the soldiers? What did they tell you?"

"I just finished the story. Can't say I'll print it. It's hardly the thing for our peace-and-prosperity sheet, but the facts are there, if you're interested."

"Very interested. That's why I came by." She was eyeing the tent flap.

"Prepare yourself for bedlam," he said, one hand on her elbow, the other pulling back the flap, "otherwise known as bachelor quarters."

Bedlam meant a book- and paper-strewn desk; clothes, soiled towels and handkerchiefs on the floor, on the back of a chair, on the unmade cot, and alongside the cot a rough-hewn table supporting three bottles of tequila, two empty, a couple of medicine bottles, two glasses, and a tin of saltines. It was like seeing the poor man turned inside out. In a flash, the terror returned: trembling body, nausea, racing heart, vertigo.

Yancy was coming toward her, saying, "Here it...." As she was slipping to the ground, he caught her around the waist and guided her to the cot. "Just look at you, you're green as grass."

Perching on the edge, she dropped her head between her knees for several seconds, straightened, inhaled several deep breaths and looked up. Yancy was watching as if she were about to expire.

"I don't know what hit me."

"Bedlam, no doubt."

She laughed as if at a hilarious joke, then abruptly stopped. "Let's see what you have there."

Dos Cacahuates, Arizona Territory
June 24, 1880
        Private Tracy Spoonover, 19, of Fort Lowell, A.T., who is wanted in connection with the murder of Henry Jameson, a Negro porter at Branson's Dry Goods Store in Tucson, A.T., and the murders of Corporal O.T. Sampson and Private Steven Butte, was captured Thursday evening, June 24, at the home of Mr. and Mrs. Bennie Goldson in Dos Cacahuates, A.T. According to the deputies who made the arrest, Spoonover, a native of Milwaukee, Wisconsin, was said to have been acting peculiarly for some months previous to the murder of Jameson, and the subsequent murders of the two soldiers who were trying to arrest him. The accused man escaped and was re-arrested a month later in Yuma. He got away a second time and was thought to be heading for Mexico. He was found hiding in the

Goldson residence in the new community of Dos Cacahuates, on the Arizona-Sonora border.

"This won't appear in the San Francisco papers, will it?" Frieda asked.

"Hardly. You may be its only reader," Yancy answered.

"My folks would have a fit. My father would—" More wild laughter.

"I can't tell whether you're laughing or crying," Yancy said, placing his hand on her shoulder, as if to still her.

His concern alarmed her. "I'd better go." She tried to get up. Yancy caught her arm and eased her back down onto the cot.

"You wouldn't make it across the clearing," he cautioned. "Stay. You've had quite a shock. You need a drink."

Hand over her face, she waited until he returned with a bottle of tequila and two glasses. "I could use one myself," he murmured.

The first gulp seared her throat; she coughed. By the second she could feel the liquid heat coursing through her body, untying knots. Yancy lifted the bottle in her direction again. Afraid to move, for fear she might touch one of his personal effects, she gripped the side of the cot with one hand and she raised her glass. He filled it, his gaze shifting from her to the work on his desk, then back to her. "I'm doing the second issue of the *Selah*."

"Don' mind me, I'll leave in a minute."

"You look like a bird poised on the edge of a fouled nest. Let me straighten out that cot. Get up for a minute."

She rose, head whirling. He gathered his whatevers, smoothed the old army blanket and invited her to stretch out for a while. Refilling her glass and his, he retreated to his chair.

As Yancy wrote, she sipped the tequila and let her thoughts wander. Pond and desert sounds mixed with the scratch of Yancy's pen. The kerosene lamp cast a circle of light on the papers; the rest of the tent was in semi-darkness.

An image of the boy pulled along like a stubborn dog by Lollie's bewigged lover appeared. "So what's new in Dos Cacahuates besides tonight's fracas?" she called out to her host.

"We've had a big week," Yancy responded. "Twenty-three guests in town including the man from the United States Customs Service here to consider Dos Cacahuates as a port of entry and the evangelist minister from Kansas carrying Bennie's handbill." Yancy laughed. "I told him to come back in October when we'll have a batch of souls to save."

The tequila bottle clicked against Yancy's glass. Frieda extended her arm for a refill. After downing the third drink, she thought about getting up but couldn't move. A stray thought surfaced and tumbled out of her mouth.

"You wanted to become a rabbi."

"I did," Yancy answered, without looking up.

"I never knew a single American-born rabbi," Frieda said, with a drunken giggle, "or a rabbi who was single." She was slurring her words like a *shiker.* If she wasn't drunk, she was on her way.

Yancy's pen scratched on. "Maybe that was why I quit rabbinical studies, that and religious reasons."

"You're not a believer?"

"Yes and no."

"Like me."

"Like you? Miss Frieda of the kosher boardinghouse?" He was back in his chair, when she reached for her glass again.

Frieda drank, set the glass on the floor, then dropped back to the pillow.

"When I was about sixteen, I started having doubts about my religion. I spoke to the leader of the Sisters of Service, and she urged me to read the Holy Scriptures, in English, of course." Frieda was giggling again. "The ancient Hebrews had as much trouble getting along as we do." Head nodding, arm waving, she struggled to sit up. "The German Jews think the Polish Jews are trash, and the Polish Jews think the German Jews are shnobs." "Snobs," she tried again.

Yancy laughed and put down his pen. "And the Spanish Jews look down on both the German and the Polish Jews. When I was twenty, I was madly in love with a beautiful German Jewess. My mother took to her bed at the thought that her precious son would consider blending his aristocratic blood with an infinitely inferior German strain."

Frieda leaned forward, peering at his pale, handsome face through a tequila fog. He'd never spoken of his personal life before.

"What happened?"

Yancy was laughing again. "Mother's objections kept me enthralled two months longer than usual, but by summer a lovely English widow's eyes did what maternal disapproval could not do."

"Didn't marry her either," Frieda said, eager to pierce the mysteries of their able partner.

"No."

Had she gone too far? Frieda dropped back on the cot out of sight, embarrassed.

"I prize my freedom," Yancy decided to add.

Frieda was back on her elbow. "Emansha...emanshapashun for everyone." She lifted her glass, spilling its contents over the front of her dress.

Yancy's pen was moving again.

"I want Dos Cacahuates to be a new kind of place. A place where people are kind, and have reshpect for one another." A wracking sob broke from her. "I tricked that crazy boy, Yancy. He was so scared of the black bulls. Scared for me as well as himself. I can't forget how he looked at me when Old Wally grabbed him." Frieda was quivering and crying.

Yancy got up and sat alongside her on the cot. He took her trembling hands in his.

"He was insane, an accused murderer. You had to defend yourself."

"There's something else. Wally isn't Old Wally." Her tequila-glazed eyes rolled in anguish. "He's Lollie's lover."

He nodded, as if to say, "So?"

Tears streamed down Frieda's face. "It's not right. "Lollie's deceiving Morrie."

"No use thinking about that now," Yancy soothed, patting her hair and cheek.

She pointed to the glass on the floor. "Just a drop more." Like an ailing child dutifully downing her medicine, Frieda gulped her fifth tequila, then lowered her eyelids and settled back against the pillow, her hands nestling in Yancy's.

The bright morning light stabbed at Frieda's closed eyelids. Her head throbbed like an open wound. Her mouth tasted bitter and dry, and the hot morning air singed the inside of her nose. She opened one eye to see Yancy standing with his back to the cot. He was undoing his trousers and tucking in his shirttail. Embarrassed at witnessing so intimate an act, she squeezed her eyes shut. A rush of hot air hit her, as the canvas flap opened and closed. How considerate of him to leave before she woke.

Through aching, half-closed eyes, she searched the disheveled tent trying to fill in the night's missing parts. The last thing she remembered was Yancy seated alongside her, their hands entwined. He must have returned to work after she fell asleep. A new litter of crumpled papers lay on the floor around his chair. Her eyes shifted to four empty tequila bottles between the desk and the cot, lying between a row of overturned boots. Four? She remembered two empty and one half full. Had Yancy finished another bottle on his own? Where had he slept? In the chair? Alongside her?

Frieda bolted upright. A new pain shot up from the point where her spine entered her skull. Her hand on her forehead, she rose as if from a sick bed, adjusted her skirt and smoothed down her hair. She had to leave sometime. Breathing slowly and deeply, she summoned the courage to pull back the flap and peep out. No one was in sight. She slipped through the opening, ran a few yards, then slowed her pace to a nonchalant amble.

Inside her house, she fell back against the closed door and

inhaled. Clutching the door knob for support, she scrutinized every inch of the room. Would she ever enter her house again without expecting someone to leap out at her? Or, for that matter, see Yancy Nunes without recalling his kindness to her the night before? She hated to think of what a less principled man might have done in similar circumstances.

As Frieda served Yancy breakfast at the First Lady that morning, he behaved as if nothing unusual had taken place between them. Her head bowed, she apologized for intruding on him and thanked him for his brotherly concern.

"Don't hesitate to call on me whenever you need help," Yancy urged. "We're partners, aren't we?"

The heat, the heat, the heat. During the next two weeks the temperatures soared. Day after day, the thermometer rose past the hundred mark—105, 106, 107, 110 and on several days even up to 115 degrees, sucking up everything—air, water, vegetation, appetite, talk, ambition, energy. Frieda moved slowly, wearing a wet cloth around her neck, sniffing at smelling salts and lying down whenever she did not have to stand. Nothing and no one mattered that did not help her get through the suffocating days and the endless nights.

Fortunately, the number of diners dwindled at the First Lady. Passers-through stopped coming, and some of the locals no longer cared to travel fifteen to twenty miles for a meal. Harrigan and his crew took off on July first, saying they would be back after the rains came.

Then Angelina appeared one day with a woman she introduced as Guadalupe, who was nearly black-skinned and almost as round as she was tall. Two of her children were sick, Angelina told Frieda. She had to go to Los Mochis for a while; Guadalupe would work in her place.

Of course. No one was hungry anyway. She'd cut the meals down to the simplest fare—eggs, coffee, tortillas, canned fruits, vegetables, beans.

Frieda stopped looking at herself in the mirror. Her brown curly hair was frizzled with the daily soakings in the pond and scorched by the heat. She was staying under cover most of the day to avoid the sun and had turned paler than when she arrived in Dos Cacahuates. When cooking, her blanched-looking skin turned wet and pink as the inside of a watermelon. Dark circles had formed under her blue eyes, and her lips were dry and cracked, as was the skin around her nostrils. Insect bites dotted her forehead and arms, and a cruel burn on the inside of her arm—got when she grew dizzy one day and fell against a coffee pot—refused to heal.

When she was not struggling through the preparations of the meals, or fruitlessly trying to explain chores to Guadalupe, who was slower, less willing and less comprehending than Angelina, Frieda retired to her house and her bed.

There she lay, her pulse racing, her head throbbing, her body sticky with sweat, too hot to read, to write letters, to study hotel furnishings catalogs. Cursing the heat and wishing that the rains and Bennie would arrive (they were inextricably mixed in her head, Bennie and the rains), she thanked God for her protector, Yancy. At least, she had one person to turn to. Almost nightly, she went to his tent to discuss one matter or another.

What should she do about Guadalupe?

"Be patient," Yancy counseled. "Angelina will return, or Guadalupe will catch on, or both. In the meanwhile, you have to have someone to help you."

She received a letter from Bennie. He was in Omaha, Nebraska, and was doing so well; he was extending his trip two weeks.

"Two more weeks," Frieda told Yancy, "and I'll be handing out bags of dirt and calling it gold dust, like Mad Mabel of Market Street."

"You've survived this far. You can hang on for another two weeks," Yancy reasoned.

And what should she do about Lollie? They used to be as close as sisters, closer. Since that night, they've barely spoken a word to each other. Is it her duty to tell Morrie? He is her brother-in-law.

Morrie has as much sense and as good a pair of eyes as
you," Yancy said. "If he chooses to allow Lollie her *assistant*,
you have no right to interfere."

Some nights Frieda knew Yancy was in no mood to receive her and feigned absence. She tried to restrain herself,
but each night, sooner or later, she was on her feet and starting across the clearing to his tent. The bit of companionship
she got from him had become as essential to her existence as
water. When with him in his tent, she tried to emulate his im-
personal, but amiable manner. Though outwardly proper, she
was aware that she was secretly inhaling the fragrance of his
hair pomade, studying the way his eyebrows grew over his
long brown eyes, noting the color in his cheeks (was there
more, was there less), measuring his cough, one day's against
the next. She was also examining his writings, searching for
clues about the half-known man behind the pen, and puzzling over the sharp contrasts that divided him: a native-born
American, a northerner and a southerner, a poet and a promoter, exacting and slovenly, forthright and secretive, optimis-
tic and despairing, inviting and evasive, euphoric and de-
pressed, an intimate friend and a business associate.

Yancy was a puzzle to himself too, Frieda realized, reading
a poem he had written on a scrap of paper, left on a corner
of his desk.

I'd like to know the reason why
Our Maker, deemed master at his craft,
Would press together under one thin skin
A peacock, a fox, a rabbit, a snake, a goat.
Even a simple-minded farmer knows
That such an assembly
Would lead to mayhem in the barnyard.

When he dropped bits of information about himself, she
hungrily picked them up. His father had died when he was a
small boy. His maternal grandfather, the Rhode Island spice

merchant, had tried to father him. The stern old man, a lay rabbi, longed to make a scholar of him. But Yancy had been equally drawn to his richer, more fun-loving Charleston relatives, with whom he'd lived when his father was alive. When his mother had remarried, he moved back and forth between the southern and northern households. The elders were long since gone, and he had lost interest in the rest of both clans, and they in him.

He'd been in love a half-dozen times, but never able to bind himself to one and forsake all others. About his work, he was equally irresolute. He tried poetry, but introspection and solitude heightened his distaste for the human condition in general, and himself in particular. Teaching English literature bored him, and newspaper reporting was a scalawag's trade. He'd joined forces with Colonel Leighton because he had to make some money, but he was barely earning enough to sustain himself. This last morsel Yancy let fall one night in the middle of July.

"Until Dos Cacahuates," Frieda said, reflecting on how the project had gilded all of their lives with new promise.

Yancy's lips tilted in a sardonic smile. "It's not wise to invest too much hope in any townbuilding scheme."

"*Hope* is what you need most," Frieda countered. "Believe you're going to recover your health and find in Dos Cacahuates the success and happiness that has eluded you elsewhere, and you will. Yancy, you could end up in a history book."

"Or," Yancy mocked, "in a mug book."

CHAPTER THIRTEEN

For the Greater Good

FOR SEVERAL NIGHTS thereafter, when she came to call, Yancy was absent, or pretending to be. Nor did he have much to say to her during the days. The first night she noticed his lantern burning in his tent, she hurried across the clearing to see him. He didn't respond to her call. She listened to his labored breathing. Was he asleep? Stricken? Unconscious? Extending her kerosene lantern in front of her, she rushed in.

"Who's there?" Yancy asked. His voice was wan, querulous.

"Are you all right?" Frieda asked.

"Right as rain. Where'd that expression come from? Not from around here."

"I need to talk to you."

"Not tonight."

"Can I get something for you?"

"No."

"Sit with you for a while?"

No answer.

She felt like a stubborn child who, upon being ordered home, refuses to budge. "Please."

"Turn off that lantern; my head aches."

Frieda doused the light and felt her way to the chair. An acrid, medicinal smell dominated the hot dark air. She sat still, monitoring his wheeze, coughs, groans. Pity for him swelled, along with pity for herself.

"I've missed you so much."

No reply came from the cot.

"I thought you were angry with me." Frieda knew she

was shifting the attention from him to her, but couldn't help herself. "Your friendship is my only comfort, Yancy." She was speaking from her heart to an unseen presence as she would not have dared speak to him eye-to-eye.

"Nonsense."

"You keep me going." Frieda's voice was plaintive and damp with new-born truth. "I must have *someone*." She listened for a response, none came. "The truth is...."

"No truth tonight." The cot creaked as he coughed.

One sob, then others, drowned all other sounds in the dark tent. She knew she ought to take her distress back to her own house, but she couldn't return to that empty room loaded down with misery.

"Say something, please. Anything." She rose as if lifted out of the chair and slid to her knees alongside the cot. Fumbling in the dark, she wrapped her hand around Yancy's bare arm.

His hot, damp hand dropped over hers. He heaved onto his side and groaned, "Oh, Frieda, leave, leave now."

Startled by the urgency of his plea, she started to rise. He reached up, pulled her back onto the cot, clasped her to his chest and rocked her to and fro. Her arms circled his bare back. They clung together like lone, lost souls who'd collided in the dark and were afraid to let go for fear they'd never find each other again. She flung herself alongside him, a thin sheet separating her from his nakedness. The evidence of his hunger for her pressing against her hip, she heard him cry, "Frieda, Frieda, Frieda."

The sound of her name, uttered in desire pulled her out of her phantom state. Her beating heart and panting breath told her what she wanted, wanted now.

What of him? She pulled back to see. His eyes were closed and his head was tilted so that his long, straight, black hair touched his thin shoulders. "Yancy," she started.

"Shush." His mouth fell on hers.

He wanted her. The unapproachable prince, the scholar, the gentleman, wanted her. With an unrestrained cry, she pulled back the sheet and slid down onto his naked body, her dress rising and her bare legs tangling with his. Her hand un-buttoned the front of her dress, then reached for his hand. Her lips found his again.

Frieda woke before sun-up. She was lying on her side, her back pressed against the tent canvas. One of Yancy's arms pinned her in place. She lifted the arm as if it were a bar over a door and climbed over his sleeping body feet first. Then she straightened her clothes, smoothed her hair, crossed her fingers and slipped out of the tent into the pre-dawn dark.

Back in her own house, she washed her face and hands and replaced her crumpled dress with a thin nightgown. Lying on her bed, her eyes closed, she relived their coupling, marveling at its intensity, and even more at the absence of shame. The emotion she was feeling was so new, it was difficult to name. Satisfaction? Triumph? Exaltation?

From their first meeting, Bennie's admiration and desire for her reached out like a cresting wave and swept her to him. In their lovemaking too, the impetus invariably came from him. He was constantly studying her as she tied her shoes, arranged her hair, read a book, or lay at his side in their double bed. She often stretched her desire to accommodate his, as a wife was expected to do.

Last night, she was the aggressor; she wanted Yancy, and made him want her, Frieda recalled, astounded at the lingering thrill of seduction. No misgivings, no sorrow, no regrets. She, Frieda noted incredulously, was an unrepentant adulteress. It served Bennie right. He left her in this inferno while he gallivanted through the middle west, enjoying cool breezes, good food and God knows what other pleasures.

Clinging to her reverie, Frieda did not rise until Guadalupe summoned her to start cooking breakfast. Then she drifted through the day, oblivious to the dreaded heat, the insects, her aching legs. In front of others, Yancy permitted himself only a customary nod. And his words to her were brief and confined to business. But her blood surged, when he spoke them, as if he were uttering endearments. Like a nocturnal animal, her body and mind daydreamed, waiting for nightfall, when she could return to his tent and savor again the unexpected rewards of waywardness.

When she entered his tent that night, he was sitting in his chair pen in hand. He rose, his face somber, and came to her. Frieda turned off her lantern and went to meet him. In moments, they were again on the cot locked in each other's arms, retracing the steps to last night's lovemaking. She nuzzled against him, drawing his thin arms around her, the way a rock climber secures himself to a staked rope. Her hands played over his body and to her renewed amazement, she again had her way with him. Once more, it was in Frieda that rapture radiated longer, and Frieda who babbled of joy and gratitude. While Yancy, once his passion was spent, began to speak with misgivings of their conduct. His tone was tender and his fingers wandered over her face and body, but he was clearly trying to reconstruct a fence between them.

"We're living in each other's pockets, Frieda. We're bound to be discovered, just as you found out about Lollie and her man. Last night was an accident, Frieda, a lovely one; tonight, its aftermath. We must take hold of ourselves."

"All I care about is this incredible thing that has happened to us," she responded.

Yancy unloosened her arm and sat up. "Are you possessed? What's become of the righteous woman I know?"

She heard his words, but they didn't seed in her. She'd sped from despair to delight in his arms. By comparison, all other journeys were inconsequential.

The next night, when Frieda arrived he was not in his tent. Unwilling to go home, she sat in the dark, inhaling the traces of Yancy in his writing tools on the desk, his boots at her feet, his jacket hanging on the rack above her. Time, possibly two hours, passed before he returned from Lollie's, unsteady on his feet and drenched with the odor of Mexican cigars and tequila. He stepped through the tent flap, belched, then noticed her sitting there.

"Where were you?" Frieda asked.

"I was talking to Abe Beisel. He's leaving for Guaymas to-morrow with a load of merchandise. You shouldn't have waited."

"I had to," Frieda said, moving out of the chair and onto the cot. She seized Yancy's hand and tried to pull him down alongside her. He sidestepped her and made for the chair.

"Just as well, I need to talk to you. Abe Beisel was camping up on the slope near the hotel last night. He wanted to know who the woman was he saw leaving my tent just before dawn. Lucky for us, from his bedroll he couldn't see where she went. I assured him he was dreaming. Beisel is playing poker and won't be bedding down for an hour or two, but it would be hard to convince him he had the same dream two nights in a row. He's a good friend of Bennie's, Frieda. You'd better leave now."

"It's too late, Yancy. I don't care anymore." She tried to pull him out of the chair. He resisted. She rose and settled herself on his knees. She could feel his body stiffen with anger as she slipped her hand inside his shirt. He grabbed her hands and restrained them.

"You're not yourself," he reasoned. "Heat and loneliness have undone you. I can't let you destroy your future—and the project to boot—for a few nights of madness."

Frieda covered his face with kisses. "You put everyone's interests before your own." Her lips settled on his tight mouth for several seconds before she said, "The only thing I can do now is to tell Bennie the truth. I hate to hurt him, but you and I—"

Yancy sprang from the chair, throwing Frieda to her feet. "There'll be no you and me ever, Frieda. Do you hear me? Not ever. There will be no me and anybody." As if on cue, he began to cough. Reaching for his handkerchief, he rocked back and forth, his face reddening, his eyes bulging.

When the attack passed, Frieda continued. "I've tended consumptives before. I've seen men brought back from death's door. I'll look after—"

"Control yourself. If you are not ashamed, I am ashamed for you."

"I can't deny what I feel for you, Yancy."

He clamped his hand over her mouth. "Hush. If you can't deny it, then bear it in silence as countless noble people before you have borne their illicit desires. What is nobility but the strength to overcome unworthy impulses? We lost our heads; now we must find them again." Yancy's voice had climbed to prophetic authority. His large brown eyes held her blue ones as he uttered his final injunction. "We must sacrifice our base desires for the greater good. We'll both be stronger for what we have denied ourselves."

The feeling of wrongdoing, absent until that moment, whooshed through Frieda like blood rushing out of a newly opened vein. Chuted to her proper place, she was again looking up at Yancy, from the vantage of someone inferior, powerless and clearly at fault. "You're a remarkable man, Yancy," Frieda whispered. "I hope I can make Bennie believe how little of this was your doing."

"Frieda," Yancy commanded, "I order you never to mention a word of this to Bennie. Soon, the memory of this mishap will dissolve like smoke in the air. From this moment on, you are the wife of my business associate, nothing more." As Yancy talked, he guided Frieda to the tent flap. "Don't say another word. Go while we still have the strength to do what is right," Yancy said thrusting her out into the hot, moonless night.

Frieda hesitated in front of the tent. How dare he put her out like an annoying child? She should go back in and force him to hear her out. The voices of men leaving Lollie's and heading her way convinced her otherwise. As she rushed across the clearing, head bowed, Yancy's cough followed her like a round of gunfire. She turned and looked over her shoulder. His tent, like his diseased lungs, seemed to be expanding and contracting laboriously. His pain gladdened her.

After that, Frieda avoided Yancy. Bereft of his intoxicating presence, her perception gradually cleared. Several nights later, she lay awake in the black heat overcome by her treachery and its consequences. She'd broken her marriage vows before her first anniversary and could unburden herself to no one. That would be her punishment. No confession, no making amends, no forgiveness. Frieda's throat clogged with self-loathing.

CHAPTER FOURTEEN

Desert Rain

JULY ENDED WITH no rain. It was a bad year, a drought year. In the south, Angelina reported on her return, many people were leaving their homes in search of water and food. Guadalupe insisted on staying after Angelina's return. At least with the Señora, she would have something to eat and drink. Then two more uninvited helpers joined Frieda's staff: a girl of about fifteen, as small as a child of ten, and her husband, who was close to her age and height. Guadalupe brought them to Frieda and introduced the girl simply as her cousin, and the boy as the husband of her cousin. They'd walked up from Rancho Santa Ana hoping their cousin Guadalupe would take them in. Too weary to resist, Frieda allowed them to stay. She would be needing help later for the Big Day, if they survived until then.

Word came that the Papago Indians, native to the area, had gathered their cactus fruit, brewed their ceremonial liquor and held their usual rainmaking ritual early in July. Failing to get the prayed-for rain, they decided to try again. Yancy, accompanied by Ramón, went to a Papago village to watch. He spent the next day in his tent writing an account of the ceremony, with particular attention to the poetic prayer visualizing the massing of rainmaking forces. Reading the account, the Papago plea for rain rooted in Frieda. That night as she lay in the black heat, she saw small white clouds growing into fat, dark thunderheads, and frogs and spiders creeping forth to summon the rain. Then, at long last, the rain.

Ranchers and miners had started coming to Dos Cacahuates to fill pots and cans with water from the pond.

And interest in Morrie's artesian wells heightened noticeably throughout the area. Two wells had produced a show of water, then dried up. And two others were yielding enough to irrigate the ranch truck garden and orchard. Morrie continued to drill, hoping to tap a lasting supply after the rains came and the water table rose. Cocooned in the heat, Frieda took one step after another, day by day, counting each as Angelina did, as otro día encima.

Clouds began to appear during the first week in August. They drew lower and darker for about a week; then one day right after lunch, Frieda noticed that the entire southeastern end of the sky was dark gray and dripping like a dark gray watercolor wash. During the meal, claps of thunder sounded, quickly silencing the tent. Not a word was spoken after the first roar; then, one by one, the diners began to move outside. Someone left the tent flap pulled back, and Frieda could see lightning zigzag through the cloud-darkened sky. She hurried to finish cleaning up, eager to join the expectant group outside.

The air outdoors was heavy with the smell of ozone. A soft, hot wind swept up yellow-white dust from the ground, which was as hard as brick and cracked with parched fissures. Each of the Dos Cacahuatans wordlessly took up his own station to wait. Lollie and Wally fussed around the saloon, fastening the flap, restaking the sides. Yancy carried a tarpaulin from the store to cover his printing press and supplies, then, pen and pad in hand, sat down to absorb the incoming storm, his features twitching with excitement. Morrie was busy corralling the horses and the cow.

Frieda brushed a broom aimlessly across the threshold of the First Lady. And Angelina and Ramón quickly gathered up the wash drying on surrounding bushes. A heavy cover of warm air settled in the clearing, and the sun, submerged in clouds, radiated a dawnlike aura. Lightning crackled on the western slopes of the Mohawks, and claps of thunder resonated with earthshaking fury. Everyone present, Frieda sensed, was filled with the same emotion: anticipation of relief—life-giving, long-awaited, beautiful to behold. She'd never felt anything like it.

The first drop fell at one thirty-six p.m. (according to the Dos Cacahuates *Selah*). Frieda first felt a round pellet splatter on her forehead. She looked down. They were hitting the ground feet apart. The big drops fell on the dry earth, making dark circles the size of two-bit pieces that sizzled for several moments, then disappeared, sucked up by the parched soil. Drip, drip, drip. Stepping out of their waiting positions, Frieda and the others moved toward the center of the clearing, their heads tilted toward the dark skies, their hands stretched forth, and their tongues extended to catch the cool, sweet water.

"*Heeeejaaaaa,*" Ramón cried.

"*Jaaajaaaa,*" carried on the husband of Guadalupe's cousin.

"*Aaaaay, ca-ca-ray,*" Guadalupe added.

"*Hallelujah,*" Wally shouted.

Their faces wet and beaming, they turned to each other, exchanging wondrous looks. It had actually come. Within minutes, the intermittent drops became a solid downpour. Everyone in the clearing was soon soaking wet and dancing, first alone, then joining hands and spontaneously circling, their feet splashing in the water accumulating on the surface of the baked ground.

After a few minutes of shared exaltation, the circle broke, and the group split back into clusters and singles, though no one left the clearing until the rain was over an hour later. After the ground was dry again, the delicious aroma of the creosote bush, greasewood, and damp sand permeated the warming air. Unable to get her fill, Frieda kept inhaling. The scent seemed to circulate through her, reviving dormant cells. Like all the other creatures who'd been in hiding all that dry summer, she felt like jumping, croaking, running, flying.

By evening, the air was almost as hot and thick as it had been that morning, though the unbearable edge was gone.

Territory veterans assured Frieda there would probably be more rain the next day, and then every day throughout August, turning the desert fresh and green. In a celebratory mood, Frieda baked some pies, the first in weeks. By the time she took the last one out of the oven, everyone else had left the cook tent. As she walked back to her house, she noticed people had divided into groups and were continuing to celebrate. The largest had congregated at Lollie's. It was all male and more numerous than any gathering she'd ever seen in Dos Cacahuates. Where'd they all come from? Had they crawled out of earth and from the bottom of the pond, like the rest of the desert's thirsty amphibians? The rise and fall of their raucous talk, punctuated by wild laughter, had a companionable ring. No trouble tonight, Frieda thought. Everyone's too happy. The Mexicans were having their own fiesta. They—Angelina, Ramón, Guadalupe, Guadalupe's cousin, and the husband of Guadalupe's cousin—had gathered around a campfire at the side of Angelina and Ramón's lean-to. Alternating between song and laughter, their voices added their distinct strain of good cheer to the exhilarating night.

Alone in her room, Frieda restlessly paced, returning every few minutes to the front window to see if the light still burned in Yancy's tent. He and she seemed to be the only two people in the settlement alone in their quarters that night. She had taken so much from Yancy, and given so little. Just once she wanted to go to him, not with her problems, complaints, or illicit longings, but as an act of charity.

She washed, changed into a clean blue cotton dress, and with newfound energy brushed her hair. Arranging a freshly-brewed pot of coffee, a pie, a cup and saucer and silverware for one on a tray, Frieda set out, prepared to deposit her offering and leave.

Halfway across the clearing, she noticed Morrie standing near the wagon in front of the store watching her. Frieda stepped along briskly. A coyote yowled. Even the coyotes are happy tonight, Frieda thought. Was she adapting? Coyotes had become no more alarming than the nocturnal chiming of the bells of Grace Cathedral near the boardinghouse. Someone was calling her name.

Frieda looked over toward the store to see Morrie hurrying toward her. Where was she going? He stood in front of her, his sandy hair covering his forehead, his hazel-eyed gaze nervously darting between her and the ground. She was on her way to Yancy's tent. He was working late and she thought he'd like some coffee and pie.

"Yancy's out," Morrie stammered.

"His lantern is lit. He would have turned it off had he left his tent."

"I saw him go out," Morrie piped.

Frieda bristled. Morrie was keeping an eye on her. Morrie, of all men. Why didn't he keep an eye on his own wife? "I'll just go see."

Her brother-in-law shrugged. "I'm going over to Ramón's," Morrie said, moving past her without another glance.

Two feet from Yancy's tent, a woman's giggle stopped Frieda. It was followed by a man's voice, loose, drunken, speaking Spanish as only Yancy spoke it. A tinkle of glasses sounded, then a husky, countrified girlish voice croaked with pleasure, "Don Yawncee."

Projected against the side of the barely lit tent, she made out the shadows of two figures drawing together in a swaying embrace. Transfixed, Frieda watched until the shadow, now one, slid down out of sight. The light went out. Rooted in place, listening to the murmur of voices and the creaking of the cot, she shuddered, then whirled around.

As she walked back to her house, she saw Morrie with the group at the campfire in front of Ramón's.

"Coffee, pie anyone?" Frieda called, heading for the yellow circle as if it were her original destination.

"Yancy was just retiring," Frieda informed Morrie, "I decided not to disturb him."

Later, as she tossed in her bed, her simmering shame

boiled up into anger, this time at Bennie. Had he not brought her to this hellhole and abandoned her here in the blazing summer, none of this would have happened.

CHAPTER FIFTEEN

Bennie and Friends

FRIEDA WAS AT THE cookstove in the First Lady tent preparing the midday meal when Ramón lifted the flap and called excitedly, *"Doña Fridita, venga. Don Bennie llegó—con amigos."* Bennie. She dropped the empty pan in her hands and started to run. Bennie. Heart thumping, tears rising, Frieda stopped. Her eyes went to the marked calendar hanging alongside the cookstove. August nineteenth. He was three weeks late. From Bennie, her mind shifted to the letter she'd just received from Tehama Street with that humiliating news clipping.

Frieda returned to the cookstove, picked up the fallen pan, set it down on the table with a bang and dipped her spoon into the huge pot of *chile con carne* bubbling on the burner. "Shush," she heard Bennie signal to Angelina. His boots padded through the dust behind her. Frieda's body tightened. When his thick hands fastened to her waist and spun her around, she resisted, pivoting in place.

"Frieda, darling, sweetheart," Bennie said, before his lips landed on hers. She allowed him, and herself, a hungry kiss before she pushed him away, cautioning, "Bennie, we're not alone."

Undaunted, Bennie's mouth roamed over her cheek, her ear, her neck. "I don't give a *damn*. I'm so glad to see you."

By then Frieda was beating him on the back with her wooden spoon still damp with chile. Bennie laughed, pulling away at last to say, "Let me look at you." His hand reached up to grasp her chin. "I've dreamed of that face in a hundred different beds." He was starting to embrace her again. "Bennie," Frieda protested, "you'll make me ruin lunch. The men are hungry."

"I've brought another five. Can you feed them? They're big shots—three mining operators, a cattleman and an importer. I practically roped them to get them here. Got something good?"

"Just chile con carne."

Bennie leaned over the pot and inhaled. "No matzah ball soup, roast chicken, carrot tzimes?" he teased. "I've been bragging about my wife's Jewish cooking all the way down here."

"The management needs notice for special meals."

"Well, you tell the management that we're starving and will be glad to take whatever there is. Come on," he took her hand, "I want to introduce the beautiful First Lady of Dos Cacahuates."

Frieda struggled from his grasp. "Don't be insane, Bennie. I can't come out to meet anyone looking like this." She drew up her shoulders stiffly. "I'll meet whomever I have to meet, but after I've had a chance to tidy up. And, please, don't introduce me as First Lady of Dos Cacahuates. I'm not, never was, and don't want to be."

"Sure, Frieda," Bennie answered, his arm on her shoulder again. "Didn't mean to offend. I'm just so danged happy to see you, and anxious to show you off." He was looking at her, hoping for some response. When none came, he asked, "Didn't you miss me at all?"

"We've been awfully busy again in the last couple of weeks after the rains, and before that the heat and...." Her voice was starting to quiver. She turned away, afraid she was going to burst into tears.

"It must have been hard for you," Bennie said, his hands cupping her shoulders.

"Can't talk now, or there won't be anything to offer your important guests. Give me thirty minutes," Frieda said, mustering a stern tone.

"I'll take them over to Lollie's for a few drinks."

Frieda finished setting out the lunch, chile, canned fruit, coffee, tortillas, salad, then left Angelina to tend to the rest of the preparations. She peeped out of the tent to make sure no one was in sight, then dashed across the clearing. Locked in her house, she washed her face, recombed her hair, set out a fresh city dress. All the while, she constructed a case against Bennie. Didn't he know any better than to leave a hat on a bed? It's bad luck. Wasn't it just like him to come trooping back with a herd of big shots, expecting to find a San Francisco spread, and her looking like a grande dame. If she heard First Lady of Dos Cacahuates again, she was going to bellow.

She turned for a last look in the mirror. Grande dame, indeed. She looked like she'd been lost in the desert for forty days. Her skin was splotchy; her lips cracked, and her hair as dry as Mexican hay. Maybe some earrings, Frieda thought. Alongside the golden circles in the bureau drawer lay the last letter from her family and the article from the *Alta California*. She hadn't answered the letter yet. The sight of it brought a new surge of anger, first in the direction of San Francisco, then at Bennie.

Frieda slammed the bureau drawer, then walked briskly out of the house and toward the First Lady. The moment she and Bennie were alone, she planned to demand an accurate assessment of International Improvement Company and the people behind it. She'd lent her name to the enterprise, urged people to invest, not only her family, but Miss O'Hara, the Sisters of Service, friends, San Francisco businessmen.

During lunch the afternoon rain drummed on the canvas walls. Despite Bennie's urgings, Frieda insisted on playing proprietress, instead of taking her place as hostess at the table. Harrigan, his crew, and about fifteen regular customers took seats and quietly ate, watching and eavesdropping as Yancy, Bennie and Morrie wooed the affluent visitors. The old Ajo mine, a magnificent copper mine, only thirty miles away, could be brought into profitable operation once the short lines were built. And there were other mines in the locale— silver, lead, gold, and copper—ready to go into full operation as soon as the Gulf of California and the Pacific Coast were in easy reach. They'd had serious inquiries from English and Scotch mining interests as well as from some of the largest mine operators in the United States.

Hot air, suggested the *Alta California*, not only described the climate but the new development on the Arizona-Sonora border too, Frieda recalled, shuddering.

What about water? the cattlemen asked. Morrie's pale, narrow face leaned into the circle.

"That's my brother's specialty," Bennie explained proudly.

When Morrie started to review the water report for the third time, Yancy interrupted, saying he wanted to show them the plans at the sales office before he took them to the townsite and up to the hotel. Commerce, he turned to the importer, between Mexico and United States, had fantastic potential, as did tourism. The hotel site, with the hot springs and the pond below, set in the midst of a desert, was a natural for a winter resort. Yancy's voice dropped to a confidential tone. It was public knowledge that a railroad had been started in Guaymas in May. Work was going slow because, Yancy's voice dwindled to a whisper, the termination point on the border was being reconsidered. The new choice, Yancy indicated silently, his index finger pointing to the sawdust floor.

A handful of tin plates fell out of Frieda's hands, clattering against the cookstove before falling to the ground. The men's eyes shifted to her. Reminded of her presence, they began complimenting her on the chile, the pies, the salad.

They hadn't tasted anything yet, Bennie assured them. He hoped they'd have a chance to sample Frieda's roast stuffed chicken, noodle pudding and pound cake. She made a honey nut cake, Bennie confided, the memory of which had brought him out of a sound sleep in Fairfield, Kansas. The men's laughter made Frieda want to crouch behind the cookstove.

"Got some more coffee, Frieda?" he called. As she poured, he pointed out her other attributes. She was from a fine San Francisco family and was well-educated. She could outspell and outwrite him by a mile. She did a lot of charity work up there in San Francisco and was already planning a school, a hospital, a kindergarten for Dos Cacahuates. Frieda tried to catch his eye, to signal him to stop. Instead of silencing him, her pained expression elicited new praise.

"Mrs. Goldson is clearly one of Dos Cacahuates' major selling points," an amused visitor interjected.

"That is the truth," Bennie responded. "One hundred midwestern farmers are coming out to the lot auction, just to feast their eyes and feed their faces. And that ain't all...."

The coffee pot Frieda held in her hand was almost empty. She tilted the spout and let the remaining hot liquid pour on to Bennie's thigh.

He jumped up with a yowl. Yancy seized the chance to urge the visitors to return for the last auction on October fourth.

Before he left with his guests, Bennie came back to speak to her. "See you just as soon as I can, sweetheart."

"Very well," Frieda said, sounding stern even to herself. "There are a number of things we must discuss."

"Don't I know it," Bennie said, with a broad grin and a blown kiss.

That evening, after supper was served and sleeping arrangements for the guests were set, Frieda excused herself. Bennie rose to escort her across the clearing. He would have to accompany the men to Lollie's—they were going to be discussing business over brandy and cigars. "Wait up for me," Bennie begged, his arm slipping around her waist.

Frieda nodded silently, her own agenda in mind.

It was almost twelve o'clock when Bennie tried the door. Finding it closed, he knocked, calling her name. She rose, let him in, then returned to bed, where she'd been waiting for him, her father's letter and the newspaper article within reach. The smell of brandy and cigars preceding him, Bennie strode to the bed, reaching out to embrace her. Extending her arm, palm flat against his chest, she held him away from her. In her other hand she waved the incriminating documents.

"From the minute I arrived, I knew something was bothering you. Let's have it," he said, taking the letter from her hand. He dropped his hat on the table and seated himself in a chair. He read the news clipping first, then looked up calmly. "So?"

"What does it mean?" Frieda demanded. "Is the Dos Cacahuates development legitimate? I must know. If there is anything faintly dishonest about the enterprise, I want nothing further to do with it. I accepted your proposal and came to this Gehenna with you. I've worked, enduring hardship, incredible discomfort, assaults on my person, the cruelest loneliness, and all of it willingly, believing I was helping to 'Make the World a Better Place.' Only to have my father send me this clipping from the *Alta California*. Is it true, Bennie? Are the International Improvement people shady operators?" Frieda's voice had risen to a platform volume. She was shaking her finger, and the rest of her shook involuntarily.

"Hold it," Bennie ordered, after having tried to interrupt several times. He rose, took her remonstrating finger in one hand and clamped his hand over her mouth with the other. "Now, listen to me for a minute. Yancy already showed me the article. Someone sent him a copy. I can explain everything. The Southern Pacific is trying to block the Santa Fe's drive to the Pacific Coast. They got wind of our project and suspected that it was a Santa Fe ploy to get a line through to San Diego. They're the crooks, not us."

Frieda listened, unconvinced.

"I'm surprised at you, Frieda. I thought you'd see through that newspaper trash instantly. A big city girl like you. You should know how unreliable newspapers are."

"Are you sure, Bennie?" Frieda asked.

"I told you Yancy and I already discussed it. Why didn't you tell Nunes what you were thinking?"

"He was too busy with other things," Frieda said, her rage dissolving.

"Let me see what else you have there." Bennie lifted the letter from the table. He read through it quickly, then folded it and handed it back to Frieda. Tears shimmered for a second in his eyes. "You poor kid, the Levies hit hard."

Unhinged at having an ally again, tears flew from Frieda's eyes. His arms dropped around her and she sobbed like a child. "Oh, Bennie, it was awful here, awful. The heat was unbearable. A crazy man hid himself in the house, Angelina had to go to Los Mochis, business slowed to a standstill...."

Kissing her wet cheeks, smoothing her hair, he apologized over and over. What a fool he had been to leave an inexperienced girl in the wilderness alone. He should have known the others in the camp would have their own concerns, yet he had expected more of them. Especially Morrie. Bennie shook his head again.

"Morrie?" Frieda said. "He's been hiding out like a hibernating bear. Lollie and that Old Wally, who isn't old at all," Frieda blurted, "have been carrying on right out in the open."

"I should be horsewhipped," Bennie said. "Listen to me, Frieda. If you can forgive me, I swear I'll never leave you alone again. Not even for a day." His face brightened. "I'll tell you what. To heck with the First Lady. You come with me to San Francisco next week. I am going up there to break up these malicious rumors and to speak to Mrs. Cohn. She's back from Europe, and Mendel and Minnie are with her. We'll have a nice holiday, and you can cool off and visit with your family."

"Oh no," Frieda said, drawing back. "I can't do that. Not now. I'll go home later, after October."

"Then I won't go either," Bennie decided. "Let Yancy go. He'd do the job better than I anyway. You know how charming Yancy can be."

Frieda nodded, she knew.

"No, siree," Bennie said, "I'm not going to go off and leave my little girl for more than two hours at a time."

Frieda wiped her eyes with the front of her nightgown, sighing wearily. Bennie drew her into his arms. Frieda nestled her cheek against his, then offered her mouth to be kissed.

Her hands rose to fondle his ears, the back of his neck, his hair.

"I missed you so very much," Frieda whispered.

"I'm here now," Bennie whispered back, pressing his body against hers.

Relaxing against him, Frieda silently recited a prayer of thanks.

At the Pond

LIFE BECAME BEARABLE again for Frieda with Bennie back. Her sanity reemerged like distant mountain slopes after an obscuring cloudburst.

The clientele of the First Lady started to grow again. Despite the continuing heat, the rain-filled arroyos and the rutted roads, each day new people arrived to sample the best bill of fare between Tucson and Yuma. Frieda managed to turn out no less than sixty meals a day; on Sundays, over a hundred, with the help of Angelina and Ramón, Guadalupe, Guadalupe's cousin, and the husband of Guadalupe's cousin. Income from Lollie's, the First Lady and from Bennie's sales tour had paid for the completion of the construction of the hotel. Everything was going to be all right. Frieda smiled, knowing where those words had come from. Problems did seem to be straightening out. Though it took him two weeks, Bennie even made good on his promise to speak to Morrie.

Tuesday, the last week in August, Morrie was spending a rare day in the settlement waiting for the well driller to arrive with his repaired equipment. (Lollie paid for the repairs with earnings from the saloon.) At lunch, Frieda heard Bennie tell his brother he wanted to talk to him, in private. As she passed through the clearing on her way to her siesta, Frieda saw them on the store porch: Don Fuego and Don Agua. She marveled again at the differences between the two brothers. They were seated side-by-side on the edge of the rickety porch, their legs extended out in front of them so that their muddy boots edged on a puddle, residue of that afternoon's rainstorm. Morrie bent forward to stir the water with a stick; Bennie leaned back, puffing on a cigar. Frieda started to wave, but noting that neither of the men were looking in her direction, she decided they had already commenced their long-delayed talk.

Stretching out on her bed in her embroidered wrapper, Frieda lay fanning herself while she waited for Bennie to return with a report on the outcome. The next thing she knew he was sitting alongside her, his cigar smoke billowing.

"Well?"

"Morrie don't seem inclined to pay a mind."

Frieda couldn't believe it. "What did you say to him?"

"He shouldn't be leaving Lollie alone so much."

"Is that all?"

"No. When he asked why, I told him that maybe there was something going on between her and Wally. 'Old Wall'?" Bennie imitated Morrie's soft voice.

"But Wally isn't old. Did you tell him that?"

"He didn't give me a chance. He jumped all over me, his voice shaking, near tears."

"But everyone knows, Bennie."

"Morrie's convinced he never had it so good."

"That was his answer?"

"More or less. He said that all his life he's been looking for a woman just like Mama—hard-working, capable, uncomplaining, good-natured. Lollie was all those things and a lot more. So he had no intentions of aggravating her with jealous gossip. I tried to get him to talk to her about Wally. Just ask her, I told him," Bennie said. "But he wouldn't hear of it. Said he wasn't like me, making up to every man, woman and child he came across. He was close to one person—she was his wife, friend, business partner. He's happy. Lollie's happy. That's all he cares about."

"You let it go at that," Frieda concluded.

"Morrie did say that once the ranch got going and the townsite and hotel were paying off, Lollie wouldn't need to run the store and the saloon. He was planning to build a real nice ranch house and move her and the baby out there."

"So he knows about the baby."

"Appears so. Things have a way of working themselves out, Fried," Bennie said.

On a half-dozen occasions Frieda started toward Lollie, but each time drew back. She rehearsed opening lines— "There's a personal matter I want to discuss with you, Lollie." "Lollie, I want to talk to you about that Old Wally." "As your sister-in-law, Lollie, I have a right to know...." The words sounded leaden, superior, nosy, begging a rebuff. How could she discuss trouble with a woman who looked as carefree as Lollie? In the store, during the day, Frieda could see her leaning across the counter wearing a loose Mexican dress, her hair in braids, swapping stories and jokes with the customers who straggled in. And in the evenings, in unbelted, brightly colored silks, her hair done up in a pile of curls, Mexican silver earrings dangling, she was the genial hostess at Lollie's, greeting customers, serving drinks, from time to time picking up a mandolin to play and to sing, as though she didn't have a problem in the world.

She and Lollie were as different as Bennie and Morrie. Lollie's smiling face was as puzzling to Frieda as the white powdered faces framed in the windows in Dupont Alley, or the girls in the saloons on Kearny Street. Girls who spoke first to a man, who did not flee when a strange man reached out to touch them, who did not seem to mind it at all when the mashers in front of Picken's Drug Store flung lewd invitations at them. The same invitations, when directed at Frieda, made her question what in her face or dress had incited such liberties. Lollie spoke right up to strangers, "Drop in at Lollie's. Our motto is the same as at the store—if we ain't got it, we'll get it." She and the potential customers invariably broke out in knowing laughter.

One afternoon, Frieda found herself at the pond alone with Lollie. Guadalupe and her cousin had come with Frieda, but they decided to wash their faces and leave. Frieda hesitated on the edge of the pond for a moment or two, studying the back of Lollie silhouetted against the rose-washed sky. How lovely the pond was in the late afternoon. Between the open spaces in the cottonwoods and willows, the purple ranges walled in a small world. Birds chirped happily and the frogs cheerfully croaked. Unself-consciously, Lollie dipped the water onto herself with a tin cup she held in her hand. Then she lowered herself into the water and slowly straightened. Her wet cotton dress outlined her protruding abdomen. As Frieda watched, Lollie ran a hand meditatively over the hard swell. Her chin tilted and she gazed upward.

Slipping out of her sandals, Frieda stepped into the pond. The mossy slime on the bottom squished up around her toes, and she felt the thick, green water drag around the edges of her skirt. She advanced slowly. Lollie had greeted her earlier, but seemed to have forgotten that Frieda was still there. Her face registered surprise at the sound of Frieda moving toward her through the water. Arriving at Lollie's side, Frieda smiled shyly. She lowered herself into the water; it was warm but cooler than the air. She squeezed her eyes shut, stopped her nose with her fingers, then ducked her head in, too. The hot springs drained into the pond, giving the fresh water a sulfuric taste. When she straightened up, Frieda was dripping from head to toe. She turned to look at Lollie, who was gathering her skirt up and tucking it into a loose woven belt that hung below her waist.

"I've been wanting to talk to you," Frieda blurted.

Lollie's green eyes appraised her sister-in-law guardedly, as if expecting an assault.

"What about?"

Frieda's hand drifted through the water. "I've seen so little of you lately," she hedged.

"The store, the saloon," Lollie said, her eyes fixed on a red-throated cardinal hopping across a huge, rotting cottonwood trunk that lay like a plank into the pond.

"I've been thinking that we ought to talk."

Lollie was beginning to edge toward the log. Her face had the closed look of a girl accustomed to being called onto the carpet.

"I'm going to sit up here," Lollie said, as she stepped onto the branch of the fallen tree and seized another branch to hoist herself onto the log.

Once she was settled, Frieda followed, wringing her skirt out as Lollie had. Then she sat herself in a shady spot. "Until this summer," Frieda said, "I've always loved the sun. Now the most beautiful day I can imagine is a cloudy one. I would have never believed heat could be so awful."

"The heat's nothing to get excited about," Lollie responded lazily.

"I'm glad we're alone," Frieda started again.

Lollie's eyes were noncommittal. She wasn't going to help but she wasn't going to hide either.

"It's about that man, the one who works for you, Old Wally." She had not meant to sound sarcastic, but that was the way the words came out.

"Ray Blackstone is his name. Is that what you wanted to know?" Lollie focused her green eyes on Frieda and kicked at the water so that it sprayed their legs. It was Frieda who dropped her gaze when Lollie said, "He's my lover." Her tone was only a little defiant.

All Frieda could manage was, "Oh."

"He's been my lover for more than two years. I'm crazy about him, and he's crazy about me." She looked away, then looked back at Frieda, "and it will probably be the death of both of us."

A hawk swooped down over the pond and circled, looking for his evening meal. Both women watched the bird in silence.

"Even before you married Morrie?" Frieda asked. She was still approaching Lollie with care.

"I married Morrie because of Ray. I thought I could put an end to the affair that way."

"The two of you couldn't marry because he's not Jewish," Frieda deduced.

"Oh God, no. He has a wife and three children," she paused and sighed, "and four mean brothers-in-law. His wife's two brothers and her two sisters' husbands are all in law enforcement in the Arizona Territory. They live in Charleston, Contention City and Tucson, and they're determined that Ray is going to stay with his wife, Emily, and stop fooling around with that brazen Jewess Lollie Friedman. They locked Ray up and drove me out of Charleston. That was how I got to Tucson that weekend. Morrie and Yancy thought I was there like everyone else, to celebrate the new railroad, but that wasn't true. Ray's brothers-in-law had forced me on a stagecoach in Charleston, then two of them had followed the coach to Tucson, to be sure I got there, and from there out of the Arizona Territory."

Frieda listened, trying to conceal her shock. Driven out of a town, trailed, and threatened.

"How did you meet Morrie?" Frieda thought to ask. Bennie had told her Yancy's version, but she wanted to hear it from Lollie.

"I saw Yancy and Morrie early one day at a small table in front of the hotel. Joe Wiss, one of Emily's brothers, was following me, so I stopped in front of the table and started a conversation. Yancy gave me his finest sales talk, and I was pretending to be interested. He asked me to sign a list so he could send me an announcement before the lot auction. I wrote my name, and they began to ask me questions. Was I married? How long had I been in the territory? Where was I from? When Yancy invited me to dine with them at the Bella Union Hotel, Wiss moved off into the crowd.

"The next day, though, there was Lester Wiss, in front of the hotel when I came out. He had just come up from Charleston and had promised Emily that he was going to put me on a train for the coast. He started calling me ugly names—Jew bitch, Delilah, whore—then he seized me by the arm and started rushing me up the street. A deputy sheriff was standing right on the street, watching him and not doing a thing. He was a relative of the Wisses. I started to tell Lester he was making a big mistake, that I was finished with his dumb *goy* of a brother-in-law and was all set to get married to a nice Jewish gentleman who was in Tucson on business. I told him that he had better keep his hands off me, because I was finished taking their abuse. My fiancé knew people in Tucson, important people. We were walking in the direction of Yancy and Morrie's table. When we got within hearing range, I called out to Yancy. God bless him, he picked up the cue and greeted me by name.

I told them that Lester didn't believe I was engaged to be married to Morrie. Yancy bawled out Lester and told him to be on his way. As he was leaving, Lester warned me he'd be watching the newspapers for a notice of the marriage."

"You weren't really intending to get married, though?"

"Good God, no," Lollie cried. "But Yancy hustled us off to the restaurant in the Cosmopolitan Hotel. There he started to sell me on Morrie and Dos Cacahuates. Morrie," Lollie said, smiling, "just sat there nodding his head as Yancy all but drew up a marriage contract on the spot."

"Why did you agree?"

"I was scared. I thought if I married a fine Jewish gentleman like Morrie, I'd get over this madness for Ray." Lollie was leaning over and absently cupping the warm water in her hands and letting it drip down the front of her already wet dress. "I really thought that I'd never see him again." Her green eyes moved from Frieda to the dusky sky, and then back to Frieda. "They were keeping him locked up like a corralled stallion."

Frieda sat back listening, her eyes drawn down to Lollie's midsection framed against a wall of green shrubs on the bank of the pond. March, April, May... she found herself counting.

"You know how Yancy gets," Lollie was saying, "once he's hooked on an idea. He had us standing in a local Jewish gentleman's parlor surrounded by a group of *our people* that afternoon. They even had a *huppah,* canopy, left over from a Jewish wedding the year before. We had quite a party, considering: some local Jews, others in Tucson for the railroad celebration.

"Whatever made you return to Charleston?" Frieda asked.

"Morrie had started his first well, and was in a hurry to get back to Dos Cachuates. But I was dead-set on going to Charleston before I settled in. I'd left all my things there. Those oxen had shoved me onto the stagecoach without so much as a handbag. I wanted my dresses, dishes and the tablecloths I had embroidered."

Frieda shook her head—one minute Lollie sounded like Lola Montez, the next like Frieda's mother.

"Besides," Lollie added, "I wanted to be sure stories appeared in the Charleston *Sun* and the Tombstone *Epitaph*, so Emily's family would let up on Ray. Morrie and I went to both papers; we even talked up Dos Cacahuates while we were at it. Ray told me they let him out two days after we left town."

"Poor Morrie." Frieda regretted the words as soon as they were out.

"We were getting along just fine, Morrie and I." Lollie's eyes begged Frieda to believe her. "And I really figured Ray Blackstone was out of my life forever. Then he popped up the day of the Seder. The Jewish peddler with the Beisels, that was Ray. One of the merchants in Charleston had received an invitation from Bennie. Ray decided it was his chance to sneak into Dos Cacahuates. So he got himself all done up, like an old Jewish peddler, and waited on the road just outside Dos Cacahuates to hail one of the guests."

Frieda couldn't believe it. She thought she had heard the old peddler chanting the prayers in Hebrew.

"When we were clearing up after the Seder," Lollie went on, "I stepped behind one of the tents to shake a pebble out of my shoe and adjust my stockings. I thought I had heard the birdcall Ray uses as a signal, but with all the birds at the pond, I didn't pay any attention. I was on my way back when this old geezer comes up behind me, whirls me around and presses his dirty old beard into my face. I struggled as if I had been seized by a grizzly bear.

"But he was stronger than me, far too strong for a bent old man. He kissed me hard, I bit his lips and was about to defend myself with a well-placed kick, when he let me go and started to laugh like a hyena. Then I knew who it was."

"And he's been here ever since?"

"In and out, mostly in, wearing different disguises until he settled on Old Wally. Ray gets a bang out of dressing up. He's been a Mexican beggar, once a lady and once a man. Another time, he was a Mexican rancher in Dos Cacahuates to buy tools. He spent the whole day in the store with me. Done up like a miner, he got Bennie to grubstake him. And another day he really had Yancy going, playing an inspector from the bank who came down to see how they were using the money they borrowed for the construction of the hotel."

Lollie's face was lit with amusement over Ray's antics. "I'm stuck, Frieda. It's no life for me without him. I've tried every which way. I'm his." Lollie saw Frieda's eyes darting to the mound rounding out the wet muslin. "So is it." Several emotions tangled in the three words.

"Then tell Morrie," Frieda said.

"I've tried. I can't do it yet. He's counting on me, thinks I'm his lucky charm. Because of me, the wells are going to come through, the townsite and the railroad are taking shape."

"The longer you put it off, the harder it's going to be."

Lollie's eyes shimmered with surfaced misery. "If I tell Morrie, Frieda, I'd have to leave. He needs me right now. Who'd run the store and the saloon? We're not making a lot of money, but we're using all we can put our hands on. Morrie is committed to maintaining the well driller's equipment, and it's costing plenty. My family is involved, too, now that they're sending the furniture." Lollie paused. "But Morrie himself makes it hardest. He cries, Frieda, when he talks about how empty and lonely life was for him here before I came."

Contrary to her carefree look, Lollie had been circling her mountain of trouble. "How long can you go on like this?" Frieda asked, suddenly concerned for her.

"I'm trying to hold out until after the lot auction."

Frieda understood.

"Besides," Lollie added, "once Ray and I leave here together, we're open game. The Wisses have come through Dos Cacahuates several times already. Lester Wiss came in and had a drink at the saloon. He was reasonably polite to me but never stopped looking around. We'd have a rough go, Frieda. I don't think I could make it pregnant. Nor would I exactly enjoy giving birth on Devil's Highway."

Frieda could see the sense in Lollie's thinking.

"The truth is, Frieda, I care for both of them. I have a real affection for Morrie; he's like the brother I never had. But I'm crazy about Ray. Could you possibly understand that?"

Frieda flushed and nodded.

"I haven't done it with Morrie for several months. I told him it was because I'm pregnant." Lollie's eyes sought Frieda's. "I thought you might wonder about that."

Caught, Frieda looked away. She had.

"The few nights he's home, he snuggles up to me as if he's drawing nourishment. He lays his hand on my stomach and dreams out loud about farming on the ranch and building a ranch house for the baby and me." Lollie stopped, kicked fiercely at the water. "Maybe you're right, Frieda. Maybe I should tell him and leave right now—take my chances about getting out of the Territory alive."

Frieda was no longer sure.

"Just get it over with. I'm getting so I can't stand to listen to him, or look at him drawing pictures of a ranch house and a town house." Lollie's shoulders drooped. "He'd cry and carry on, I know he would. I can't stand to see a man cry," Lollie said.

Tears filled Frieda's eyes. "Maybe," she told Lollie, "it would be best to let things ride for a while. Later, after the lot auction, when the town is underway, and there are more people...." Her voice dwindled off, unable to imagine Morrie's future without Lollie.

"You really think that's best, Frieda?" Lollie's words trembled with uncertainty. "You don't think I should tell him now?"

Frieda was certain. "It would be a terrible thing to do

now. Things have a way of working themselves out."

Lollie reached for Frieda's hand and squeezed it. Then she eased herself off the log and back into the water. She waded toward the shore, with Frieda following. Several steps along, Lollie slid on the slippery pond bottom and lurched forward. But Frieda was there to seize her arm and draw her upright. The two women separated at the shore, each finding her own bush and pile of dry clothing. Dressed anew, they stood together on the shore brushing their wet hair into the still hot air. Then silently they settled on the edge of the pond to smoke the Mexican cigarettes Lollie had taken from her pocket and to watch the black clouds gathering for the next day's storm drop over the hot colors of the sunset framing the blue, black and purple mountains. New understanding drew them still closer.

"I think I'm pregnant too," Frieda whispered into the near darkness. Bennie's child, she silently thanked God. In retrospect, the obvious symptoms had started in May, but she had been too misery laden to contemplate another change in her already tattered life.

"*Mazel tov,*" Lollie registered her delight and concern. She reached out and gathered Frieda's head to her shoulder. Drenched in the strangeness of her new condition, Frieda edged closer to Lollie, nestling against her. San Francisco was worlds away in space and time. Neither the teachings of her family nor those of Miss O'Hara appeared to apply. Now Lollie was her sister and supporter, and she hers.

CHAPTER SEVENTEEN
Unforeseen Forces

BENNIE WAS OVERJOYED about the baby. He waltzed Frieda around the room until they both collapsed breathless on the bed. Clutching his hand, she confessed she thought it was a little too soon. He disagreed. Their child would be the first American born in Dos Cacahuates. Lollie's child was due in late October; theirs, not until March, Frieda reminded him. Then theirs would be the first girl or boy, Bennie persisted. Or the second, if it's the same sex as Lollie's, Frieda said. First or second, he was glad they were getting off to an early start. He hoped they'd have ten children, one a year. In twenty-five, thirty years there'd be Goldson houses up and down the main street, Goldson Avenue. Give him five or six sons, and they could sew up the town—general merchandise, hardware, furniture, banking, mining, railroads. Once Dos Cacahuates was going full blast, they'd start other towns all over the southwestern Arizona Territory. One or two might want to do something in Sonora—mining, ranching, farming.

"Our daughters," Frieda joined in, half-teasing, "will marry high-principled, well-educated men, bear a horde of healthy children and keep the town's schools, libraries and charities humming."

"And," Bennie added, "carry on their mama's reputation as the prettiest and the best cook in the county."

The two paddled in the golden waters of their imagined future until Frieda's sole regret bobbed up again. She wished they had another year or two to get the town going. By next March, Bennie assured her, they'd be settled in a proper three-bedroom, frame house on the prized southeast corner opposite the plaza, and they'd be surrounded by friendly neighbors, willing to help out in a pinch. The short line would be in, and her mother could come from San Francisco to Dos Cacahuates with one change of trains. As Bennie named and cleared obstacles, Frieda was struck by a second misgiving. She was going to give birth in Dos Cacahuates. Assisted by whom? When she was a child, portly, balding Dr. Holheim attended the mothers on Sutter Street. She'd often seen him drive up to the expectant household in his one-horse carriage, if the patient could afford it, with a nurse at his side. The neighbors throbbed with anticipation until the business had been accomplished, and the doctor came down the front steps announcing the outcome to all in earshot. It was a boy, a girl, twins, an easy delivery, a difficult one. Once, Frieda saw him, exhausted and grim-faced, report he'd delivered a healthy baby boy, but the mother had died of unforeseen complications.

South of Market, Jewish ladies were attended by a midwife who lived on Howard Street. *Meshuganah* Mrs. Copperman, as she was called, moved as if propelled by her flying hands and flapping tongue. Her abrasive voice, spewing orders and curses in English and Yiddish, blew assisting relatives and friends in and out of the labor room to boil water, get towels, hold down the laboring woman, gag her mouth. Once Mrs. Copperman asked Frieda to help with a delivery. She did that time, but never again.

Now it was she who had embarked on that inescapable journey and would not be released until she delivered. The day-long nausea (why did they call it *morning* sickness?) had stopped, and was replaced by new discomforts. Her breasts swelled and ached, a light crust appeared on her nipples anew each day and a pain settled permanently on her lower left side. Also, new pleasures. She was drowsy most of the time, particularly in the afternoon when she surrendered to sleep as though it were a forbidden passion. Food, too, brought new delights; she wolfed it down like a beggar left alone at a laden table. In the dark, warm nights, and sometimes, much to

Frieda's embarrassment, in the morning or afternoon, she was moved by bouts of sexual longing she could not ignore. Like a drunk after a hair of the dog that bit him, Bennie teased. An unprecedented laziness also slowed her; Frieda could have sat watching her stomach grow, sewing baby things and day-dreaming her way into motherhood. Instead she was working all day at the First Lady (except for that delicious daily siesta) and all evening with the women sewing tablecloths, napkins, bedspreads and curtains for the hotel.

Along with these pains and pleasures was the recurring question: If not Dr. Holheim or Mrs. Copperman, who will deliver her baby? Or, for that matter, Lollie's? Bennie knew. Sadie Silverstein was not only a cook and veterinarian of sorts, but a midwife. Frieda couldn't believe she'd come from Gunsight to deliver a baby. For five dollars, food, lodging and hay for her horse, there wasn't much Sadie wouldn't do. That dilemma resolved, Bennie returned to more pressing concerns: the Big Day, one month away.

Yancy was in San Francisco, where he'd failed to obtain retractions from the newspapers but had succeeded in getting the *Alta California* and the San Francisco *Chronicle* to print articles about the lot auction, and to promise to send reporters to cover the event. He was also meeting with investors—most beneficially, the Miners and Minnie's mother. Rosamund, wrote Yancy, was a shrewd woman, with numerous influential business associates and friends, as well as experience in the conduct of commercial and social events. Continued Yancy:

> You will be pleased to learn Rosamund has agreed to travel with the Miners and me to Tucson, where she will oversee the Big Day arrangements: transportation, accommodations, food and entertainment. Her generous offer will allow you, Morrie, and what remains of your crew (now that Harrigan and his boys are gone), to get the hotel furnished and ready to accommodate thirty to fifty discriminating investors.

Ten days later, Yancy wrote again, this time from Tucson. He was the houseguest of Isaac Aaron, a longtime friend of Rosamund Cohn. Aaron was introducing him to Territorial legislators, newspaper editors and some of "Arizona's most substantial investors." The rest of the letter consisted of detailed instructions on the work to be completed by the Goldsons and "what remained of their crew." Bennie insisted on reading Nunes' letters aloud to her with a jubilance she could neither match nor feign. He appeared oblivious to the fact that Nunes, Rosamund Cohn and the Miners were doing the planning and the politicking—leaving the dirty work to them, the humble locals.

One night as they flopped into bed exhausted, Frieda suggested that in the rush of Big Day preparations, Bennie had forgotten about the baby. He swore he was as excited as ever, but they had so much to accomplish before October 4, he couldn't do or think about anything else. His response hung over the bed unanswered.

"Damn it, Frieda, the baby won't be here 'til spring. We still have to get through the fall and winter."

If he had not convinced her that Bennie Goldson took things as they came, she would have thought he sounded worried.

On September third, a caravan of eleven eight-mule-drawn wagons, led by Abe Beisel, pulled into Dos Cacahuates laden with linens, tableware, glassware and kitchen utensils from San Francisco; furniture from Los Angeles, including a piano (to Bennie's glee), and three boxes from the Sisters of Service. The freighters rested a day, then on Tuesday afternoon began to prod and push the mules and wagons up the slope to unload. Once the supplies were in the hotel, it would be Frieda and her helpers' task to arrange the furnishings and store the supplies.

After the midday meal, Frieda stood in front of the First Lady deciding whether to struggle up the slope to see the Waverly upright and the other furniture, or to take her customary nap.

In her house with the door locked, Frieda took off her clothes and stretched out on the bed with a worn sheet thrown over her perspiring body. The sky had cleared rapidly after that afternoon's rain, and the thermometer at the *First Lady* was registering 102 degrees when she left. She'd sleep for an hour, write and thank Miss O'Hara for the food, clothing and medicines the Sisters of Service had collected, then go up to the hotel and see what Beisel's men had hauled in.

"Get up, Frieda! Now." Bennie was pulling her hand.

She sat up, clutching the sheet. "Stop, I don't have anything on."

"We've got to get out of here. Everyone else has already left." He was racing around the room looking for something for her to wear. "Throw this on," he commanded, tossing a flowered wrapper at her. He yanked her to her feet and began stuffing her arm into one sleeve then the other. "Get moving," he ordered.

As they burst through the door, Frieda looked around. What were they running from? Indian attack? Bandits? Revolutionaries? The clearing was empty, abandoned. Her chest was pumping as if it were all heart, sweat was pouring off her face and she was moving as fast as she could, but not fast enough for Bennie.

"Come on," he growled, dragging her along. "We've got to get up on the hill."

She tried but couldn't move any faster. Sharp-edged rocks and twigs cut into her feet. As they started up the slope, a thought crossed her mind, and with it a glimmer of anger. She'd heard stories about fake Indian raids and robberies staged to scare tenderfoots. Bennie wouldn't do anything like that. Or would he?

"What's going on?" she called. "Bennie, *tell me.*"

"Flash flood," he answered without turning.

The sky was blue and unblemished. The afternoon storm

was long since over, and the ground was dry. She stopped in her tracks, digging her bruised feet into the rough path. "I don't believe you."

Bennie yanked her so hard, she fell to one knee. "Do you want to drown? Listen, damn it! You can hear it."

A rumble like a roll of thunder sounded from afar.

"Where's that coming from?"

"Over there. See?" Bennie pointed to a sheet of black hanging over the distant mountains.

"That's miles away."

"It's heading in this direction and moving fast. It's going to pour out of the draw that runs on the west side of the slope and come tearing down into the clearing. We'd better be on the hill before it does."

A sharp stab in her heart matching the pain in her side, her face streaked with tears and sweat, Frieda picked up her pace. Halfway up the hill they passed mule teams still attached to loaded wagons tied to steel stakes driven into the ground. Both looked back but neither halted.

As her bare feet reached the plateau, Frieda collapsed, gasping, clutching her wrapper. There were nearly fifty people milling about: Lollie, Ray (out of disguise), Angelina, Ramón, Guadalupe, Guadalupe's cousin, the husband of Guadalupe's cousin, Abe Beisel, some of his men, and assorted Mexicans and Americans she'd never seen before. Not Morrie. He'd left for the ranch that morning, Frieda saw him go. Bennie wanted him to wait to see the piano, but Morrie refused. He had customers coming to buy water.

"Here it comes," a man shouted, as if announcing the arrival of the circus. The group swarmed toward him on the western edge of the plateau. Frieda rose and followed, trailing blood from her cut feet. They were looking north.

"Where?" she asked.

"Over there," came a half-dozen responses. Arms rose pointing toward a layer of mountains, spliced by a barely detectable stream. A minute or two later, a muddy avalanche of water came through the draw, racing and roaring below the plateau, deep brown against the dun-colored hills, carrying up-rooted junipers from high in the mountains, boulders, yucca trunks, cacti, dead animals, several corrugated tin roofs. Frieda watched the leaping, tumbling, splashing water, hypnotized. After several minutes, her eyes swerved to the faces around her. Their expressions mirrored her feelings: fascination mounted on fear, awe in face of mighty forces—powerful, uncontrollable, pitiless—mowing down anything or anyone daring or dumb enough to remain in its way. Turning back, she watched the waters descend into the clearing.

"*Baruch atta adonoy, elohaynu, melech ha olom, dayan ha emet.* Praised be thou, oh Lord, our God, King of the Universe, judge of truth," Frieda chanted. Paling before news of a disaster, crimson with outrage, atremble with bad tidings, she'd heard her father utter those words, acknowledging then, as at no other time, the possibility that he had erred and was being punished.

She watched the raging waters pour into the pond, staining the clear green water. Then the structures began to collapse—the First Lady, Lollie's, Ramón and Angelina's house, the sales office, Yancy's tent, the store. As its flimsy walls gave way, bolts of cloth, sacks and barrels of provisions, tools, the sign—Goldson Brothers, General Merchandise, *If We Ain't Got it, We'll Get it*—sailed off toward Mexico. Bringing up the rear was Ramón's chicken house, with a rooster mounted on the roof.

Their house. What about their house? The adobe dissolved like a cube of sugar, giving up to the waters their bed, table, chairs, cupboard, her trunk—everything she'd brought from home—clothes, linens, candlesticks, menorah, *mezuzah*, all gone. She should have nailed the mezuzah to the door frame as her father had instructed her. *I'm sorry, Papa, I was waiting until we built a real house.*

Trembling, she turned from the wreckage below to the hilltop hotel, rooted in place, untouched. Around her she could hear the men counting their current losses and matching them against previous ones. "Back in '67," she heard one of Abe Beisel's men say, "it took us a whole month to dig out proper. We lost every goddamn itty, bitty thing—washed out. No food, water, shelter, and up to our assholes in mud and mosquitoes. Wait and see, every goddamn creeping, crawling, croaking critter is going to be hoppin' all over us."

"We'll have to be hustlin' right out for water and provisions," said another of the freighters, a spry older man with shrewd lizardlike eyes. He was peering out across the valley. "Didn't hit the Mexican town a'tall. Now I see why the Mexicans settled on the other side of the butte."

He was right. The flood waters were pouring into Mexico along the west side of Dos Cacahuates, Sonora. She'd heard there'd once been a Mexican town due south of the pond, opposite American Dos Cacahuates. How could Bennie and Morrie have been so foolish as to settle in the path of flash floods?

The wagons and their teams on the slope were caught at a mid-point, half in the water, and half out of it. The mules, their heads flung back, were braying, seemingly for help.

Where was Bennie? She spotted him just above the swirling cauldron of water with Beisel and some of the other men struggling to pull the wagons and animals up the hillside. Bennie had taken a position shoulder-deep in the water, his head flung back like the mules.

"Move, you sons-of-bitches, or your bloated carcasses will be in Huatalobampo by morning," she heard him yell.

Frieda could barely make out his face, but she could tell from his hoarse, exhilarated shout that there was no place he'd rather be. All they owned swept off in a deluge, and Bennie was having a helluva time. Frieda turned away, unable to watch. Her legs aching, her feet sore, she limped to the hotel. Inside she sat on a still-wrapped chair uncertain as to what to do next. Several minutes later a call went up for all hands. Frieda went outside to see if she could help. The men had released the teams and were leading the reluctant animals to safety. Others had tied long ropes to the wagons and were hauling them up the hill. She joined them.

CHAPTER EIGHTEEN

We're Fine

A MOSQUITO BUZZED. Frieda ducked her head under one of the lace curtains Angelina brought with her when she fled the sewing tent. Bennie was lying alongside her under a curtain too, his mudcaked boots and pants all but standing on end alongside the mattress.

"Beisel and his men are leaving in the morning," Bennie said.

At the word *leaving* Frieda eased her pained body away from her husband. They had already fought that battle, and she lost. She could leave if she wanted; he was going to stick it out and salvage what he could. Cross the desert with Beisel and a half-dozen teamsters, wearing Bennie's shirt and Angelina's petticoat under her flowered wrapper? She'd rather die in Dos Cacahuates and presumed she would.

"We've got to get a letter off to Yancy." He was eyeing the last of the candles Harrigan's crew had left at their hilltop campsite.

"No paper," Frieda responded from under the curtain.

"Wrapping paper, from the furniture."

"Pencil?" She poked her head out.

His bruised and blistered hand pointed in the direction of the three boxes sent by the Sisters of Service. They'd already opened the one labeled medicine and took out bandages and camphor for their injuries. Bennie eased himself up off the mattress and limped first to the box, where he found a pencil, and then to the lobby for a piece of paper.

He resettled himself with a groan.

"Can't it wait until morning, Bennie?"

"They're leaving first thing. You'll have to write. I can't hold the pencil."

"I don't know if I can either."

"Try."

"My left hand hurts more than my right. Maybe I can."

"Good."

"But make it short. I've got to get some sleep if we're going down to the settlement tomorrow."

"We are, and early. We've got to pull what we can out of the mud before it dries."

"Then start."

"September fifth. Mr. Yancy Nunes, c/o Mr. Isaac Aaron, Tucson, Arizona Territory."

"Tucson will do."

"Dear Yancy," Bennie inhaled, then eased out a long breath, his hand massaging his hipbone. He'd slipped in the mud and fallen on the head of an ax, bruising his side. "Excuse this crude letter. We suffered a flash flood, but we're all fine."

"Not so fast," Frieda said.

"Just about everything went except the hotel and, thank God, the new furnishings."

"I'm only taking down the essentials."

"No human lives lost, but Abe Beisel is out eight mules and one wagon. Fortunately, I cleaned out the strong box that morning to pay Abe freight charges, so we had no cash losses."

"Tell him what we need."

"We're flat busted and desperately in need of food, clothing and bedding. The pond won't be of use for a while, but we have water from Morrie's wells and, God bless him, fruits and vegetables, too. We'll start digging out tomorrow."

Frieda switched the pencil from her right hand to her left, then back to her right.

"We're going ahead with our plans for the Big Day and advise you to do the same. Sorry about your Washington hand press, also your ink and paper. Must be in Hermosillo by now."

"I'm leaving out the part about the press."

"We'll be back in business in a week or so. When can we expect you?"

"That's it. The candle's almost out."

"Thanks, Fried'."

"What for?" She folded the paper and dropped it on the floor alongside the mattress.

"Everything." He started to lift himself up to kiss her. Straightening with pain, he fell back on the mattress. "Tired?" Bennie asked.

"Dead."

His hand crept along her side searching for her hand. Finding it, he hooked his pinkie finger through hers. "Don't worry about a thing. Everything is going to be all right."

The next day Frieda dragged herself up at dawn and wearily prepared a breakfast of the coffee, bread and fruit Morrie had brought up the back slope. Then she found some shoes one of Beisel's men had left for her, picked up several curtains to use as bags and, too heartsick to talk, followed Bennie and some of the others down the slope.

Calf-high in watery mud where her house used to be, Frieda suddenly regained her strength. Ignoring her sore hands and her aching side, she bent over and began searching the ooze for something, anything. The linens her mother had brought from the old country; the tablecloths the women of the Levie household had embroidered before her wedding; the silver Sabbath candlesticks that had belonged to a grandmother she'd never seen; the spice box, the Seder plate, the kiddish cup, the Chanuka candelabra, the mezuzah and the prayer book her parents insisted she take to her new home— her trousseau, such as it was; her books and letters. All gone. She'd been entrusted with her family's cherished possessions and had lost them. Chiding faces reprimanded her; tongues clicked. They'd warned her what awaited her in the wilderness. But she had been too stubborn, too willful to heed them. Her midsection churned with fear of dark consequences.

Hours later, her hands and legs water-wrinkled and mud-coated, she'd collected several plates, a couple of cups, a few knives, forks, and spoons, but none of the irreplaceable things she'd hoped to find. Like a dog rooted to homeground, she kept searching around her vanished home until Bennie shouted to her. She looked up and saw him beckoning from near the pond. Slushing through the mud, she made her way to him. He'd found their cupboard and propped it up against the trunk of a fallen cottonwood. Frieda fell on the contents.

From its water-logged interior, she drew forth soggy petticoats, underdrawers, skirts, a shawl, the tallis and yarmulke her father had pressed on Bennie, and other ceremonial objects she'd feared lost. Each recovered piece, she clutched to her breast and kissed as if it were the last of its kind on earth.

As she emerged from the waters and started up the slope, her back bent under the weight of her lace curtain sack, a strange thing happened. She felt herself split into two separate beings. One half continued trudging up the path, painridden, spent, inching along. The other darted ahead, light-footed, unencumbered, looking back with a pitying smile at the weary climber clutching her load as if they were reclaimed parts of her body.

Bennie promised no more water, and none came. Even the daily rains stopped. By the fourth day, the only signs of the disaster were two rectangular foundations where the house and store had stood, and the ground was still several shades darker from the clearing to Devil's Highway. The pond looked as it had before, except that the trunks of three more cottonwoods reached like fingers into the water.

When Frieda and the others were finished below, clearing away and burning what could no longer be used, Bennie called them together. The hotel was as sound as a well-built ark, so why didn't they all move in? With their other obligations out of the way—the store, the restaurant, the saloon—they could concentrate on getting La Cíbola ready for the Big Day.

As he talked, Frieda restrained an urge to scratch his face and pull his red hair. Yet, once they got started, she saw the merit of his thinking. In a few days, they managed to unload the boxes and unpack and arrange the furnishings. In two weeks, they'd be ready: the landscaping would be in, the curtains hung, the rooms whitewashed, the pictures up and the kitchen in working order. Each day they grew more comfortable in the hotel. At night after a supper prepared of whatever Morrie brought from the ranch or from across the line, they gathered in the saloon—Bennie, Frieda, Lollie, Ray (his disguises abandoned), occasionally Morrie, Angelina, Ramón, Guadalupe, Guadalupe's cousin and the husband of Guadalupe's cousin. Together they planned the next day's work, Bennie played the piano, they sang, then trudged off to sleep, surprisingly content, given their circumstances. Frieda was still waiting for the next disaster but was beginning to consider the possibility that none might come.

By September tenth, Yermo's stagecoach was again pulling into the clearing with provisions and mail. Yancy was doing so well in Tucson, Phoenix and in the Territorial capital Prescott, he would not be returning to Dos Cacahuates until September twenty-first. He urged them not to concern themselves about the Big Day arrangement. Rosamund had hired Leo Hammerstein to bring in the food, a Tucson band, several entertainers for the banquet, a barbecue and a hunt breakfast. She'd also agreed to cover the Big Day expenses with the understanding she would have first claim on the day's returns. Colonel Leighton would be arriving in Dos Cacahuates on October third with a party of eastern investors. Yancy suggested they prepare hotel accommodations for Leighton's people and Rosamund's San Francisco friends, and the rest of the crowd could sleep in their wagons, tents or bedrolls.

On September twelfth, a letter came from Alejandro Ramirez, who obviously had not heard about the flash flood and was bringing a party of six visitors to Dos Cacahuates. Would Doña Fridita outdo herself with a special feast? The guests were likely investors, including Ramirez's cousin, who was associated with the Sonora Railway, Limited.

Bennie was elated; Frieda, downcast. She rose, left the table, and headed for her room. Lying on her bed, Frieda stacked up a brick wall of objections.

Several minutes later, Bennie arrived carrying a pitcher of warm water. "About time for me to start shaving again," he said, rubbing a week's growth of red stubble.

Frieda watched him lather his jaw with a yucca root dipped in water. (Soap was one of the numerous items no one had remembered to send them.) Talking out of the side of his mouth, stopping to grimace as he scraped at the heavy beard with the straight razor he'd found near his vanished store, he said, "You don't want to cook for Ramirez?"

"Let them come on the Big Day when we're ready for them."

"They're already on their way."

The room was silent except for the scrape of the razor and Bennie's groans. "Get something together for them; then you can take it easy. Mrs. Cohn will be here with her crew in a week or ten days."

"I'm not lazy, Bennie," Frieda said, annoyed that he would press her. "We've been through one ordeal and are facing another."

"Don't worry about a thing, Fried'," Bennie said, not turning. "Lollie said she'd cook if you didn't want to. She's not the cook you are, but in a pinch—."

"Bennie," Frieda flamed, "Lollie could go into labor any time. The baby's dropped. She'd better start thinking about how she's going to get Sadie Silverstein down here." Near tears, her voice cracked. "I'm not going to deliver that baby, Bennie," she warned.

"Hell, it's only a three-hour drive from Gunsight. But if Sadie can't make it, I'll deliver the baby. I've done it before."

Frieda clutched her skirt to keep from throwing a nearby hairbrush at him.

"If need be, I'll cook the supper, too."

"That's the trouble with you, Bennie. You think you can do everything. You may have super-human powers, but the rest of us poor mortals don't."

"Cooking a supper and delivering a baby are not exactly extraordinary feats. Women do them everyday and everywhere."

Frieda gritted her teeth. "Stranded on a plateau in the desert, without so much as a bar of soap, or a stitch of clothing for a baby?" As she spoke, it occurred to her that there might be baby things in the Sisters of Service boxes.

"Morrie will go for Sadie."

"Who will go for Morrie?" Frieda countered. Since the flood, Morrie'd been out at the ranch most of the time. He claimed he was picking up much-needed money selling water, but Frieda suspected Ray's undisguised, young face had asked for an accounting Morrie was not prepared to demand.

Bennie ran his hand over one clean-shaven cheek, then turned the other. "If need be, I will," he said.

"Deliver the baby, cook the supper, go for Morrie?"

Bennie nodded.

"I thought you were going to peddle water for Morrie."

"True."

"Then you tend to your business. I'll get some kind of supper together," Frieda snapped. "And if need be, Ray will go for Sadie."

Bennie was combing his hair. He set down the comb and turned to face Frieda, his brown eyes aglow with affection. "Just what I always needed, a woman with a head on her shoulders." He started for the bed.

"And a constitution of iron," Frieda added.

"You're a wonderful wife, Fried'," Bennie said, lowering his cheek to hers.

"But will I last?"

"Wish you were back on Tehama Street?"

"Yes."

"You mean it?"

She did not respond.

"I'm crazy about you." His hand tenderly covered the rise below her waist, "And it."

Her arms started around his neck, then stopped. "Things will be better after the Big Day, won't they?"

"They will. I promise."

"How do you know?"

"They couldn't get any worse."

CHAPTER NINETEEN

The First Citizen

BENNIE KNOCKED ON the white linen tablecloth. "Señor Ramirez is speaking to you." Frieda was looking back over her shoulder through the open door to the corridor leading to the rooms. She turned, and upon finding the eyes of her six guests fixed on her, flushed. "Dispénsenme, Señores," Frieda whispered, her eyes circling the table to include Ramirez and his traveling companions—Señores Gonzales, Monteverde, Hildalgo, Rosales, and most important, next to Ramirez himself, Ignacio Flores of the Sonora Railway, Limited. The men, all prosperous-looking dons in their thirties and forties, graciously excused her.

She'd tried to beg off, but Ramirez had insisted his hostess's lovely face at the table would add flavor to the meal. Acquiescing, Frieda chose the seat nearest the corridor. Perched on the edge of her chair, head tilted toward the door, she strained to pick up sounds from the room at the far end of the hall, the one where Lollie lay in labor.

"The gentlemen are discussing the color of your eyes, Frieda," Bennie prompted. "Señor Ramirez insists they're as green as—"

"...dos piedras de jade."

"Jade stones?" Señor Flores scoffed. La Señora's eyes were as blue and gentle as Guaymas Bay on a cloudless day.

Señor Monteverde agreed with Flores. Her eyes were blue and gentle, also, intelligent and compassionate. Gonzalez thought he detected the pride of a lioness in her eyes—not only in her eyes, but in her carriage and in her alertness.

Smiling and nodding, Frieda forced herself to face the group as they spoke of her to each other. Sadie was with Lollie, assisted by Guadalupe and Guadalupe's cousin. Frieda promised she would join them the moment she could tear herself away. Angelina and Ramón had cleared away the main course dishes and were serving the cointreau their guests had brought from Guaymas.

"*A la independencia y el poder de México,*" Flores toasted.

"*A la independencia y el desarrollo de México,*" Gonzales seconded.

From the corner of her eye Frieda watched Guadalupe pad to Angelina's side and whisper in her ear. Angelina's features registered something short of alarm, concern. Surveying the table, Ramón and the guests, Frieda heard her tell Guadalupe, "*Vendré despues del café y el postre.*"

After coffee and dessert. There was still time. Frieda raised her newly filled wine glass as Monteverde rose.

"*A la independencia y la belleza de México.*"

"*A la amistad entre México y los Estados Unidos,*" Bennie chipped in.

"*Todo está bien?*" Frieda mouthed as Angelina placed a peach pie, a knife, and plates in front of her. Doña Sadie wanted more hot water, Angelina whispered back. Frieda started to get up, but once again Bennie summoned her attention. Forcing herself back in the chair, she looked up, barely able to conceal her impatience.

"Señor Ramirez wants to know if challah is the holy bread of the Jews?" Bennie asked, his gaze shifting from her to Ramirez, who was holding a piece between his index finger and thumb.

"More holiday bread than holy bread," was her response. "The Jews of San Francisco and elsewhere bake and eat challah on the Sabbath and other holidays." She reconsidered. "In a way it is holy. The baker says a blessing as he or she prepares the dough, and people recite a blessing before the first bite."

"*Sí, es pan sanctificada,*" said Gonzales, a rosy-cheeked, portly man, "made by blessed hands." He punched a wad of bread into his mouth and chewed with relish.

As the guests ate the dessert, the conversation centered on the pie crust, then on the fruit. Without hearing a word, Frieda knew Bennie was telling the Mexicans that the fruit came from his brother's ranch. From there he'd slide into other ranch products, the daily output of their artesian wells, the prospects of additional wells adjacent to the ranch. Footsteps and rumble of hushed voices drifted from the corridor. Frieda turned to see what was going on. The hall was empty. After the auction, Bennie was telling his guests, they plan to add poultry and livestock. Then Rancho Cornucopia will lack nothing.

Ramón was refilling the coffee cups and serving second helpings of pie. When he picked up Frieda's plate, she rose and stepped back from the table. Her fingers nervously plucking at the skirt of a red bombazine dress borrowed from Lollie, she stammered in Spanish, *"Dispénsenme, Señores. Mucho gusto en verles."* Not waiting for their responses, she went to tell Angelina to join her in the back room as soon as the men left for the saloon.

As she conversed with her helper, she heard Ramirez ask Bennie if la Señora was ill. She was so rosy-cheeked and cheerful back in May; now she seemed nervous, wan. Ramirez hoped Bennie was not misusing her. *Pobrecita*, she must be lonely, so far from her home and her mother. Bennie assured Ramirez she was entirely well and never happier. She loved Dos Cacahuates and was as eager as ever to pursue her good works there. But, Ramirez cautioned, he mustn't let his little treasure work too hard. Never, Bennie swore. He was doing everything in his power to guard his beloved. Ramirez approved. Men were obliged to protect the delicate angels God provided for their delight.

Fighting down rage, the *delicate angel* hurried toward the corridor. As she approached the room where Lollie lay, her steps slowed. Her guests' banal talk stirred one kind of pain; the prospect of re-entering the scene she'd witnessed that afternoon, another.

As Frieda stood summoning her courage, the door opened and out came Guadalupe with a pair of scissors and four cuts of string in her hands. Doña Sadie wanted the scissors and string boiled, she said, answering Frieda's questioning gaze. Relieved that a midwife was on hand and in charge, Frieda went to welcome her. Sadie had on a blue Mother Hubbard, and her gray hair was bound in a towel that pulled her sagging cheeks tight to her temples. She was seated on the bed alongside Lollie, her big hand spreading across her swollen, nightgown-covered midsection. Frieda stood near the door, hoping to remain a bystander.

"They're about two minutes apart now," Sadie called brusquely. "Still got a bit to go. Why'd you let her drink all that whisky? I hope she don't get sick along with everything else. I never delivered a drunk mother before."

Lollie lay still, her eyes closed, her open mouth exuding whiskey fumes.

"I took one bottle away from her. I don't know where she got the other," Frieda said, thinking, but choosing not to add, probably from Ray.

Lollie's eyelids rolled back, and she looked up with the dazed expression of a child who hurt and didn't know why. "Frieda? Is that you?" Her hand beckoned, then drifted toward the night table and a nearly empty whisky bottle.

Sadie seized the bottle. "No more of that for you, little mother."

"Bitch," Lollie muttered, falling back against the pillow.

"You city girls," Sadie complained, "All sparkle and no grit. What a way to bring a baby into the world. Dead drunk."

"She scares me, Frieda. Don't leave me, please," Lollie whispered, searching the room for her sister-in-law.

"Don't worry, Loll'," Sadie called loud enough to get through her patient's alcoholic stupor. "I ain't about to let her go." She turned to Frieda. "I'm going to need you. Especially if she starts vomiting."

The room rocked like a ship in a storm. "Angelina and

Guadalupe know more about having babies than I do," Frieda
replied lamely.

"I want you. I don't talk Spanish that good, and I need
someone who understands me and can move fast when I tell
them. Ooo, that was a good one," Sadie said, her hand riding
the contracting abdomen. "Maybe the whisky wasn't such a
bad idea," Sadie said. "That one would have brought a yell
from a sober lady." She looked up at Frieda again. "Listen,
honey, you'd better get into something you won't mind spoil-
ing. We're going to have a mess on our hands." She looked
down at her watch again, her hand pressed against Lollie's abdomen. "Only a minute apart now." Sadie dropped her watch
back in her pocket, casually threw back the covers with one
hand and held up the kerosene lantern with the other. Separating Lollie's knees, she peered between her fragile-looking
legs.

"Thought the head might be showing. Not yet." Sadie's
hand dove under Lollie's thighs and felt the sheet. "The water
bag broke. She could have floated away, but she wouldn't have
knowed the difference. Lands," Sadie groaned, "delivering a
drunk woman is just like delivering a cow." She spread Lollie's
legs again. "Come here, Frieda. You want to see something?"
When Frieda didn't answer, Sadie looked up again. "Sakes,
girl, you better get out of those clothes. There's not much
time left now. Wash your hands, too, with a strong soap. Get it
out of my bag."

Soap in hand, Frieda left, hoping the baby would be born
while she was gone. She didn't want to witness that birth—
Lollie thrashing about like a mindless creature, Sadie handling
her as if she were a dumb animal. Like Aunt Chava cleaning a
chicken, Frieda thought pulling off her red dress and gold
earrings and reaching for a fresh wrapper. She could see her
spread the chicken's legs; thrust her hand into the gaping cav-
ity between them; pull out red, yellow, and pink clumps, un-
mindful of the slippery tissue, her thoughts far from the operation she performed.

To get back to the women, Frieda had to pass the saloon,

now occupied by Bennie and his guests. She could hear him at the piano accompanying one of his guests who was singing a familiar *ranchero* in a sweet, boyish tenor. It was a popular song; she'd heard it frequently. The rancher had all he could wish for—cows, pigs, a dog, a woman. She scurried passed the open door, chased by that tenor braying of male ease and contentment.

As she stepped into the room, she was assailed by Lollie's groans. Sadie, Angelina and Guadalupe surrounded the bed, their lantern-lit figures casting long shadows on the walls.

"What were you doing, dressing for a ball?" Sadie said, her voice strained with exertion. "Come here, I need you. The head's in place and she's contracting hard."

Frieda threaded between the other women and stationed herself alongside Sadie. For several moments she stood silent, unwilling to look at Lollie, trying not to hear her cries.

Sadie straightened, grunting with frustration. "Look, I have to turn her around, so's I can get to her. Help me. Get over on the other side of the bed. We'll move her head over there. You take her shoulders; I'll take her legs." Angelina came to help Frieda; Guadalupe assisted Sadie. As the women lifted her, Lollie unfurled a long, sharp cry, flailing her arms and kicking her feet.

"I'd give her a touch of chloroform if she wasn't drunk. Quiet, you," Sadie reprimanded, as if she were talking to a naughty child. "I don't dare with her in this condition. You tend her arms and head, Frieda. Get a basin first, in case she vomits." Sadie had Lollie's nightgown up out of the way and was down on the floor before Lollie's bent knees.

Frieda nestled her sister-in-law's head against her shoulder, trying to hold down her arms as well. Lollie's whole body stiffened. Frieda looked down and saw her white abdomen jerk like a mountain hit by volcanic action. She yowled like a wounded dog.

"Three more of those, and we'll have our hands on the first American citizen born in Dos Cacahuates." Sadie pronounced the name Dose Ca-ca-wad-ies.

Her mouth open in shock, her hands thrashing, Lollie's body shook with another powerful contraction.

"The next one's going to do it. I can see the head. I can practically take hold of it. Just look at her belly jerk."

Frieda raised herself to take a peek. The hard ball of flesh tightened and squeezed, as if gripped by invisible hands ejecting some alien matter.

"Push, push. For God's sakes, Frieda, tell her to push. Just once more," Sadie urged, pressing herself onto the moving mound.

"There, there, there it is," Sadie cried, triumphantly.

Frieda looked up to see Sadie tugging, then laboriously rising to her feet with a pair of ankles in her hands—a skinny, blue and red-streaked thing hanging head down, a long appendage dangling from its midsection.

"It's a girl," Sadie cried, happily.

Poor little thing, Frieda thought.

Angelina stepped forward, her face wreathed in a bright smile, her arms covered with a white towel as she stretched forth to receive the crying infant.

Freed from the child, Sadie dropped back to her knees to "finish her off." Lollie lay still, exhausted, her lips moving but no sound emerging.

"It's a girl, Lollie," Frieda whispered.

Lollie opened her eyes and looked at Frieda. Her expression seemed to say that she knew, but she didn't care much yet.

"Here, pass me that basin," said Sadie brusquely, holding up another clump of tissue, the afterbirth. "Now give me that scissors and string." That job done, Sadie sighed with relief and rose wearily to her feet. With the ordeal over, she turned gentle. "Now let's get this poor, little mother cleaned up."

Using a stack of towels, witch hazel and a basin of warm water, she washed Lollie's legs. Then, calling for clean water, Sadie cleansed her hands, face and arms, and smoothed down her hair. Then she sent Guadalupe to the linen closet for a clean nightgown and clean sheets, and Angelina to the kitchen for some herb tea. "With laudanum, tea and all that whiskey and hard work, she's bound to sleep tonight," Sadie said, as she spread a blanket over Lollie. "I could use some of that tea myself. And I'm hungry, too. Missed my supper."

Frieda gazed at Sadie in wonder. *How could anyone be hungry after that revolting event?*

"Starved," Sadie said, as she packed her bag. From her pocket she drew her big watch. "Delivering babies is hard work. Got here a little after nine. It's eleven-thirty now. I ain't had a bite since two."

On shaky legs, Frieda made her way down the hallway at Sadie's side. Bennie and his guests were still in the saloon. The sound of the piano and the singers filled the passageway.

"Don't you want to tell the father what he got?" Sadie asked.

"He's not here," Frieda hedged. "Besides I don't want to go into the saloon."

Sadie shrugged, her eyes appraising Frieda curiously.

Seated at the table, a piece of challah in one hand and a turkey drumstick in the other, Sadie asked, "Who's Ray?"

Frieda thought for a moment before answering. "The blonde gentleman who brought you here."

"She called for him a few times when you were out of the room."

"Where is Ray?" Frieda asked, aware for the first time that she had not seen him since he set out for Gunsight.

Munching away, Sadie said, "On the trip over, Ray was acting pretty nervous. He kept looking around as if someone was chasing him. When I asked him what was bothering him, he said he wanted to get me to Dos Cacahuates pronto. I took him at his word. When we got to the hotel and I was getting my things out of my saddlebags, I noticed three men talking to him. The girls were waiting to take me in to Lollie, so I just went along with them. When I came back to the yard to get something I forgot, I saw them riding off together. I don't like to make that journey alone unless I have to, so I called to Ray to be sure to come back for me. 'Sure he will,' one of the men answered for him. What was that all about?"

Sadie was eyeing Frieda, waiting for a response.

"Beats me," Frieda lied.

Sadie shoved her cleaned plate away and said, "Alone or escorted, I've got to be on my way. I'll have fifty men lined up for breakfast by seven in the morning. If I'm not there, I'll lose $12.50. By the way, I charge $5.00 to deliver women. For cows, $2.50, unless there are complications." Sadie pulled a handkerchief out of her pocket and wiped her face. "Having a baby sure does remind a woman who and what she is."

Sadie rose and stood waiting. Frieda tried to get up but her legs wouldn't support her.

"What's wrong?"

"Just a little weak," Frieda confessed, embarrassed before the older woman's vigor.

"Your first time, I forgot. Come on," Sadie said, hooking her strong arm under Frieda's armpits and pulling her to her feet. "I'll put you to bed, too, and keep an eye on the both of you for a few hours. But I've got to be on my way before dawn. You city girls sure ain't worth much in a squeeze," Sadie muttered, as she led Frieda to her room.

From the saloon came the sound of Bennie teaching one of his Mexican guests to sing "Buffalo Girls." Sadie jerked her head in the direction of the music. "I'll collect from Bennie after I get you to bed and give the boys something to celebrate about. Just listen to that Mexican."

"Bah-fah-lo gahs, wontjew con out tonight, con out tonight, con out tonight, ahn weel dahnce by de light of de mun."

CHAPTER TWENTY

Down in Dos Cacahuates

SOON AFTER MRS. COHN and the Miners arrived in Dos Cacahuates, Minnie inveigled Frieda to her room to show off the dresses Miss Francy of A La Mode Dressmakers in Tucson had created for her and Rosamund. Her cheeks rouged, her wiry hair drawn back in a cascade of curls, her small brown eyes luminous with self-satisfaction, Minnie looked healthy, almost pretty. Holding up a white satin dress with a beaded bodice, she whispered conspiratorially, "Mendel says I'm going to be the most beautiful woman at the banquet in this."

"You will," Frieda loudly agreed.

Minnie set down the white dress and drew from the clothes piled on the bed the lavender gown she planned to wear for the Hunt Breakfast. Laying that one down, she peered at Frieda, her forehead furrowing. "Are you all right, Frieda? You look like you're going to faint."

"No I'm not. I've never fainted in my life."

"You don't look well. My mother's worried about you."

"We've been working day and night to get everything ready," Frieda said, eyeing the door.

"My mother thinks you and Bennie aren't happy together."

"Quite the contrary," Frieda protested, again too loudly. "We've never been happier in our lives."

"Like Mendel and me," Minnie crowed. "My mother says I was incredibly lucky to find him. He's going to be the most prominent mine operator in the west. And he worships the ground I walk on."

She's gloating like the new heavyweight champion. "How nice for you," Frieda murmured.

"My mother says with a man like Mendel, I'll never want for anything. What are you going to wear to the banquet?"

"I haven't decided," Frieda answered. "Now, I really must go, before I-I-." Tears threatening, she dove for the door. Minnie followed, calling, "Don't work so hard, Frieda. You'll make yourself sick."

On the eve of the Big Day, Bennie paced outside their tent dressed in his green suit, his wide, ruddy face clean-shaven, his polished boots in one hand and a cigar in the other. He called to Frieda again, urging her to hurry. Harry Felixson had come down with half the Tucson City Band, and the musicians had already started to play. It sounded like the Fourth of July at Levin's Park.

She turned for a last look in the small hand mirror. The green satin dress from one of the Sisters of Service boxes was worn and outmoded. She'd taken in the sides, but there was nothing she could do with the plunging neckline, except cover it. Across the line, Angelina found her a black shawl embroidered with red flowers. Hideous as it was, Frieda draped it over her bare arms and swung a fringed end over her exposed bosom.

Her hair was also beyond repair. She'd washed it that afternoon and brushed it dry in the sun. Then she'd built a small fire, heated a curling iron and—holding a hand mirror—arranged her curly, brown hair to resemble Minnie and Rosamund's coiffures. Later in the afternoon, as she stood in the First Lady stirring steaming pots of soup and stew, Frieda felt the curls slide onto her forehead and down her back. Her only recourse was to collect the limp strands into a workaday topknot.

"Frieda, we've got to get going," Bennie called.

Exhaling a resigned sigh, she stepped through the tent flap carrying her black dress shoes in one hand, and in the other a floral headpiece which she could not decide whether to wear or leave behind. Instead of his usual unqualified approval, Bennie studied her as though she'd forgotten something, and he was trying to decide what. He finally suggested, "A little powder or rouge?" Frieda started walking. Bennie strode ahead, all but running up the slope, eager to be with the crowd, hand extended, introducing himself as he always did: "Bennie Goldson, Dos Cacahuates." He'd be busy all evening, laughing, talking, clapping people on the back, embracing men and women alike in a two-armed Mexican-style abrazo; then, sooner or later, he'd be seated at the piano, singing and urging others to join him. Maybe she and Minnie could sit together, Frieda thought, and whisper about other guests as they used to do in San Francisco.

As they threaded through the noisy, crowded hotel, Frieda clutched Bennie's arm. The Cohns were not the only grand ladies at the banquet. Two days before, Colonel Leighton (a huge and marvelously dignified-looking man) had helped from his stagecoach two well-decorated eastern fashion plates. Each of the other parties—from San Francisco, Los Angeles, Tucson, and Hermosillo—included one or more elegantly attired women. In comparison, Frieda felt like the miner's daughter, Clementine.

Bennie went straight to their hostess, Rosamund, who stood behind the head table. Holding one of each of their hands, and speaking in a low, intimate tone, Rosamund told them she was counting on them to play host and hostess to the Territory people out in the patio. Minnie and Mendel were handling the mining people, eastern and western; Yancy and the Colonel were caring for the railroad investors. She would be looking after the San Francisco guests. Nearly fifty had come out on a Silver Palace car—railroaders, real estate investors, agricultural and ranching people, a few newspaper men. Everyone would have a chance to mix during the dance, Rosamund said, squeezing Frieda's hand.

"Doesn't everything look lovely?" her hostess asked, her outstretched arm claiming the dining room as her own.

A nod was all Frieda was willing to grant the elated Mrs. Cohn.

Places for Bennie and Frieda waited at one of the six tables on the brick-paved patio. Theirs was on the far side of a fountain that spewed water in coughs and spurts. Their tablemates were already seated. To the left of Frieda sat Lollie and Morrie. Lollie was dressed in the red satin gown Frieda had worn the night Rayina was born. Her blonde hair in an upsweep, her face powdered, she looked almost like herself. All that was missing was her flashy, every-seat-in-the-house smile. Lollie kept turning to peer through the open doors to the main dining room, hoping, Frieda suspected, to spot Ray in some disguise. Brushed and polished, Morrie wore a black suit with a very long coat out of the Sisters of Service boxes. Sadie and Sam Silverstein, Abe Beisel, and his nineteen-year-old son (his wife was in San Francisco again) were the other familiar faces at the table.

The remaining twosome were seated at Frieda's right. "Jake Plotzman, Tubac," the gentleman introduced himself as he took Frieda's hand and drew her down into the chair alongside his. "See you're not sitting with the aristocrats either," he said, as he scrutinized Frieda's face. Without turning, he tossed his hand over his left shoulder, "My wife, Rachel." Frieda leaned toward the table to smile at the pretty, impassive face.

Jake was a short man with a big chest and a two-inch mat of straight black hair that started low on his lined forehead. A red, bulbous nose dominated his face. His voice was hoarse from shouting at mules, someone told Frieda later. He provided most of the conversation at the table, while his wife noted she was from Liverpool and was silent thereafter.

Rachel's face was fresher and prettier than any Frieda had seen since she left San Francisco. Her gleaming white skin made her blue eyes stand out like larkspurs against a white fence. But there was an uncomprehending porcelain doll-like quality about her that reminded Frieda that this lovely Englishwoman made her home in Tubac, an outpost almost as remote as Dos Cacahuates.

"What are you doing in Tubac?" Frieda asked Jake. General merchandise, freighting. Hadn't Bennie told her about his old friend Jake Plotzman? He leaned over to chide Bennie, who was just rising out of his chair to go to Yancy, who was beckoning from the dining room. Plotzman settled back to tell Frieda of his friendship with her husband during the years Bennie and Morrie had a small store in Tubac. Jake hinted at youthful exploits—running after wine, women, song, gold and a decent meal—and running from Jew-haters, competitors, Indians, bandits, parasites and sly women.

As course followed course, the Territorial people at Frieda's table pinpointed the origin of each of the delicacies: the turkeys were from old man Grayson's ranch; the oysters, from Guaymas; the smoked hams, from Pete Kitchen's ranch; the bread, from Striker's bakery in Tucson; the beef, right off the San Leonardo Ranch; and the fruit pies, chocolate cakes, and blanc mange were prepared in Hammerstein's kitchen in Tucson and transported to Dos Cacahuates. They ate with gusto, noisily lauding each dish and the banquet overall. Each seemed to take personal pride in participating in so grand an event in a remote corner of the reputedly uncivilized Arizona Territory.

Smoking his after-dinner cigar, Plotzman turned to more intimate subjects. "There's one thing Bennie's got that I ain't. That's luck. I guess he really made it this time," Plotzman told her. "Truth is, I got it all over Bennie for brains, but who needs brains with a lady like you? This Rachel here," his tone continued at the same resounding volume, "a beauty, right? I fell in love with that face. Listen, after four years in Tubac, I would have fallen in love with a picture." He tapped his head. "I don't know if she's just stupid, frightened, or what."

"Shush, she'll hear you," Frieda cautioned.

"I don't even think she can hear." Plotzman leaned over in what Frieda guessed to be deference to the delicacy of the subject and said, "I try to stay away from her—you know what I mean. What would she do with children?"

Frieda drew back further, afraid of what he might say next. Plotzman leaned in after her. "I got a few consolations, though. She's Jewish, believe it or not, and she doesn't cry or complain like Beisel's wife and so many of the others. She's an orphan, thank God for small favors. But I do get lonely. A man has to have someone to talk to." Jake drained his sixth glass of wine.

Frieda kept turning to look for Bennie.

"I should have married a Mexican girl. I lived with a beauty, a member of the Alonzo de la Torre family of Hermosillo. Heard of them?" he demanded of Frieda. "She lied to her family about me—told them I was a rich, Polish nobleman, a devout Catholic, married to a duchess with leprosy, and that I'd marry her as soon as my duchess, the leper, died." Plotzman grinned: "And they accepted it. We got along fine until we had a falling out during the Pesquiera-Gándara dispute. I was in the Gándara camp; they were in Pesquiera's. Her brother and some of his friends kidnapped me, brought me to Tubac and dumped me. After that, I didn't dare go back to Mexico."

Frieda fidgeted nervously in her seat.

"Seeing Bennie Goldson make it after so many disappointments and failures does my heart good," Jake confided, his worn, ungainly face wreathed in a childlike plea. "On the drive over here, I kept thinking, if someone like Bennie Goldson can make it, why can't I?" His eyes fastened hopefully on Frieda's. "All I need is one more chance. I've had a million of them, but something always went wrong."

When the band struck up a waltz, Jake, ignoring pretty Rachel, invited Frieda to dance. Hating herself, Frieda accepted. She was eager to be in the dining room and was too reticent to go there unescorted. Jake, who was exactly the same height as Frieda, was a sure and graceful dancer.

"Doña Eufemia's work," he answered proudly when Frieda complimented him. Never a skillful dancer, Frieda was having trouble with Jake's intricate steps. When she spotted

Bennie in the group clustered around the Colonel, she asked to be taken to her husband to be introduced to the president of the company.

"A pleasure, madam," the colonel drawled.

As Leighton drew out the word "playsure," his eyes held hers in a warm, magnetic gaze that seemed to reach down and draw her up to his considerable height. "Ah've heard of your fine works in this rapidly growing international community and assure you, madam, your contributions have been entered alongside those of your husband's." He had reached for her hand and held it up in a firm grip as he spoke. Her hands were trembling; she hoped the Colonel did not notice. Someone took his arm. The Colonel bowed to Frieda, then turned to be introduced to someone else.

"Isn't he something?" Bennie exclaimed.

Frieda didn't answer. Her hand hanging in mid-air, she glanced at the patio, then at Bennie. "Is there anything I can do to help you?"

Bennie reflected, brightening. "Several ladies are afraid of snakes and insects and won't go to the outhouse alone or allow a man to escort them."

Frieda's first charge was an eighteen-year-old girl, wife of a boyish-looking lieutenant. "He's so disdainful of any show of timidity," the girl explained.

As she waited, Frieda sighted a shovel against the outhouse. She'd killed three snakes since she'd been in Dos Cacahuates and was confident she could deal with another should the necessity arise. On her fourth trip, Frieda spotted and assaulted with the shovel what turned out to be a harmless king snake. When her charge emerged from the outhouse, straightening her skirts and smiling, Frieda showed her the dead snake, earning herself a respectful look and a quick trip back to the dining room.

For the next two hours, as the band played and the guests danced or talked, Frieda escorted other women to the outhouse. Rosita, a lively Mexican girl who had come with her father from Hermosillo in a stagecoach; the wife of a merchant from Tucson (Frieda could not remember his name, though his wife assured her he was famous throughout the Territory); the companion of a Washington, D.C. Customs Service official; a widow who operated a dress shop in Denver and was thinking of making a move; the bride of a San Francisco newspaperman who had come along on the free trip and was paying for it with an unremitting case of diarrhea.

A little after midnight, leaving Bennie surrounded at the piano, Frieda slipped out and returned to her tent. Away from the excitement of the crowd, the music, the food, the drink and the need to appear to be taking part, Frieda's spirits plummeted. Alone in the dark, she dug out the evening's slights and snubs as if they were bullets embedded in her flesh.

When you feel down, girls, as everyone does at one time or another, she could hear Miss O'Hara say, turn your gaze upward to the fixed star of Service. Let those who would demean you, do so if they must. Nothing they can say or do will deflect you from your course. You're striving to become Elevated Feminine Spirits, and to "Make the World a Better Place."

Those, and all the other uplifting words Miss O. had lavished on her youthful disciples, failed to ease Frieda's misery that night. It was as if the earth had tilted, and she lay alone down in Dos Cacahuates, unseen, unheard, writhing in the dark.

CHAPTER TWENTY-ONE

The Big Day

SOMETIME DURING THE long, lacerating night, Bennie had popped in, told Frieda he had things to do and disappeared. Soon after dawn, she forced herself out of her cot and into clean cooking clothes. As she stepped into the clear morning air and looked around, her dark mood lifted. Bennie had promised her a Big Day worthy of the name: investors and lot buyers from near and far, swarms of peddlers eager to hawk their wares, and entertainment-starved locals looking for excitement. All week long, people had been trickling into Dos Cacahuates; now, seemingly overnight, a large crowd had materialized. Buggies, horse- or mule-drawn wagons and buckboards, even a few pushcarts littered the area from the townsite to the pond several hundred yards away. Others had ridden in on horses or burros, and some, mostly Mexicans and Indians living within a fifty-mile-radius of Dos Cacahuates, had walked in. In the center of the townsite, in the area marked "The Plaza" on the town plan, not far from the First Lady and Bennie and Frieda's tent, waited a roughly constructed platform with a big banner across the front that read:

LOT AUCTION TODAY.

INTERNATIONAL IMPROVEMENT COMPANY,

DOS CACAHUATES DIVISION.

Below, in smaller print, were the names of the company officers: President, Colonel Jack Leighton; First Vice President, Alejandro Ramirez; Second Vice President, Yancy Nunes; Secretary-Treasurer, Bennie Goldson. On the stand were chairs and a table with a gavel on it. In two rows perpendicular to the stand, about thirty feet apart, Ramón and his helpers were spreading bear grass mats for the peddlers to display their merchandise.

Frieda watched as the Papago who had set up camp alongside the pond several days before laid out their wares: baskets made out of willow and devil's claw, woven string bags, carrying nets, cowhide sandals and coils of rope.

Other peddlers, some with merchandise-loaded wagons— a medicine show among them—began unloading and arranging their goods, and a dozen or more Cacahuatans from across the line had erected cloth-shaded booths, and were bringing out fruits, vegetables, clay pots, baskets, serapes, and silver jewelry.

Musicians—mariachis, fiddlers, banjo players and an accordionist—were unpacking their instruments, and a pair of Mexican dancers were shaking out their red, white, and green costumes. On the other side of the pond, behind a thicket of cottonwoods and tamarisks, three tent establishments—a saloon, a sporting house and a gambling house—had been in operation for several days. Customers were already moving in that direction. A far larger group, maybe twenty or thirty, were waiting in front of the First Lady.

Frieda strode toward the dining tent as if she were going onstage, had the star role and was confident she would play her oft-rehearsed part well.

The large stove was red hot and loaded to full capacity. Frieda inspected the contents of the pots simmering on the burners and the pans baking in the two ovens. Satisfied, she filled a mug with coffee, cut herself a piece of cornbread, and signaled Angelina to pull back the tent flap and ring the triangle. Hungry customers filed in and without a grumble submitted to the proprietress's instructions. They stood single-file waiting their turn at the serving table; dropped their two bits in the bowl; took the plate of eggs, beans, corn bread, and stewed fruit and the cup of coffee handed them; went outside, found a place to sit, and ate.

From the starting clang, Frieda was on her feet, giving orders, cooking and serving at top speed. What little she learned about what was going on outside the First Lady she gleaned eavesdropping on her customers' conversations.

"Heard that President Hayes was coming down to Dos Cacahuates."

"Yuma newspapers said he was in Maricopa to speak to some Indian chiefs just the day before yesterday."

"He just might turn up, being it is an election year."

"The President of the United States come to Dos Cacahuates, Arizona Territory? Hah."

"Weaver's the only candidate who gives a damn about the Territory. Tucson papers had a nice little piece about the Greenbackers last week. Said the Territory had enough of taxation without representation, and I do agree."

"Did they invite Hancock? He's my man. Democrats are for the people. It's about time we got another Democrat— Lincoln, Grant, Hayes—now if Garfield gets in, we wouldn't have had a Democrat in office since Franklin Pierce."

"Someone said our devoted governor is going to kick off the auction."

"Governor Fremont couldn't find his way to the Arizona Territory."

Hoots of laughter ensued.

"Think that flash flood they had down here last month was part of his plan to flood the desert?"

"Old Charlie Poston, Father of Arizona, was on the stand waiting his turn to speak. Probably dedicate Dos Cacahuates to the Sun God."

More laughter.

"Did he have a pretty little girl with him?"

"That's what Poston knows most about, pretty little girls."

"I'll say this for the Goldsons: They sure got out their fair share of dandies."

"A reporter from San Francisco interviewed me and then had me set down to have my picture sketched," bragged one man.

"What did he want to know?"

"If I was down for business or for a good time. Did I intend to buy."

"Whatcha tell him?"

"I told him I was here for business and pleasure, and I intended to buy and sell."

"Buy and sell what?"

"That I didn't say."

Bennie ducked his head in and waved on the way to the auction stand. At noon, the lunch customers discussed the progress of the sale.

"Got off to a fast start."

"One lot right after another."

"Goldson knows how to keep things rollin'."

"A set-up," grunted a half-full mouth.

"What do you mean?"

"Those are shills, dummy. Ain't you ever been to an auction before?"

"What's a shill?"

"Hired bidders."

"I think the railroad's a bluff, too."

"Not so. The Sonora Railway already has a line to Dos Cacahuates in construction. Read in the Tombstone Epitaph—"

"Hot air. Get enough hot air out this way to know hot air."

"It's not hot air. I bought three of those lots."

"I can't help it if you're a fool."

"I'm not a fool. I'm just gettin' on board early."

"For a long, lonely ride nowhere."

"You say."

"I say."

"You say."

The two growled, then lunged at each other. The husband of Guadalupe's cousin and a brawny customer seized one brawler, two other customers grabbed his opponent, and they dragged them out of the tent kicking and cursing.

As Frieda served the midday meal, the babble inside the tent mixed with the continuing fracas outside: enraged shouts, knuckles landing on bone, animal-like grunts, wisecracks and jeers from onlookers. Cutting up lettuce, slicing bread, transferring buckets of stew to big pots to heat on the stove, Frieda kept listening for someone to break up the fight and send the troublemakers on their way. No one did. The crowd outside was growing larger and more contentious.

"What's going on out there?" Frieda called to a man coming into the tent.

"They're still disputin'."

"Isn't anyone going to stop them?" she snapped.

"Nope," he replied, as if answering a ludicrous question.

"Well, I can't stand anymore," Frieda cried. She seized a huge pot of water she had set on the flame several minutes before and started outdoors, shouting, "Out of my way, out of my way." When she reached the combatants, one man was sitting on the other's midsection, his arm was drawn back, and his fist clenched. Standing alongside them, she watched the fist fly through the air and land with the force of a hurled baseball in the middle of his opponent's face. Blood spurted from the prone man's nose and mouth. Still, no one moved. The crowd had hushed, waiting for the next, possibly definitive, blow.

"On your feet now, you dogs," Frieda shouted, "or I'm going to empty this pot of boiling water all over the both of you."

In a flash, the two were on their feet and on the run in different directions.

"And the winner is Mrs. Bennie Goldson," came a referee-like call from the crowd.

Laughter, wisecracks, and more laughter followed Frieda as she headed back to the tent, stern-faced, steaming pot held out in front of her. At the entry, she turned. Addressing no one in particular she announced, "Supper won't be ready for forty-five minutes. Anyone who can't behave, stay out. I'm running out of patience."

By the time she was serving the roast turkey, cranberry

sauce, mashed potatoes, apple pie and chocolate cake, results of the lot auction began filtering into the First Lady.

"I hear it was a sell-out."

"Sell-out in hell."

"Why so?"

"Any yokel can take a chance on a five-dollar down payment."

"There were a hundred lots spoken for before we even got here."

"Maybe."

"Well the girls at the pond did right well," a new voice piped up.

Mild laughter.

"They had a pretty nice assortment."

"I seen better."

"On the hoof."

"I spotted three Pima County lawmen."

"Looking for anyone in particular?"

"Take your pick. Billy's been real active in New Mexico. Victorio's on the run around Safford. And what's the name of that Mexican bandito that's been raising such Cain over in Agua Prieta and San Luis?"

"I can't tell one from the other."

"I used to see Billy in Tucson. That boy was a first-class monte dealer."

"Anyone try their luck with the monte dealer here?"

"I couldn't get near him," exclaimed one disgusted voice. "Five or six of those fine eastern ladies walked right in and took over."

"Can't tell the ladies of quality from the fancy ladies out here today."

By eight-thirty that night, all the American food had been consumed, and Frieda had dispatched Guadalupe's cousin and her husband across the line with a twenty-dollar bill to bring back more beans, tortillas and anything else edible they could find. When the Mexican food was gone, Frieda scrawled CLOSED with a piece of charcoal on the back of a tin plate and clipped it to the tent flap with a fork. By then, the carnival din had dwindled, the hotel guests were enjoying a buffet supper in the dining room, and most of the campers had cooked and eaten their suppers and settled down for the night around their campfires.

Like a long distance runner sliding across the finish line, Frieda stretched out on one of the wooden benches and was instantly sorry. The pains in her side, which she had refused to acknowledge all day, leaped to life like a flame hit with a gust of air. Her legs throbbed with a dull ache from her thighs to her toes, and she had to jump up twice to walk off excruciating cramps in her calves.

It was her feet that hurt the most. They were black with dirt and splattered with grease, spilled coffee, beans, squirts of chewing tobacco—she refused to identify what else—and they were so swollen that the straps of her sandals had cut red welts around her ankles. When she closed her eyes, the daylong din roared in her ears and tin plates flew at her like a barrage of stones.

Concerns set aside during the hectic day resurfaced for consideration. Where was Lollie? Dozens of customers had asked for her. Bennie had stopped in several times but she'd been too busy to talk; and he, too busy to wait. Several hours had passed before she saw him again starting up the hill to dine with the guests. She'd filled three cigar boxes with cash. Now what should she do with it? A customer warned her that a pack of ruffians were acting up, galloping their horses around the townsite and camping grounds, shooting off their rifles. Lawmen were supposed to be keeping an eye on them; still, she ought to hide the cash. And what about the package from her mother and father that man from San Francisco brought for her? He had come in the middle of the suppertime rush, and she had taken it, thanked him, and put the brown paper wrapped box in the dish cupboard. It took her several minutes to bring herself to rise and limp to the cupboard. She was reaching for the package when two, heavy hands clamped either side of her waist. She shrieked, turned around, and there was Bennie grinning at her and pointing to his mouth. After shouting above the noise of the crowd all day, his voice was reduced to a hoarse whisper.

"You sound like Jake Plotzman."

"He lost his voice yelling at mules. No money in that."

"How about lots?"

"We sold all but four. The colonel was so happy he kissed me on one cheek and then the other," Bennie croaked.

"Better than you expected?"

"Much. You're not pleased?"

"I will be when I'm back from the living dead."

"How'd the First Lady do?"

Frieda tossed her head in the direction of the cigar boxes. "Count what we took in, if you like. I'm too tired to care."

Bennie emptied the boxes on the table, stacked the coins like poker chips and counted every one, discarding an occasional wooden two-bit piece. "Two hundred and thirty-three dollars and fifty cents," he reported, impressed. "That's four hundred and sixty-seven meals."

"More than that. Some wise apples slipped through without paying, and a few filched coins from the pay bowl."

"You must have cooked up everything but the canvas."

"And sent out for more."

"What do you have there?" Bennie asked, as Frieda hobbled back to the bench, box in hand.

"A package from my parents. Open it for me. I don't have the strength."

He ripped off the paper, pulled back the top and passed it back to her.

Frieda pulled out a blue and white box marked *Yahrzeit* in Hebrew letters containing memorial candles to light on Yom Kippur Eve, and a list of whom to light them for: her four deceased grandparents, and Uncle Chaim, Aunt Chava's late husband. There was also a Jewish calendar in Hebrew and English, and a *lulov*, a palm branch, and an *estrog*, a citron, for the *Succos* service, the fall holiday following Yom Kippur. At the bottom of the box was a letter to her from her father.

Dear Frieda:

I made a mistake about Bennie's townsite and hotel. Maybe because I, myself, had a lot of bad luck
with real estate investments. The newspapers here ran
the names of very substantial San Francisco investors
who traveled to Dos Cacahuates for Bennie's lot sale.
I would buy lots too, if I had some cash. But I don't.
What I do have is some Bluebell Mining Company
stock. I bought it when I was doing good business in
Virginia City, Nevada. I don't know what the stock is
worth now, but I paid $350. Would the company take
the stock in exchange for lots? Maybe Bennie can arrange it, since it's in the family.

Regards,
Abram Levie

She looked up at Bennie, tears starting down her grime-
stained cheeks. From his wary expression, she guessed what
he was thinking. "It's not bad news, it's good news. Papa
wants to buy in," she said, handing him the letter.

He read it, his tongue searching the inside of his mouth
as if trying to pinpoint a sore spot. The troubled-area located,
he sought Frieda's eyes. "The company has a firm rule: all
cash or time payment, no trades. But I'd hate to see the old
man miss out." His gaze turned to coins on the table. "Would
you be willing to buy your father's stock with the First Lady's
earnings?"

Frieda waited to hear more.

"You'd be doing him and me a favor. I could let him have
the last four lots for $332.50, and I could do what I was hop-
ing to do: report a sell-out."

The Bluebell Mining Company stock was worthless.
She'd heard her father say as much. Even so, the fact that he
now wanted to support their efforts in Dos Cacahuates elated
her. She'd believed she no longer cared that her father had
obstinately refused to bless their marriage. The urge to throw
her arms in the air, shout with joy and dance around the tent

told her otherwise.

"Why not" she cried. "It would be worth a day's take, just to get out of here and go soak my feet."

"Come on," Bennie said with a laugh. "I'll carry you down to the pond."

He handed her the cigar boxes to hold and lifted her in his arms. Carrying her as if she were a tired child, he strode across the campfire-dotted clearing toward the pond. Nestled against his chest, Frieda inhaled the sweet midnight air, mixed with her husband's powerful aroma—brandy, cigars, and self-satisfaction. The Big Day was over. She no longer had to hold herself together and keep moving. Her hand curled tighter around Bennie's neck. Closing her eyes, she relaxed and let herself be carried.

Seated on the edge of the pond, Frieda dipped her feet through the reeds into the cool water lapping at the shore. Pushing herself forward, she let the dark moonlight-silver water cover her calves, then her thighs, extinguishing the fire, dulling the pain. Bennie's arms around her, supporting her, she lay half-submerged, eyes closed, drifting in and out of sleep. What a delight after a day like that day and a night like the night before.

CHAPTER TWENTY-TWO
En Route

BENNIE WAS AFTER HER to attend the shareholders' meeting in Tucson with him. Frieda balked. Who'd tend the First Lady? They were serving fifty to one hundred meals a day, and the operation was still their main source of cash. Leave Dos Cacahuates for a week or so, and the German widow from Kansas who'd started selling meals out of her tent would scoop up all her regulars. Besides, her hair was frizzy, her skin was peeling, and a ragpicker would turn up a nose at her clothes.

Bennie knocked off her excuses with sharpshooter precision. Angelina and Ramón could keep the First Lady going for a week. As to the widow, locals might go for her sauerbraten and Gesundheitskuchen once or twice; after that, they'd be waiting on the road for Frieda. As soon as they got to Tucson, he'd drive her straight to Zeckendorf's to buy a new dress, shoes, stockings, and whatever else she needed to doll herself up before going to the Miners' for the meeting.

Her objections demolished, Bennie argued his case. He wanted her with him when he announced the success of the lot auction and presented his plans for the next stage of development. They needed to relax and store up some fun before the work piled up again. Once the company paid him his back salary and cash layout, they'd start building a new house and store. Then, before they knew it, she'd have a baby to look after. This was her chance to visit with her friends in Tucson and shop for herself, the house, and the baby. Besides....

Bennie wasn't going to stop until she agreed. She agreed.

"Now you're talking. We'll take the southern route, along

the international border. It's rugged, but it's passable this time of year, and we'll be as alone as Adam and Eve."

At dawn, on October nineteenth, they had the wagon loaded and were about to depart. As Bennie hitched up the two horses, Tomaso and Tomasina (his new teammate), Frieda checked the food basket in the back of the wagon: hard boiled eggs, roasted chicken, a noodle pudding, coffee grounds, dried apples, bread, raisin and nut strudel, butter cookies. Then she examined the rest of the supplies: canteens of water, a coffee pot, firewood, four khaki-colored blankets and, under the blankets two rifles, and a cigar box containing seventy-three dollars, the First Lady's earnings since the Big Day. She patted the box tenderly, then slipped it back under the blankets, imagining herself shopping at Zeckendorf's, the White House, maybe even at A La Mode Dressmakers.

For the first hour, they rode in near silence, closer to the solitude of the night than the companionship of the day. By the time the eastbound wagon entered a wide valley flanked by a towering mountain range to the north and a wide desert plain to the south, the desert day had begun. Frieda loosened her rebozo, stretched her legs out in front of her and tilted her face to catch the morning sun. As she relaxed, she picked up the rhythm of the wagon as it jerked and swayed along the uneven, hard-packed sand road.

Bennie was already taking in his beloved desert. He inhaled the clear air, then exhaled a satisfied "aaah." Holding the reins lightly in one hand, he gazed about, calling to Frieda's attention the sights that delighted him. Old Diaz Peak had a cloud caught on its point. There was an elephant tree. The Papagos used its bark for curing hides. Had she seen the bobcat darting across the arroyo? That dark gray-green plant was called ironwood. The feathery tree was a honey mesquite—the locals ate its berries.

The miles mounting, they moved deeper into a green valley and dipped down to follow the Papago River. As they rode, their talk changed from the scenery to people and events, especially the Big Day and its aftermath.

"I've never known as commanding a figure as Colonel Leighton," Bennie reflected.

"Big men are always impressive," Frieda replied.

"Six-foot-two, at least," Bennie calculated.

"He did look elegant at the banquet."

"More than elegant," Bennie said. "There's something prophetic about that man. Just standing alongside him made me feel bigger, stronger, wiser."

She'd felt that way about Miss O'Hara—when she was seventeen, Frieda thought, but didn't say.

"It's forward-thinking men like Leighton who make America great."

"A few things bothered me about him," Frieda confessed.

"Such as?"

"Some parts of Leighton's banquet speech made me uneasy."

"Which parts?"

"'*Ah* can do business with any white man *alahve,*'" Frieda imitated.

"The man was a colonel in the Confederate Army," Bennie objected. "What do you expect?"

Frieda thought of something else. "I was expecting him to stay longer."

"He'd told Ramirez he'd come to Guaymas to settle up with him right after the auction."

"Is Yancy going to stay in Tucson?" Frieda asked hoping the answer would be yes.

"He's doing the company a lot of good in Tucson working on the newspaper, standing for the legislature, moving with the swells. I'd as soon see him stay where he is."

Frieda nodded accord.

"Mrs. Cohn and him are quite a team," Bennie noted. "I don't know how we would have made it without her. She's some woman."

"She certainly is." A moment later Frieda modified her endorsement. "I just wish she and Minnie paid more attention to Mendel."

"I don't hear Mendel complaining," Bennie said.

The two sank back into their own thoughts, until further down the road a woodpecker drilling at the top of a giant saguaro brought a hoot from Bennie. "Reminds me of old Morrie."

Frieda was glad Bennie finally got around to speaking of his brother. He hadn't uttered a word about him since Lollie and the baby disappeared.

"How's Morrie doing?" Frieda gently probed. "He hasn't been in Dos Cacahuates since the Big Day."

"He's fine," Bennie answered.

"I thought he'd be upset."

"He was, but he's taking hold."

"You never told me what happened at the ranch," Frieda said, "after Lollie left."

"No, I don't suppose I did."

They rode in silence for several minutes. "Bennie?" she finally prompted. In their seven months together, she'd learned her husband treated painful personal subjects the way he did rabid animals: approach them only when absolutely necessary.

"I *am* part of the family," she prodded.

"I don't know much more than you," he responded. "Lollie was gone for more than a week before I found out."

"Who told you?"

"Ramón heard there was some kind of trouble at the ranch but it didn't sound too serious. I figured I'd ride out and see what was going on when things settled down in Dos Cacahuates."

He had been busy, Frieda remembered. A number of the guests—railroad people, mining company representatives, a few cattle ranchers—had stayed on at the hotel. So had a half-dozen politicos—two from Washington, D.C., who had come to discuss a customs house, and four from the territorial capital in Prescott, who were there to oppose it. Bennie had to look after them and oversee the couple Rosamund had hired to run the hotel. There were also new settlers to counsel—two German families from Kansas; the doctor and his

family, including a tubercular daughter; the four Chinese from
Tombstone; the two peddlers, one Irish, one Jewish; a retired
Negro soldier and his wife; several Mexican families who had
moved from across the line; also the occupants of the three
tent establishments who'd bought lots facing the plaza opposite the Goldsons' tents and had moved from their semi-con-
cealed locations in the cottonwood grove to the townsite
proper.

"Lollie running off must have hit Morrie hard," Frieda
persisted.

"Sure it did. Morrie don't take to a lot of people, but he
sure took to Lollie."

"He must have said something, Bennie."

"He said nothing."

"Nothing?"

"Nothing."

"Then how did you know he was upset?"

"Rosalia, the baby's nurse, told me."

"She was still there?"

"Yep."

"Why?"

"He kind of went crazy."

"What did he do?"

"He went tearing around the ranch with a shovel, digging
in one place, then in another."

"Why?"

"Rosalia thought he was digging himself a grave and was
going to shoot himself like her last *patron* did. She was determined to keep him alive, mostly because she had no other
place to go. So she brought her baby and her little boy outside and they followed Morrie around the ranch all that first
day. She tried to coax him to come inside when it turned
dark, but he wouldn't."

"Poor Rosalia. What a fix?"

"She sent her six-year-old boy back to the house for
some tortillas and beans, then she and the kids settled down
for the night near him. A little before dawn, a wind came up.

The baby began to cry. Morrie yelled at her to take the baby indoors, but he wouldn't come with them, so she refused. The baby yowled so long and so miserably, Morrie finally gave in. He went into the house but insisted on remaining in the kitchen. Rosalia put the kids to bed, then sat alongside Morrie at the table near the cookstove. They just sat there, Rosalia said, not saying anything, like a jailor and a prisoner. He finally collapsed on his arms and fell asleep. A few minutes later, he awoke crying for Lollie. Rosalia tried to massage his back, thinking it would calm him down. When she touched him, he jumped as if her hands were fiery pokers. She kept talking to him and rubbing his back, and after a while, he kind of let go."

"Poor Morrie. He counted on Lollie for so much," Frieda said.

"Near dawn, Rosalia got him to go into the bedroom and lie down on the bed. She sat alongside him, holding his hand. He finally fell asleep and didn't wake up until noon. She cooked breakfast for him, then she and the children went back outdoors with him. They just sort of wandered around the ranch all that day. The next day, she got him to help her water the trees in the orchard. They've been working together side-by-side ever since."

"She's going to stay on with him?" Frieda asked.

"Looks like it."

"As his housekeeper?"

"And then some."

They rode in silence for a while, Frieda remembering how Lollie had tormented herself about leaving her husband.

"What is it, now?" Bennie wanted to know.

"Lollie, Rosalia, what difference does it make as long as he's got a woman to take care of him."

"I wouldn't say that," Bennie said. "Living with Rosalia is a big step for Morrie. I never knew a man in the Arizona Territory more determined to resist the favors of the Mexican women. Morrie was with my father when he was robbed and murdered by Mexican highwaymen. Morrie's known all kinds of Mexicans—good, bad, and in between, since then—but he can't seem to get over being scared of them." Bennie sighed. "One way or another, things always seem to work out, don't they?"

Do they? Her family would have a few things to say about Rosalia. What happened to the other one, the Jewish girl whose family were solid business people in Los Angeles? What kind of name is Rosalia? Mexican? Indian? When did he marry her? You mean they live together and they're not married?

She'd argue that some married people weren't really married, and some people who weren't married really were. Lollie married Morrie, but she was never *married* to him. Lollie is *married* to Ray Blackstone. And Ray Blackstone is *married* to Lollie, not to his wife, Emily. Emily is *married* to her brothers, not to Ray, just as Minnie is not married to Mendel, but to her mother, who is still *married* to her ex-husband Leopold, who is *married* to his French Catholic wife. Wild animals, her Aunt Chava would conclude.

Bennie seemed relieved that Morrie's new living arrangement was now out in the open. His face glistening with perspiration, his Stetson lowered over his eyes, he was whistling through his teeth. Easy, good-humored, slow to judge, he was so different from the men she had known in San Francisco, particularly the men at Levies' Kosher Boardinghouse. She studied his broad, rosy face, his full lips, which were pressed against his clean teeth. Little things didn't bother Bennie. She couldn't imagine him getting upset, as some of the boarders did, over the amount of soup in his bowl, whether he had been given one or two pieces of chicken, who had and who had not said hello to him on the street. Nor could she see him gloat when he succeeded or collapse when he failed.

Frieda edged closer to him. The sparkling freshness of the air, sunlight and shadows playing on the craggy mountain ridges, the soul-swelling warmth of the sun—this desert was Bennie's gift to her. Tears started. Bennie traced the trickle with his index finger.

"Sad? Happy? What?" he asked.

"Happy. I'm so happy I'm married to you."

Gazing down at her, his own tears sprouting, he tied the reins to the brake, and drew her into his arms. They clung to each other, lips locked in a thought-blotting kiss, until the wagon dipped into a deep pothole. With a surpised laugh, Bennie straightened, released her, reclaimed the reins, and directed the straying horses back to the trail. Frieda stayed close to his side, her hand resting on his.

"See that clump of cottonwoods up there?"

Frieda looked ahead, and nodded.

"Up there, little city girl, I'm going to introduce you to what Maizie Green at the Birdcage in Tombstone used to call the delights of love *au naturelle.*"

"There must be a Jewish law against it," Frieda said, sitting down on the rough Army blanket. "If not a law, then a blessing."

Laughing, Bennie stretched out at her side. "I'm starving for you," he said, bending to rub his nose against hers. She lay back on the blanket, her arms rising to draw him closer. Bennie pulled his head back for a moment to gaze into Frieda's eyes. "Don't you ever leave me," he whispered.

"Leave you? Never."

His lips were on hers again, one hand lifting her skirt, as her body arched to meet his. *What joy,* Frieda thought, just before she thought no more.

The first thing Frieda saw when she sat up was a small gray cottontail gazing at her with round blue eyes from the base of a cottonwood, only a few feet from her head. She wanted to pick up the little creature and draw it to her naked breasts. The rabbit was gone before she moved. Later, she spread lunch on the blanket and they ate, her hands caressing Bennie's as she offered him an egg, an orange, a cookie. Time after time, she reached up to touch his face again, kiss his lips, unwilling to let the thrilling connection between them dissolve.

As they packed up, Bennie touched her glowing cheek and said, "I told you you'd feel a lot better once you got away for a while."

CHAPTER TWENTY-THREE

Shareholders' Meeting

WHEN FRIEDA AND BENNIE reached the Miners' rambling, tile-roofed adobe, the front yard was jammed with buggies, wagons, and saddled horses. To avoid calling attention to their tardy arrival, they went around back and slipped in the kitchen door. Servants, fingers to their lips, directed them to the parlor. Frieda stopped at the hall mirror for a last look at her freshly combed hair and her new blue, faille dress. As they tiptoed into the crowded parlor, Yancy called, "Here they are."

A momentary silence followed as the assembled turned to see who Yancy was greeting. More welcoming words flew at them.

"The Goldsons, at last."

"Now we can get down to business."

"We've been waiting for you."

Bennie was escorted to the board of directors' table at the east end of the room, while Frieda made her way to a stool in the southwest corner. Once she was settled between the draped window and a wiry little man in ranch clothes, she looked up to see Minnie and Rosamund waving at her. Pleased to be welcomed from the directors' table, Frieda waved back.

Tilting her head to see over the shoulder of the man in front of her, Frieda studied Yancy, who—inkstand, quill, and papers in front of him—was chairing the meeting. He bore slight resemblance to the ailing and shabby grandee she knew in Dos Cacahuates. His dark hair fell in a straight line against his stiff, white collar and he had a new, pencil-thin mustache. He wore a well-cut, black waistcoat; a wide, gray silk tie, and a tattersall vest. His expression was businesslike, and his words flowed in crisp, well-formed sentences. He looked magisterial, unapproachable.

Between Yancy and Bennie sat Rosamund and a Mexican gentleman Frieda did not know. At first glance, except for the small, inner circle, everyone appeared to be strangers. On closer examination, she recognized several more people—Hammerstein, the restaurant owner; a Tucson merchant whose wife she had escorted to the outhouse; two bank employees who had come to Dos Cacahuates to check on the progress of the construction of the hotel; a Territorial legislator; and the Pima County marshal who had ridden in to pick up the crazy boy, Tracy Spoonover.

Frieda strained to hear as Yancy introduced, "Mr. Ben Goldson, one of the first two American settlers in what is now Dos Cacahuates." *Not as Secretary–Treasurer of the International Improvement Company, Dos Cacahuates Division?*

"We're reviewing the company report, Mr. Goldson," Yancy said, pointing to the booklet on the table in front of Bennie.

From his tone, you'd think they barely knew each other, Frieda thought, her eyes moving from Yancy to Bennie. He'd picked up his copy and was leafing through it, searching for something. What? Frieda glanced at a similar booklet in the hands of the man next to her. Yancy cited another section, and pages fluttered. As the assembled read, Nunes ceremoniously attributed the success of the Big Day to the efforts of Mrs. Rosamund Cohn, her daughter and son-in-law, Mr. and Mrs. Mendel Miner, and a few others.

Rosamund shot Yancy an impatient glance. Undeterred, he stayed with the report, reading aloud the names of the illustrious guests who had come from north and south of the border, the various events staged for their entertainment and profit, the glowing statements about the region made by prominent visitors. Rosamund raised her hand and, without waiting to be recognized, urged the chairman to get to the specifics now that Mr. Goldson was present.

Yancy avoided her prodding gaze but did her bidding. "Please turn to 'Income' on page four. The total income for the Big Day lot auction was $15,300. The number of lots sold were 270. Slightly more than one half, 140, were all cash sales, grossing the company $14,000. For the remaining 130, the company received a down payment and a signed contract to pay over a three-year period. These sales brought in an additional $1,300, totaling—"

Bennie interrupted. "Those were the figures when we counted up after the auction. We sold the last four later that night. Mr. Nunes had left Dos Cacahuates by then, but I reported a sell-out to Colonel Leighton."

A light applause greeted Bennie's announcement. He responded with a grin and a wave. "In all, between January and October, we sold five hundred lots, counting the seventy lots assigned to the seven members of the board in lieu of salaries, and some operating costs."

"Thank you, Mr. Goldson. These were some of the details we have been waiting for," Yancy said. "Now, I'd like to have the accountant present his statement." He waved his hand, and a medium-sized man with a prominent stomach and a gold watch chain rose and began to read numbers. Bennie leaned forward, listening intently, making notes on the back of the booklet with a quill pen. The accountant reported the total overall income as $22,500. Bennie was on his feet again. The total should be $22,832, he corrected. He'd let the last four lots go for $332. The accountant thanked Bennie and wrote something on the paper he held. Except for an occasional cough, the scraping of feet, the creak of a rocker and the scratch of Yancy's pen doodling, the room was quiet until the accountant completed his report.

Were there any additions? Bennie rose. He wanted the shareholders to know that Dos Cacahuates already had more than one hundred permanent residents, and they were receiving new inquiries daily. His features registering annoyance, the accountant appealed to the chairman; he was asking for additional income, not a census report. Bennie nodded and sat down.

"Expenses," the accountant continued. "I've paid bills sub-mitted by Mrs. Rosamund Cohn, Yancy Nunes, Leo Hammerstein, the Borderland Stage Line, the...." When he completed the list, he invited creditors with outstanding bills to present them. Hands shot up. The accountant called on them one at a time—the stationer, the printer, the hardware man. Then Rosamund Cohn and Leo Hammerstein rose to-gether with additional items. Next came Bennie, with a list of reimbursements due Bennie Goldson, Morrie Goldson and Golden Brothers, General Merchandise. After Bennie, Ramirez's attorney stood up. The accountant asked him to wait until the other bills were submitted, since his was the largest.

"And me, what about me?" cried a man waving a derby. "I'm Friedman's representative. I have a bill for $5,000 worth of furniture."

Lollie's family must have found out she left Morrie, Frieda thought with a pang. The furniture, the accountant quickly explained, would be considered later, with the dispo-sition of La Cíbola Hotel, Inc. *Disposition?* Frieda wondered what the man was talking about. The Pima County Bank people lowered their hands. "That leaves unpaid bills totaling $6,012.94," the accountant summed up.

Yancy nodded, and the acountant returned to his seat. "Now that Mr. Goldson is here we can settle these accounts and move to the business of the hotel. Mr. Goldson."

Bennie took the floor, sent a good-will smile out to the shareholders, then addressed Yancy. "Before I give my report, I'd like to note the deficit figure is incorrect, Mr. Nunes."

"The accountant rose to ask, "How so?"

Bennie walked behind the table to where the accountant sat, picked up his report and scanned it. "Here it is. This fig-ure is wrong. I paid this bill myself."

Stone-faced, Yancy, Rosamund, and the Miners listened as Bennie addressed them.

"You remember the night of the auction, the officers of the company counted the money and we paid Mrs. Cohn the money she'd advanced us; also, Hammerstein, and Nunes, who'd run up promotional bills."

They nodded.

"There was $3,019 left in cash. And as I already told you, I collected another $332. So the total cash on hand was exactly $3,351."

Rosamund jumped to her feet.

"Now just a minute, Mrs. Cohn. Let me finish. We owed Ramirez twenty-five percent of the total lot sales, $5,708. We'd already paid him $800 back in May, right? So we still owed him $4908."

Frieda was on the edge of her stool, studying the perplexed faces of each of the directors.

"Mr. Goldson, can you please get to the point?"

"Give me a chance," Bennie said, growing impatient. "I already gave Ramirez most of what we owe him."

"What do you mean? Ramirez wasn't even in Dos Cacahuates for the Big Day," Yancy responded.

An uncomfortable flutter started in Frieda.

"I know he wasn't. I gave the money to Colonel Leighton."

Yancy rose slowly. When he spoke, his voice was quiet, controlled. "Why did you give the money to Colonel Leighton? No one told you to give any money to Colonel Leighton."

"I'm the Secretary-Treasurer, I had the money, and the Colonel asked me for it."

"May I ask you again, Mr. Goldson, why did you give the money to Colonel Leighton?" Yancy's voice had dwindled to a whisper.

"There's no need to get upset, Yancy," Bennie said. "He took the money to Ramirez. The Colonel went straight to Guaymas when he left Dos Cacahuates. He said Ramirez needed the money immediately; it had something to do with the Sonora Railway, Limited. The colonel wanted to be sure Ramirez was satisfied, so he'd be willing to turn over the next parcel of land for development. Colonel Leighton was on his way to South America and went out of his way to arrange passage from Guaymas."

Bennie searched the dubious faces before him. "A party of rurales escorted his stagecoach. I turned over the money to the head of the company. What's wrong with that?"

"How much did you give him, Bennie?" Yancy asked, his tone clipped, noncommittal.

"I gave him $3,351. We still owe Ramirez $1,557. The Colonel was hoping we'd have some expense money for him, but he understood when I explained there was nothing left for the time being...." Sensing animosity rising against him, Bennie stopped. Crimson from his collar to the roots of his hair, he cried, "If you don't believe me, ask Colonel Leighton."

Ramirez's attorney rose. He addressed Bennie in his meager English. "Ramirez saw no Colonel and no money."

"Aw hell," Bennie said, "give him a chance. He was probably delayed on the road."

A lantern-jawed, tan-faced man on the other side of the room got up. "I'm from the United States Marshal's office in Houston, Texas. I was sent here to find Colonel Jack Leighton. I have a three-year-old warrant for his arrest—"

Yancy interrupted the man. "The Colonel's past is not in question here, but his present whereabouts are. Do you know where he went after he left Dos Cacahuates?"

"Colonel Leighton traveled from Dos Cacahuates to Guaymas. On October twelfth, he boarded a ship for Peru," the Texan said.

"Without giving my client a peso," Ramirez's attorney noted.

"There's a mistake somewhere," Bennie said, "Yancy, Mr. Nunes here, knows the Colonel better than I do. Jack Leighton is too farsighted, too honorable, to take money under false pretenses. Besides, why would a rich, influential developer endanger his standing over $3,351?" Bennie looked from Yancy to the shareholders. "Are any of you willing to stand up and accuse Colonel Jack Leighton of being a common thief?"

A murmur of no's sounded in the room.

A hand shot up. Yancy called on the man, a rough-looking miner type. Avoiding Bennie's gaze, he put his question to Yancy. "How do we know Goldson is telling the truth about giving the money to the colonel? How do we know he didn't keep the money for himself?"

Several others sided with the questioner. How did they know? His face redder than his hair, his jaw muscles working, his teeth gritted, Bennie responded. "Anyone who knows me will tell you. I'm not polished, and I get carried away, but Bennie Goldson is no thief." His voice rose to a shout, his fists clenched at his sides. He looked at the doubting faces of the crowd, and then back at Nunes.

"You tell them, Yancy. I've worked hard on this development. I believe in it. Dos Cacahuates is going to be the biggest community on the Arizona-Sonora border. Right from the start, I pitched in and gave it all I had. Nunes will tell you that. Last January he fell out of a stage half-dead with consumption, but I could tell a good idea when I heard it. We took him in and gave him all the money and help we could. Tell them, Yancy."

Yancy tapped his gavel. "Mr. Goldson, this is a business meeting. There's no need to shout."

"I'm not shouting yet," Bennie shouted, "but you're going to hear some shouting if you don't tell these people what you know about me. Tell them that I'm a reliable, hard-working gentleman."

Bennie strode to Yancy's side, grabbed his hand—the one holding the gavel—and ordered him to get up.

"At this moment," Yancy said, rising reluctantly, "I could not possibly vouch that you are a gentleman."

The crowd roared agreement.

Bennie drew back a thickly-muscled arm and aimed at Yancy's waxen face. An uproar erupted. People jumped to their feet shouting, "Throw him out," "Let him speak," "Be quiet." "Throw him out" was the most insistent.

Mute and burning with shame for Bennie, Frieda waited in the corner. She watched as three men seized and restrained her husband, and others formed a protective ring around Nunes. As he was being pulled and pushed from the room, Bennie bellowed, "I'm the most honest man in this whole goddamned room, in this whole goddamned town, in this whole goddamned Territory. You sons-of-bitches think you can come out here and spin tales to the country boys, hoodwink us with your big words and grand ideas. You'll be hearing from me, Yancy Nunes, you dirty, double-crossing, consumptive dandy."

Two more men joined the eviction party. Several minutes later, the five returned straightening their clothes and smoothing their hair.

"We told him he can return when he's ready to act like a gentleman," one reported.

Hit by alternating waves of anger and shame, Frieda rose and started toward the door.

"You can't go now," the wiry little rancher next to her hissed. "Listen to me."

Head down, she waited to hear what he had to say.

"Your fool husband will need to know what went on after he made a prize jackass of himself."

It seemed like good advice. She returned to her seat.

Yancy's face was glum and his voice low-pitched. Ramirez had sent word that he could no longer participate in any transactions with the International Improvement Company and was filing a lawsuit for payment. The Sonora Railway, Limited, it was recently announced, had decided to make Nogales its terminus on the border, eliminating the possibility that there would be a Mexican railroad to Dos Cacahuates. Nor was that all, Yancy sped on, obviously eager to be finished with the bad news. A group of landowners is contesting Ramirez's title to the land grant in Dos Cacahuates, and no more land can be sold until legal title to the land has been established. The shareholders listened in grim silence.

Under the circumstances, Yancy concluded, they had no

alternative but to declare the International Improvement Company bankrupt.... Frieda's ears closed after the dreaded word bankrupt.

When her stunned mind revived, Yancy was completing the disposition of the La Cíbola Hotel. Soon after, around her, people rose grumbling. Frieda closed her eyes and waited for the room to stop spinning.

CHAPTER TWENTY-FOUR

El Gato Negro

FRIEDA EDGED ALONG the wall out of the crowded parlor. She tried not to hear what the shareholders were saying about Bennie, but she heard nonetheless. "A good-time Charlie. At the piano he can't be beat, but in business he's dense as a mule." With a single, sidelong glance, Frieda identified the speaker—a fat, pale-skinned man with a thick growth of graying hair.

"My brother-in-law knew him in Prescott and Tubac. Said he was good-natured fellow, and when push came to shove, he could shove with the best of them. It wasn't Bennie he didn't like; it was the townsite and railroad scheme. One in a hundred go and, on the border, one in a...."

In the front hall, she overheard Yancy shiftily undermining Bennie, "He who excuses himself accuses himself."

Angry enough to do some shoving of her own, Frieda lowered her head and charged for the door. Outside she searched the Miners' front yard and the street for Bennie. Neither he nor his wagon was anywhere in sight. Where could he have gone? Should she wait for him to come back for her? Or go look for him?

"Frieda. Friedaaaa," she heard Minnie call.

She looked over her shoulder. Minnie and Rosamund were rushing toward her. Frieda started for the road.

"Wait," Rosamund commanded. "We must talk to you."

I don't want to talk to you, I don't want to talk to anybody, Frieda thought, picking up her pace.

"Where are you going?" Minnie called again.

"To find Bennie." She flung the words over her shoulder.

"You can't go by yourself. We'll go with you," Rosamund offered.

"No," Frieda shouted back.

"He's probably on his way to Mexico by now."

As she was turning the corner, she heard Minnie call through cupped hands. "If you don't find him, come back here. We're your friends. You're not aloooone."

Frieda rushed passed Levin's Park along the path she and Bennie had taken that morning from the center of town to Minnie's house. Across the bridge, past Zeckendorf's, she hurried toward the plaza, expecting to find him on a bench, cooling down, thinking things over and waiting for her. He wasn't there, so he was probably at the Cosmopolitan Hotel, where they had a room, or having a drink at Goldtree's Gem Saloon.

Finding him in neither of those places, she concluded Bennie had regained his wits and was consulting a lawyer on Main or Pennington. But which? Up one street and down another, studying Attorney-at-Law signs, Frieda wrestled with her other dilemma: how to break the awful news. In her family, bankrupt was the grimmest of words, ranking with cancer, consumption, conflagration, earthquake, plague, pogrom, leprosy, the death of a first-born. The word was unmentionable, especially within earshot of Abram.

She would never forget that month when her father lay bed-ridden, broken in mind and body. As a naïve, seventeen-year-old, she'd believed bankruptcy was their catastrophe, suffered in secrecy and shame by the Levies alone. Later, she learned half of San Francisco had endured a similar or worse fate during the Panic of '75. She had to find Bennie and let him know she would stand by him, assist him, if need be, nurse him, as she had her father.

For more than an hour, she searched the streets around the plaza—Church, Pennington, Meyer, Main. Her feet hurt and the hem of her new dress was edged with a three-inch border of dust. Ignoring the curious stares of passersby, she'd chased a man in a green suit and a derby like the one Bennie had bought at Zeckendorf's. When she caught up with him and found that the resemblance stopped with the hat and the color of suit, she turned and ran in the other direction. Out of breath, she stopped in front of a small bakery, rested her head against the window and closed her eyes. One street vanished and another appeared: Tehama Street. She saw herself climbing the front steps of the boardinghouse, pregnant, alone, a rabbi's prediction realized. Frieda opened her eyes, shook out her dusty skirt, wiped her perspiring face and set out again with renewed determination. Bennie had lived in Tucson; perhaps he had gone to one of the back streets to seek the advice of a trusted friend.

At the south end of Congress and Pennington streets, Frieda picked up the strains of an out-of-tune piano playing a familiar song. Bennie often banged it out when he and his pioneer pals gathered for a few beers. She tracked it to a narrow alley, behind Congress, the words running through her head.

What was your name in the States?
Was it Thompson or Johnson or Bates?
Did you murder your wife and fly for your life?
Say, what was your name in the States?

The alley was dark and reeked of mescal. Peering into the narrow passage, Frieda could see men, several Mexicans, a Chinese, standing in front of what appeared to be a wine shop or makeshift saloon several doors from the corner. In ten, swift steps, Frieda was at the entrance. The wall on one side of the broken, swinging door was of tufa stone; the other, of adobe. An unevenly painted sign read EL GATO NEGRO. As she stood in front, eyed by the hangabouts, the piano stopped, and the sound of boisterous males at drink—laughter, shouts, curses, more laughter—grew louder.

Frieda pushed through the door. The room was dimly lit, cavelike. Along one wall was the bar, a rough board suspended on saw horses. The bartender, a short man, almost a midget— he had to reach up to serve the drinks—was pouring a cloudy liquid into dirty-looking glasses. Opposite the drink dispensary were several rickety tables, all filled. At some tables men were playing cards. The rest of the late afternoon drinkers stood or crouched on their haunches against the walls. The piano music began again. It was coming from a back room.

Frieda started toward the music. Voices in the front room quieted. She could feel eyes scrutinizing her, could all but hear silent speculations. One voice rose like a road block. "Lady, you don't want to go in there."

She folded her hands over her midsection, impelled for the first time to protect the mound just below her belt. The room was thick with the smell of mescal, cigars, unwashed bodies, and the sour odor of vomit. Swaying dizzily, Frieda spoke. "I'm looking for my husband."

Laughter sounded and abruptly stopped. Some lady was always looking for her husband, Frieda sensed. Standing in the middle of the room, she fixed her eyes on the door to the rear quarters. "He plays the piano. That's one of his favorite tunes."

No response.

"His name is Bennie Goldson. He lived in Tucson for a while. Maybe one of you know him."

They seemed to be searching for an appropriate answer. Clearly, some men wanted to see their wives; others didn't.

"It's Bennie," one of the drinkers decided to reveal.

"No 'tain't," a gravelly voice called from the wall. "Tell 'em nothin'," another grumbled.

"It's Bennie," the small bartender piped up. "Get him, someone."

Frieda turned to catch a breath of air from the half-open door. "I'd be most appreciative, if someone would," she said over one shoulder. She wished her voice didn't sound so stilted. She wished she weren't so nervous. She wished she didn't have to be looking for her husband in El Gato Negro.

One spidery little miner jumped up to play the comical messenger. Face uptilted, swaying from side to side, he got his laugh, bowed and disappeared into the back room. When he returned, he reported in an English accent that, "Mister Goldson sends word that he will be out presently."

More laughter.

The barometer rose noticeably in the room, as all eyes waited fixed on the doorway. In no more than a minute—to Frieda it seemed like an hour—Bennie appeared in the doorway. He looked indistinguishable from the rest of the patrons of El Gato Negro. His brown eyes were glazed and bloodshot, and his red hair looked like Mexican hay in a whirlwind. His stiff collar was gone, as were his hat and coat, and he swayed drunkenly as he walked. In the doorway he stopped to peer at Frieda with mock disbelief.

"It's really you," he slurred. "I thought you'd be in San Fraaaaanciscoooo by now."

Curse words in Yiddish and English banged against her sealed lips. She wasn't going to have a family fight in a filthy saloon in front of twenty or thirty drunks.

"Let's go, Bennie. I want to talk to you."

Muffled snickers sounded around the room.

"I've heard the newsss. It's all over town. International Improvement is, is...." He turned his thumbs down and made a crude barnyard noise.

"There's more to it than that," Frieda hissed.

Bennie flinched under her steady gaze. Then, rubbing a broad hand over his face and into his hair, he said, "I'll get cleaned up and meet you in the plaza."

Frieda nodded, whipped around and rushed for the door. She considered waiting in the alley for him, but the moment the doors swung closed behind her, wild laughter broke out at her back. Face frozen, legs atremble, she strode toward the plaza.

On a bench directly in front of the bandstand, she waited, cheeks stinging as if slapped. The band music kept time with her rage. Bang, bang, bang, went the drum. Clang, clang, clang went the cymbal and the triangle. Eeee, ohhh, owww, wailed the horns.

"Listen to the Mockingbird," the instruments piped and drummed. The next time she noticed it was "Where is My Wandering Boy Tonight?" Then "The Golden Hills of San Francisco." Were the musicians mocking her? When a uniformed quartet stepped forward to sing "The Daring Young Man on the Flying Trapeze," she was sure they were. "Left in this wide world to weep and to mourn," growled a mescal-laden voice behind her. Bennie plopped down at her side.

His face was washed, his hair pressed back under his new derby, his stiff collar was buttoned on his shirt and his tie was knotted. He was the same businessman she had entered the shareholders' meeting with that morning, though noticeably worse for the wear. When he leaned in her direction to speak, Frieda involuntarily drew back from the pungent odor of liquor and cigar smoke on his breath, and from the sour smell of El Gato Negro on his clothes. His eyes were still dulled with alcohol.

Thigh to thigh they sat, the band music filling the space around and between them. He took her hand. She withdrew it. She would forgive him but not at once. He leaned his face closer to hers and gazed contritely into her cool eyes. She looked the other way. His hand pounced on hers and dragged it back to his lap. She struggled to retrieve it, but he held it against his knee.

Looking straight ahead, he muttered, "Why did you stay when they threw me out?"

"I stayed to find out what happened after you were...." she couldn't bring herself to say thrown out.

"Don't worry. The news got downtown fast enough. Bankrupt, sheeeee. And foreclosure on the hotel, chrisssss, sheeeee."

"There's no need for that kind of language." Frieda drew the rest of her as far from him as her captured hand would allow.

"What is there a need for?" Bennie asked, crestfallen again.

The band was blowing and thumping "There's a Hole in the Old Oaken Bucket."

Frieda turned a steady, steadying gaze on Bennie. "An apology," she said.

"Apologize to those two-faced, sly-footed...."

"To me." She sat up firm and didn't waver.

"You?"

"Yes. For making me look for you, worry about you. For getting drunk in that filthy place when we should have been together, deciding what to do next." She could see the guilt rise and color his face. "For humiliating me before those low-lifes."

"I was so goddamned mad I could have killed."

"Me?" Frieda was indignant.

"I thought you were siding with that two-timing hypocrite," Bennie lashed.

Siding with Yancy? Smoldering guilt burst into flame. "I thought you had abandoned *me*," she countered. "I've been searching for you for hours."

"You have?" Bennie's features crumbled. His eyes pleaded. "I'm a damn fool, Frieda. Most women...."

Frieda's free hand settled on Bennie's arm. "I'm not most women, Bennie. I'm your wife."

"I should have known better than to trust those four-flushers."

"You didn't know. You did your best."

"Things didn't turn out the way I expected."

"I don't hold it against you. It wasn't your fault." Her face radiated the sympathy flooding her heart.

He looked incredulous. "You mean it. You really do forgive me."

"I do. With all my heart." Her fingers caressed his cheek.

"You are not only an Elevated Feminine Spirit, you're a hell of a sport, Frieda Levie Goldson."

Her arm slipped maternally around and drew his head to her shoulder.

His lips turned up to kiss hers.

Sitting on the park bench with her contrite husband nestled in the crook of her arm, Frieda thought of Miss

O'Hara. "Steadfastness in adversity," Miss O had counseled. "Cultivate it. It grows with use."

She could feel the turmoil whirling in Bennie. Leaning against her, he was drawing strength from her strength, calm from her calm. With his leg pressed next to hers, they sat as if joined from ankle to hip, like Siamese twins. She tightened her arm around him, and he slumped, letting his body relax against her.

"I've had my ups and downs," Bennie said. "As far as I could tell, it was a matter of luck, and there's no arguing with Dame Fortune. I never dared ask a woman to share my fate before. It was too uncertain. This time, though, I had success in my closed fist."

"And you will again, someday."

"I'm not giving up," he told her through gritted teeth. "I'm going to hang on to those lots, and we still own half of the ranch. We're in debt, but I'm not filing for bankruptcy. I haven't yet, and I'm not now. We don't have a dime, but we'll get through it somehow."

"I know what we can do," Frieda said.

He lifted his head, his eyes expectant.

Her words came slowly, her plan unfolding as she spoke. "You can sell the horses and wagon."

Bennie nodded, waiting to hear more.

"If that doesn't bring in enough, I'll go to Minnie's mother. God knows I don't want to ask Rosamund Cohn for anything, but if I have to, I will. We'll need fifty dollars for two train tickets to San Francisco."

When she offered no more, he prompted, "And then?"

"We'll go to the boardinghouse. I don't know that they'll believe us, but they'll take us in. We may have to swallow our pride, but we'll have a real roof over our heads. I'll be able to have the baby at home."

Too engaged to notice that Bennie had straightened and moved out from under her arm, Frieda raced on. "I'll be willing to work right up until my time comes, cooking and cleaning. And you can help my father with the bakery and his wine and soda pop business. You might have to go to synagogue with him, but a little religion might do you some good, Bennie." She drew back eager for his response.

"No."

"No? No to what? No to asking Mrs. Cohn for a loan? No to going back to San Francisco with me? No to working with my father?"

"No to everything."

"Why?" Frieda asked, her eyes already filling with frustrated tears.

"I put seventeen years into the Arizona Territory. I've endured hardships, mortal danger, unbelievable loneliness, but I'm not giving up. My destiny is in the Arizona Territory." Bennie straightened his hat decisively. "I am going to stay and make it in Dos Cacahuates."

"You're down on San Francisco because you're not used to living there."

"I can't live in a place like 'Frisco."

Frieda seized his hand, her eyes begging, "Please, Bennie. I don't want to have our baby in a tent in a godforsaken outpost. Come with me to San Francisco, Bennie."

When he spoke, his words sounded hollow and remote. "I've got to stay here and get things straightened out."

"When would you be free to go?"

Bennie studied the grass. "Everyone bossing you around, telling you what you can say and what you can do. I'm not cut out to live in the hive. I don't know the big words, and I don't have patience to study out the small print. It's no use. I have to have room to stretch out, to talk loud and take all kinds of wild chances. Big towns are no good for me. I get in trouble in big towns. Besides, I shiver when it gets to be under seventy degrees. In San Francisco I'd be shivering all of the time."

"There's nothing here for us, Bennie. International Improvement is finished. La Cíbola Hotel belongs to the bank. The railroad is going to Nogales."

"International Improvement may be finished, but local

improvement isn't. Let those four-flushing eastern dandies get out and stay out. I promised you Dos Cacahuates is going to be the leading international community on the Mexican-American border, and it is. There are going to be a railroad, mining, agricultural and commercial enterprises that will make their lying eyes fall out."

"When?" Frieda asked.

"Sooner than anyone thinks."

"How will we live until then? We don't even have a house," Frieda said, her voice sliding out of control.

"We'll live the way we've been living. I'll get a store going again. I'll get some kind of temporary house up for us. And mining, I'm going to get serious about mining. Look what Mendel Miner did for himself. Copper, gold, silver are all going to be big in Dos Cacahuates after we get a short line railroad in."

"I don't believe there's going to be a railroad." Frieda pushed out the sentence word by word.

"What else don't you believe?" Bennie's gaze narrowed on Frieda's face.

"I don't believe there is going to be a plaza, a theater, a school, houses, stores."

"You don't?"

"No, I don't."

"Well, I do. It would all be underway right now, if it hadn't been for Colonel Leighton, Yancy Nunes, and the International Improvement Company." Bennie spat out the last three words as if they were nails.

"What makes you so sure?"

"The idea was right. The people were wrong."

Frieda groaned and turned from Bennie.

Bennie's face reddened. "That lying son-of-a-bitch Yancy Nunes is the one I blame. He knew damn well the Colonel was a phony promoter on the run in Texas, Washington and New York."

"I don't care who's to blame. I just want to go home. I want to be with my people, my mother and father, my sisters and brother." Tears flew from her eyes. "I was a Sister of Service. I come from an honest, hard-working family," Frieda sobbed. "I'm not used to associating with crooks," Frieda cried, tears wetting her face from her forehead to her chin.

Bennie jumped to his feet and yanked her to hers. His face was ablaze again; his mouth was set in an uneven snarl. His eyes were narrowed, almost closed. He looked like a madman Frieda had once watched being wrestled to the ground by four San Francisco policemen.

"Come with me," he growled, jerking her along as she struggled to break away. "So it's me who's dishonest, is it?"

"Bennie, you're hurting me," Frieda pleaded, stumbling along.

Outside the plaza, he shoved her toward the wagon, then picked her up and threw her onto the seat. As he started for the driver's seat, Frieda jumped up, hoping to flee. Seizing her dress in one hand, he shoved the butt of the rifle that lay across his knees at her with the other.

"Stay there," he growled, "and keep your ears open. If you have to tell this story on Tehama Street, you might as well tell it straight."

CHAPTER TWENTY-FIVE

The Way Home

ACROSS THE STREET from the Cosmopolitan Hotel, Bennie tugged at the reins and guided the horses between two other wagons fastened to a hitching post. He lifted his derby, resettled it low on his forehead, picked up his rifle, tucked it under his right arm and jumped off the wagon.

"Stay right where you are, Frieda. Don't get off that seat, no matter what happens," he instructed her.

Frieda looked straight ahead, refusing to dignify his orders with a look or a response.

"No matter what happens," he repeated, pounding the empty driver's seat to get her attention. "Hear me?"

To show her disgust, Frieda turned her back to him. Good God, Minnie and Rosamund were coming around the corner, just in time for the big show. She turned to see what Bennie was up to. Where was he going?

He had crossed the street and was climbing the steps to the hotel porch. She watched him approach a chubby, tow-headed boy of about nine, then hand him a coin. The child darted into the hotel, and Bennie backed off into the dusty road to wait. Several loungers on the porch greeted him. He gestured, hand raised, fingers spread, that he was otherwise engaged. She kept her eyes fastened on him until she heard Minnie call her name. She turned. The Cohns were hurrying toward the wagon.

"We've been looking for you *everywhere*," Minnie called in her shrill voice. Bennie shot an annoyed look over his shoulder, then turned back to the hotel. The two women, their expressions urgent, were beckoning to her.

Frieda's eyes shifted to Bennie who had hoisted his rifle and was moving toward the hotel. Yancy Nunes had just come through the front entrance and was standing on the porch, blinking in the afternoon light. He said something to the boy at his side, then followed his pointed finger to Bennie, who, by then, was at foot of the porch steps. Yancy stiffened and paled. He whipped around and started back into the hotel.

"If you run, I'll shoot," Bennie, warned, his voice rose above the street noises, halting traffic. "I'm going to pull the truth out of you—if need be, through bullet holes."

Yancy turned to face Bennie, fright smearing his features. "The truth about what?"

Had Yancy's terrified gaze shifted from Bennie to her then back to Bennie? Or had she imagined it? Frieda couldn't tell, but her heart was thundering as if it had. Was her husband going to expose her infidelity on a Tucson thoroughfare, before dozens of people? Her gaze darted from the men to Rosamund and Minnie, who'd come to a dead stop in the middle of the street, as had other passersby. Catching Frieda's eye, they frantically gestured to her to join them. Frieda slipped out of the passenger seat and, half-crouched, crept toward Minnie and Roasamund. They drew her between them, each curling an arm around Frieda's quaking shoulders.

"The truth about what?" Bennie mimicked Yancy. "You, don't you know, uh?"

"Not unless you tell me." Yancy had recovered from the initial shock and was trying to steady himself.

"Not this time, Nunes," Bennie snarled. "This time you're going to do the talking. And I want it straight, you hear me?"

Yancy's eyes were fixed on Bennie.

Dear God, spare me now, Frieda prayed.

"About you, you two-faced, consumptive cur."

Loungers on the porch were quietly slipping out of Bennie's range. People behind him on the street waited, entranced with the enfolding drama.

"What do you want to know?" Yancy asked, his face glistening with sweat.

A bluffer to the core, Frieda thought. *Or had he confronted so many irate husbands, he knew just what to do?*

"I want you to tell...." Bennie ventured a glance back at the wagon. Finding it vacated, he searched the street, located Frieda, delivered her a "you're going to hear about this" look, then turned back to Yancy. "...my wife and me why you didn't tell the shareholders the truth."

The shareholders. Praise be God.

"I did tell them the truth," Yancy answered.

Was he relieved too, or did she imagine his features were taking shape again.

"Not about me, you didn't."

"Nobody asked," Yancy tried.

"I asked, you lying dog. I asked you to tell them what you knew about me." Bennie stepped closer, waving his rifle.

"I-I-I...."

Bennie's eyes swerved to the three women, then back to his trembling captive.

"'At this moment, I can't vouch for you as a gentleman,'" Bennie mimicked. "You knee-knocking, face-saving, hypocrite. You can't vouch for me? Why can't you vouch for me?"

Nunes' legs were visibly buckling.

"You knew damn well that Colonel Moses-Walk-On-Water Leighton was as worthless as Confederate money, didn't you?"

Yancy lowered his head. His words rattled against each other as he pleaded. "I was sick, penniless, alone."

Bennie stepped still closer. "Speak up, damn you. You knew the Colonel was a cur, didn't you?"

Yancy hesitated, weighing his response.

"Didn't you."

"Yesss."

"And you worked for him anyway."

"I wrote handbills for him."

"The International Improvement Company, Dos Cacahuates Division, was your idea."

"The Colonel wrote from Mexico about Ramirez's land

and asked me to work up a scheme."

"You dreamed up the short line railroad, the townsite, the hotel, then hustled down to bamboozle the Goldson boys. 'All we need is good women and good water. Find some nice Jewish girls and get married.'"

"The doctor told me I had to get out west or...."

"How could you live with us and lie like that?"

Yancy met Bennie's disgusted gaze for a moment. "Once you and Morrie got to work, it began to look like a genuinely good idea." He lowered his head and coughed.

"The Goldsons were good partners, weren't they? Why didn't you tell that to the shareholders? You didn't because all you care about is your own skin."

Yancy suddenly straightened, his face angling to a haughty tilt. "I think I've answered all the questions I'm going to answer, Goldson," he said.

"You'll answer anything I ask, or I'll blow your fool head off," Bennie growled. He raised his rifle to shooting position and aimed at the middle button of Yancy's vest.

"No," Frieda screamed. Thrusting off Minnie and Rosamund's arms, she raced across the street, passed Bennie, and flung herself, arms spread, in front of Yancy. "Don't kill him, Bennie," she pleaded. "They'll hang you."

Bennie's face darkened with rage. "I told you to stay in the wagon. Get out of the way."

The end of Bennie's rifle was inches from her waist. She could feel Yancy behind her stiff as an icicle. Tears and terror mixed in Frieda's blue eyes, but she wouldn't budge. "You'll have to shoot me, Bennie."

"For chris' sakes, Frieda," Bennie hissed. "Get out of the way. This is between us men."

"A real man doesn't aim his rifle at an unarmed opponent," Yancy countered, peering over Frieda's shoulder at someone behind Bennie.

"Okay, drop that rifle," came an authoritative voice.

Bennie turned to see who the order came from.

"Drop it, Goldson." The man speaking wore a sheriff's

badge and carried his own rifle. There was a second man at his side. Two more armed horsemen came riding out of the circling crowd on the other side of the street. The sheriff dismounted and walked toward Bennie, shaking his head and muttering, "I thought you had more sense, Goldson."

Bennie held on to his rifle. The sheriff stopped several inches from him and in a low, brotherly tone said, "*Zayt nisht ah nar,* don't be a fool, drop the rifle."

"Damn it, Max," Bennie grumbled.

"What kind of *cowboyishe* goings-on is this?" the sheriff muttered as he reached over and seized the rifle from Bennie's grasp.

Noticeably relieved, Yancy watched the sheriff and his deputies escort the sullen-faced offender to his wagon.

Frieda stayed rooted in place, uncertain of what to do next. Surrounded by lawmen, Bennie lumbered onto the driver's seat.

"Now get the hell out of here, and don't come back to Tucson until you've cooled down," the sheriff yelled, loud enough to advise the crowd he was doing his job. Then he went around to the back of the wagon and slipped Bennie's rifle under a blanket, saying, "You'll need this for the trip home."

His eyes on the floorboard, Bennie didn't move.

"I told you to get going, didn't I?" the sheriff said.

Bennie ducked his head in the direction of Frieda. The sheriff turned. "Well, Mrs. Goldson, are you going with him, or aren't you?"

He clearly didn't care one way or the other, but Rosamund and Minnie did.

"She is not," Mrs. Cohn called, striding toward Frieda. "She's staying with us. I'm taking her back to her family in San Francisco."

Frieda looked at Bennie. He was slumped over the reins, his eyes closed.

"Well, I guess that's it, Goldson. On your way," the sheriff said.

The Cohn women's arms linked with Frieda's. "He's no good, Frieda. You'll be better off without him," Minnie assured her. "My mother will pay for your ticket home."

"I said get going, Goldson," the sheriff said.

Bennie flicked the reins and clicked his tongue at the horse. The wagon wheels began to turn.

"Wait," Frieda cried. She broke from her friends' restraining grasp and ran to the wagon. Bennie's face lit up as he extended a hand and drew Frieda aboard, then darkened as the Cohn women rushed to reclaim her.

"He's just like Leopold—wild," Rosamund called. "You'll be sorry."

Bennie loosened the reins and once again the wagon began to roll.

"Frieda, what shall I tell your parents?" Rosamund called after her.

She twisted to call over her shoulder, "Tell them I'm fine."

The crowd broke up into clumps to hash over the excitement. On the porch of the hotel, the sheriff and his men stood talking to Yancy Nunes. No one on the scene noticed when the Goldson wagon came to a halt near the corner, turned and started back down the street, this time on the same side of the road as the Cosmopolitan Hotel.

When the wagon was in front of the main entrance, Bennie bound the reins to the brake. Then he rose in a crouch, his rifle leveled against his shoulder, he leaned over Frieda, so that she had to duck her head in her lap. He aimed with care and fired, hitting a water pot hanging above Yancy's head. Water and clay spewed over Nunes, the sheriff, and his men. Bennie threw back his head and roared his satisfaction. Then, he fell back on the seat, untied the reins and called to the horse, "Now let's get the hell out of here."

As the wagon rolled off, the wet and ruffled sheriff came running after it yelling, "Goldson, you damned fool. If I see you in town again, I'll string you up or shoot you down, Jew or not. You hear me? Stay out of Tucson."

•

A charged silence prevailed between Frieda and Bennie as they rode toward the outskirts of town. The wagon was well beyond the environs of Tucson when Bennie's voice grumbled, "Don't you ever get in the way when I'm holding a rifle on someone."

Frieda snorted in disgust. She could see the white dome and twin minarets of the San Xavier del Bac Mission on the west side of the road when she broke her silence to lament to the desert air, "I'm married to a gunslinger."

"How else do you think I could have gotten the truth from Yancy Nunes?"

"Don't ever ask me to come to Tucson with you again. I've never been so humiliated in my life."

The sun was silhouetting the Baboquivari Mountains when Bennie decided to answer. "Stay away from Tucson?" he grunted. "Sons-of-bitches don't have to worry. I'll stay as far away as I can."

"That's Dos Cacahuates," Frieda said.

Bennie hurled a dubious look in her direction.

"Can't get any further away than Dos Cacahuates," Frieda jeered further. "It's the end of the line."

Bennie's next words were heavy with an hour of silent thought. "You're sorry you didn't stay with the Cohns."

Her words were weighted with her own hour-long inquiry. "I don't know yet."

"Mrs. Goldberg, Mrs. Goldwater, Mrs. Beisel—lots of the fashionable Jewish ladies get their checks in San Francisco, and stay clear of the Territory. If that's what you want, go back to the boardinghouse without me," Bennie said, scorn curling his words. "I'll visit you from time to time."

"Umph," was Frieda's answer.

They were still miles from Tubac, and dusk was falling when Bennie said, "You really mean to stay with me in Dos Cacahuates?"

"What else can I do if you won't leave?"

"And you won't complain?"

"Of course I'll complain. What civilized woman could live in Dos Cacahuates and not complain?"

Bennie groaned. "I can't stand a complaining woman."

"Worse than no woman at all?"

The sunset had spread from a bright red ball to a rosy wash silhouetting the dark blue mountains before Frieda spoke of still another worrisome matter. "What will we tell the new settlers?"

"That we've run into a temporary setback. That we will all have to be patient. That Dos Cacahuates is still going to be the most important international community on the border. That I intend to stay and build until I see that dream come true, and that I hope they will too."

When a first star appeared in the faded blue sky, Bennie said, "I guess we had better think about a campsite. We're approaching Tubac."

"Do we have to spend the night?" Frieda said. "I've got to get back to Dos Cacahuates as fast as possible."

"It's too dangerous to travel at night in this Apache country. Why are you in such a hurry?"

"I don't want my customers to get used to that German lady's cooking."

"Let them. You won't be running a restaurant, Frieda."

"Of course I'll be running the First Lady. We have debts to pay off, a house to build, a baby to get ready for."

"I believe I can take care of it without the First Lady," Bennie said.

"One believer in the family is all we can afford," she countered.

"I don't want my wife—"

Frieda interrupted. "I'll give up the First Lady when you buy me out."

Their eyes met. She was not giving way. Neither was he. Each turned to scrutinize his own side of the desert.

•

A half-hour later, Bennie guided the horses eastward onto a back road that skirted Tubac, on the Santa Cruz River. He tethered the wagon in a grove of cottonwoods behind the settlement, an old presidio and a scattering of houses and stores. Exhausted, each occupied with his own thoughts, Frieda and Bennie prepared a small supper over a campfire, a pot of coffee, hard tortillas and some cooked beans Frieda had wrapped and stored in a small pot. Then together they arranged a bed in the wagon.

Sandwiched between the scrawny desert and the starry skies, they stretched out alongside each other under the blankets pulled up to protect them from the chilly October night air. Alone in the dark, the events of the day began to recede as their tired bodies pressed together for warmth, comfort, consolation. His arms wrapped her against him, and she curled up, giving herself, in the dark of the night, to his protective embrace. The water trickled over the stony stream bottom, night birds called, coyotes yowled, wakeful animals rustled in the brush. All were now familiar creature sounds to Frieda. Only the thought of other people disturbed her—the Apaches, the shareholders in Tucson, her family and friends in San Francisco, the new settlers in Dos Cacahuates. A last few tears strayed down Frieda's face.

Bennie touched her cheek with his fingertips. "Please don't cry," he whispered. "I promise you, everything is going to be all...."

Frieda's hand flew up to Bennie's lips to block the word. "Don't say it. Don't ever say it again. We don't know how things are going to be."

"I won't say it," Bennie said, "but everything will be...." he stopped himself with a laugh.

Moments later, Frieda was settled again in Bennie's embrace, sound asleep.

".... all right," Bennie whispered.